In the Beginning

In the beginning there is a family. It is a very ordinary family, just like yours or mine – Ben, Rose and their three children. Then, one morning, without warning, Ben leaves and Rose is left to face life alone.

In the Beginning is the story of Rose and Ben's marriage before he leaves, and of how Rose struggles to re-invent her life when he has gone. Written with an almost artless simplicity, Catherine Dunne's brilliant first novel is at once heartbreaking, inspiring, and very true.

CATHERINE DUNNE

Catherine Dunne was born in Dublin in 1954. She studied English and Spanish at Trinity College and went on to teach at Greendale Community School. She lives on the north side of Dublin with her husband and son. This is her first novel.

Catherine Dunne

IN THE BEGINNING

VINTAGE

Published by Vintage 1998

4 6 8 10 9 7 5 3

First published in Great Britain by
Jonathan Cape 1997

Vintage
Random House, 20 Vauxhall Bridge Road,
London SW1V 2SA

Random House Australia (Pty) Limited
20 Alfred Street, Milsons Point, Sydney
New South Wales 2061, Australia

Random House New Zealand Limited
18 Poland Road, Glenfield,
Auckland 10, New Zealand

Random House South Africa (Pty) Limited
Endulini, 5a Jubilee Road, Parktown 2193, South Africa

Random House UK Limited Reg. No. 954009

A CIP catalogue record for this book
is available from the British Library

ISBN 0 09 976041 X

Papers used by Random House UK Limited are natural,
recyclable products made from wood grown in sustain-
able forests. The manufacturing processes conform to the
environmental regulations of the country of origin

Printed and bound in Great Britain by
Cox & Wyman Ltd, Reading, Berkshire

This book is dedicated to Denis.

Prologue

In the beginning there is a family. It is not in any way remarkable. It is a very ordinary family, just like yours and mine.

In this family there are five people. The father's name is Ben. He is forty-five, thinning on top, soft around the middle. He has his own business and brings home the bacon. He is fond of his children and does not beat his wife.

Rose is the mother. She is forty-two, a little weary after twenty years of war with her waistline. She is a loving mother, an efficient home-maker and she doesn't cheat on Ben.

There are three children. Their ages range from six to seventeen. They are of great importance to themselves. But for our purposes, for the moment, they are simply The Children.

This unremarkable family goes on living from day to day. Ben and Rose often ask themselves – Is this all there is? But they do not ask each other.

One day, Ben comes into the kitchen. He is looking for Rose. She is boiling eggs.

'Rose.'

He has used her name very little recently, so she looks up, surprised.

'We have to talk.'

The world collapses, years spiral into turmoil, lives are shattered. Rose knows now that all these disasters were once heralded by that phrase. We have to talk.

'I've got to get away for a bit. I think we need a break

from each other, just for a while. I'm sorry to do it like this, but I'm just not happy.'

Rose watches the eggs. She is fascinated by the way they bubble to the surface on a geyser of boiling water. One of them has just split and is oozing a gelatinous whiteness into the troubled water. She knows now that it will be all watery inside.

It is a morning made for clichés. We have to talk. My knees turned to jelly. I couldn't believe my ears. We decided on a trial separation.

Rose looks into Ben's face to see if there are answers there, any clues to explain the bag packed and ready at his feet.

'Now?' she asks stupidly.

He shrugs.

'I don't see any point in waiting. This has been coming for a good while. You know that.'

Does she? Is this what he has meant by his long silences, his growing dissatisfaction with business, his restlessness? She is aware that something has been bubbling underneath for some time, but perhaps a holiday, a weekend away together without the children . . . ? Now it seems that it is not so easily fixed, whatever it is.

She feels quite calm. She turns off the hob and wipes the splashes away, trying not to look at him.

She believes that it is so with all the great crises in people's lives. The moment passes without any great drama. The drama comes afterwards.

She is aware of the moment, of him, of herself, of the now quietly steaming saucepan of eggs. She knows all these details are engraving themselves behind her eyes, to be replayed over and over again. She pulls her gaze away from the comfortable, the familiar. She focuses on Ben.

'Can't we talk? Do you have to go now, before we've even had a chance to discuss it?'

He makes a gesture of impatience.

'I've been trying to talk to you for years. I must get away to clear my head. I'll call you when I get back.'

She knows that he is determined, also exasperated.

'Aren't you even angry?' he demands. 'Throw something, thump me if you want, but for Christ's sake, react.'

'No, I'm not angry,' she says. 'I don't know what I am, but I don't want to thump you.'

Ben starts abruptly towards the door.

'This is final, isn't it? This isn't just for a while?'

Ben turns towards her, his face white.

'I think so. I don't love you any more.'

And now he is gone. The door closes quietly behind him. Rose calls to the children that it is time to leave for school.

She puts their lunch-boxes on the table and another day begins.

Part One

Monday, 3rd April 1995; 8.00 am.

'Come on, kids, are we right?'

Voice normal, pitched as usual. Don't let out the tight scream building in head and chest. Time, she needed time.

Damien came into the kitchen, shrugging into his jacket.

'See you later, Ma.'

He had taken to calling her Ma, teasing her by elongating the sound, ever since she told him that she used to call him her little lamb.

She pretended to him she hated it, so he kept doing it. The truth was she liked it; he was growing up, but still keeping in touch.

She watched his dark head, bent over the rucksack he used for school. She felt suddenly much, much older.

'Usual time?'

Usual question. Keep it going.

He nodded, taking another slice of toast. She wondered again at the amount he ate. It seemed constant: before meals, meals, after meals. She had given up worrying about him spoiling his appetite.

This morning, that hardly seemed to matter.

'Bye, Ma!'

Back door slammed and he was gone.

Rose watched him as he pedalled down the driveway. For a moment, she had an extraordinary flash of insight, a vision of him as a stranger, not her son. Not anybody's son. Just another adult. Tall, dark hair rather long, endless arms and legs. Cycling confidently, arrogantly almost. She felt fear where she might normally have felt pride.

7

But today was not normal.

Brian and Lisa were fighting again. That, at least, was normal and Rose made a physical effort to leave the window and hurry them for school. Lethargy began to invade her knees. Her hands started to shake slightly. Her mouth felt dry.

'Come on, you two, I'm waiting!'

Still the same amount of authority in her voice. Get them out, get them gone and she could *think*. The ordinary suddenly felt strange; she needed to be in control of this.

'At last!'

The two children finally burst into the kitchen. Today, Brian was sulky and Lisa looked triumphant. Round two to her, obviously. Rose felt suddenly weary at the thought of rounds three, four and five.

She arranged her face carefully and spoke brightly, her mother's-in-charge voice.

'Let's go! We don't want to be late!'

Not for the first time, she was annoyed at herself for starting this routine. She should let them walk. Rain wouldn't kill them. But Lisa was such a slow walker and was doing so much whingeing these days. Driving was easier.

Rose could feel the tears nudging hotly, her mouth downturning. She hoped she would not need to speak.

Perhaps they sensed something. They were both silent in the back, unused to being ignored, to being put second.

Subdued, they waved from the school gates, and Rose held it all together until they disappeared.

For several minutes, she could not move.

She watched the dozens of mothers with prams and buggies, the occasional suited father. People called to each other, waved, smiled and hugged their children.

It was all so ordinary.

Rose felt utterly isolated now that the extraordinary had happened. There was no one here she could talk to. No one to whom she could say, 'My husband's just left me.'

Or was there? Was there someone here who would say, I know how it feels?

She needed a friend. She needed Martha.

Rose turned the car and pulled away slowly. She had to concentrate, her mind was everywhere, years telescoping before her eyes.

Suddenly, she slammed on the brakes.

She hadn't seen the elderly woman on the pedestrian crossing.

Angrily, the woman hammered on the bonnet of the car with her rolled-up umbrella. Some passers-by laughed. Rose had the impression of a pair of glasses and a crumpled, enraged mouth, shouting at her.

Didn't they know? Wasn't it written all over her face?

Dimly, she saw a face she recognised, looking at her in concern. Not now, Jane. She couldn't cope with kindness just now. She couldn't even apologise to the old woman who was still shouting at her, shaking her umbrella, enjoying the notoriety of the moment.

She would go home now and savour her outrage over cups of tea with her family and neighbours. She would be glad to be alive. She would be even happier to fume about rich women in their big cars, and how it was no wonder that youngsters had no respect when their parents treated the old like dirt.

All these things Rose knew as she accelerated and headed for home. She was desperate for the safety of her own four walls.

She knew how it must look, how the old woman must feel. She couldn't change that script.

Now, she had to go home and write her own.

June 1972

The phone is ringing.

It is still enough of a novelty to bring people running to the hall from all parts of the house. Kevin slams open his bedroom door, Grace runs from the front room, homework abandoned, pen in hand. Rose hangs back, sitting on the top step, not wanting to appear too eager.

Her mother gets there first. Hanging up coats under the stairs, she is first on the scene.

Rose notices how much more slowly she is walking. Everything takes a lot of effort. If she hurries, she becomes breathless. Sometimes it lasts for hours.

Kevin and Grace wait, both hopeful.

'It's for you, Rose.'

Kevin and Grace retire, defeated.

'Thanks, Mam.'

Rose sits on the bottom step, hand over the receiver, and waits until her mother finishes her slow progress towards the kitchen; waits until the door has closed with a click.

'Grace, close the door!' she says sharply.

The lack of privacy grates on Rose. She has never noticed it before; now it makes her angry. Is the hall the only place you can put a phone?

Finally, she speaks. Her heart is beating that little bit faster; her hands are clammy.

'Hello?' Just the right tone. Puzzled, as though she has not been waiting for this.

'Rose? It's Ben. How are you?'

Rose feels her colour rise.

'I'm fine, Ben, how are you?'

She can't keep the enthusiasm out of her voice. Around her heart feels tight; she notices that her fingers are leaving foggy rings on the black bakelite.

'Great – I'm in Donegal at the moment, so I can't talk for long.'

Rose feels absurdly happy. All the way from Donegal!

The rest of the conversation is easy. The tightness loosens; Ben is as nervous as she is. She chats more easily, encouraging him. She is confident now; he is going to ask her out.

Rose finishes the conversation, murmuring about the cost. She is glad that this first real contact is by telephone; it is easier than face to face. They say goodbye. Rose hangs up very gently.

Friday; they will meet next Friday. Her first real date with him. Her first real date with anyone. Ellen won't be the only one around here with a boyfriend.

Rose feels grown up suddenly, womanly. What will she wear?

She wants to be with her mother. She walks towards the kitchen.

Her mother is scraping new potatoes at the sink. It is in the days when everyone has dinner at one o'clock and doesn't call it lunch. Tea is at six; another meal to be cooked. At nineteen, Rose feels sorry for her mother and the drudgery of her life. Six dinners, six teas, seven days a week. Rose thinks there must be more to life.

'Can I help?'

'Yes, thanks, love. Set the table there. Daddy will be home soon.'

Home on his bike every day at one for dinner; back to the Corporation offices for a quarter past two. Gentle, reliable, regular as clockwork.

Rose is noticing more and more the tenderness between

11

her parents. It surprises her, that it should still be there after twenty-five years.

'Was that your man?'

Her mother nods in the direction of the telephone.

Rose feels herself blush again.

'Yes, that was Ben.'

Her mother leaves the silence for her to fill.

'I'm going out with him next Friday night.'

Forks in one hand, brushing crumbs from the oilcloth-covered table with the other, Rose watches her mother.

The older woman rinses the potatoes under the cold tap, placing the fat, waxy-yellow ovals into a large saucepan already on the gas.

'Boiling water for new potatoes, always. Remember that. Cold for old.'

Rose nods.

'Do you think this is serious, then?' After a pause.

Rose shrugs, unconvincingly.

'I don't really know. I've only just met him. But I do like him.'

'No point in reminding you that you're only nineteen, I suppose?'

Rose laughs.

'Mam, you were married at twenty.'

'I know; that's why there's no point in reminding you.'

Both women smile. Margaret wipes her hands on her blue check apron and comes into the breakfast room. Without a word, she hugs Rose to her.

She tilts the young face towards her.

'You be careful of yourself, and don't give your heart away too soon.'

Rose is a little embarrassed. She feels she has already given her heart away. She knows her mother is trying to say something else too, something about sex. Rose feels her toes curl, hoping her mother won't go any further. The moment passes.

'He's always welcome here, you know that. We'll be glad to meet him.'

Rose feels her heart fill with love. She has a great rush of sadness as she looks at her mother, back bent, knife raking through cabbage.

She is forty-five. Old. Sometimes her face is as grey as the hair she wears pulled back in a bun. Sometimes she has two high, angry spots of colour on her cheeks. Rose is afraid for her. And guilty too, as though she is responsible for her mother's lack of robustness, for her fading away from them.

She finishes setting the table, puts the plates in the oven, and takes the vegetable peelings down the garden to her dad's compost heap.

She is happy. It is June, bright and warm. The whole weekend stretches ahead of her. She is meeting Martha tonight. Rose is looking forward to spending some of her first week's pay packet.

Grace bursts into the kitchen.

'Who was that on the phone?'

She lifts the lids of the saucepans without waiting for Rose's reply.

'What's for dinner? I'm starving!'

Rose smiles to herself. Watching Grace, she suddenly knows what it is like to be grown up.

She feels sorry for Grace, who doesn't yet know.

Monday, 3rd April; 9.30 am.

Rose thought she would never get home. The image of the old woman with the umbrella just wouldn't go away. Jane's kind face made her feel ashamed. Her hand was unsteady and she had difficulty fitting the key into the lock.

She panicked when she heard her neighbour's door open suddenly. Suzanne.

She did not want to talk to anyone. The sense of humiliation was intense, physically painful. Once inside the hall, she had to stop and catch her breath. Blindly, she made her way towards the kitchen, fumbled with the kettle and the teapot.

And then she sat at the kitchen table and cried. Waves of grief and shame washed over her. Later, she moved about the house, restlessly, looking for clues.

She was driven to look at old photographs, testing herself to see how much pain she could feel. He was everywhere. Wedding photographs, photographs of the happy family on holiday, photographs of the children on their own. Ben was all of them.

She rang Jane and asked her to collect Brian and Lisa from school. Jane asked no questions and offered to feed the kids and keep them until Rose collected them. Rose couldn't speak. She hung up without even saying thanks.

She wandered around the house for the rest of the morning. At times, her heart lifted when she heard a car door slam. She had misunderstood him. He was coming back. He'd be sorry for leaving so suddenly, they'd both cry, and really start again.

The telephone startled her into hopefulness twice. Each time she dashed to pick it up. Each time it was for Ben. The second time she wanted to say, 'I'm sorry, Ben doesn't live here any more,' but she wrote the message down, as always.

The silence of the house frightened her. Everywhere was full of his presence yet still strangely empty. She knew, achingly, how much of her life, her home, her self, revolved around Ben.

By four o'clock, her eyes were swollen and red, her hair a mess and her stomach churning from gallons of tea. There was no relief in crying but it was intolerable not to. She recognised grief, but this was different from Michael. This was full of shame. She wasn't able to hold on to her husband. He no longer loved her. She was worthless, the one to blame.

When Damien came in she was lying, exhausted, on the bed. She turned her back to the door so that he wouldn't see her face. But he didn't come looking for her, assuming she had gone for her usual afternoon walk with the kids. She heard him slam around the kitchen, looking for something to eat. Finally the back door closed, and she heard him call to John next door to stall it, he was coming.

And then she slept. When she woke, her eyes were stuck together, her mouth dry and her head pounding. Slowly she got off the bed. She soaked the sponge with cold water and held it against her eyes. In the kitchen she took two painkillers and a glass of water. It was time to collect Brian and Lisa. Damien should be in by now to start his homework. She'd look for him on the way to Jane's.

Dinner. There was nothing for dinner. Ben loved his food and Rose had become an excellent cook. For twenty years, holidays the exception, she had never missed cooking a meal. Sunday dinners became a command performance. During the week, Ben liked good food, well-cooked, a simple dessert and a glass or two of good wine. He enjoyed this so much that

Rose got great pleasure out of having everything just right for six o'clock.

She didn't feel hungry now, but she knew that Damien would be starving. She pulled an emergency portion of home-made lasagne out of the freezer. The kids enjoyed eating pasta when Ben was away from home on business. Grimly, she scrubbed two potatoes and opened the door of the microwave. She heard Damien's key in the front door.

It looked like he was going to be eating an awful lot of pasta.

June 1972

Ellen is lying on the bed, reading. Rose is unreasonably annoyed that her older sister is home. She never stays in on Friday nights.

'Did you have a row with Richard?' Rose asks lightly.

'None of your business.'

Rose wishes she had a room of her own. She wants to take her time getting ready. She wants to enjoy her anticipation.

She begins to go through her wardrobe. Everything looks shabby, out of date. Nothing will do. She has nothing to wear.

Ellen continues reading. The room is filling up with Rose's frustration. Angrily, she shoves clothes on to the rail, forcing them to the back of the heavy, old-fashioned wardrobe. She has to turn them sideways to close the door.

'You can wear my new jeans and jacket, if you want.'

Ellen has put her book down and is watching her sister.

'What!'

Ellen shrugs, pretending indifference.

'I've told you – borrow the jeans and jacket if you want. *I'm* not going anywhere.'

Rose is too happy to respond to the slight emphasis.

'Are you sure?'

She feels lit up inside.

Ellen shrugs again.

'Yeah, I'm sure. I just hope he's worth it,' she says sourly.

Monday, 3rd April; 6.30 pm.

Jane opened the door almost as soon as Rose knocked.

'Come on in, Rose. Just step over the usual mess.'

Rose negotiated her way around a multicoloured pile of Lego and a garage made out of a Pampers box. Someone was screaming in the front room, and someone else turned the television up even louder. 'Neighbours' music flooded all of downstairs.

Jane threw open the door, pushing cars and boats aside with the toe of a well-worn sandal. 'Turn that down! Brian, Lisa, come and say hello to your mam.'

'Hiya, Mam. Can we watch "Neighbours" here? Jane says it's OK with her if it's OK with you.'

'Sure,' Rose agreed, brightly. This was not the time to wonder about the political correctness of Australian soaps. Jane grinned.

'Great to know how much you were missed, isn't it? Come on in; I'm in the kitchen for a change.'

Rose had sometimes found the chaos of Jane's house off-putting. Today, it was comforting. Four children under twelve and a frequently absent husband; an ailing mother-in-law upstairs and a part-time job. Rose felt she'd lose her reason.

'Sit down, Rose. We have half an hour's guaranteed peace. Jim is away and Mother is resting upstairs. Fancy a cup of coffee?'

Rose had not yet greeted Jane directly. She couldn't even look at her. If Jane noticed, she gave no indication. Now she had to reply. For the second time that day, she was speechless.

Horrified, she began to weep silently, great big tears splashing onto the table where she rested her elbows, both hands covering her eyes.

Jane waited until the great gulping sobs had subsided. She kissed the top of Rose's head and gave her a handful of tissues. Rose looked up at her, suffocated by the pain in her chest that dissolved only with the sort of weeping that invaded every space inside her. Once dissolved, it seemed to gather again and again, needing to be released through eyes, nose, mouth, every pore.

Then she half laughed, trying to make light of it.

'Ben walked out on me this morning. He said he didn't love me any more.'

The pain in her chest renewed itself in waves.

Jane held her until she'd finished crying. Then she sat beside her at the kitchen table, and quietly took her hand.

'What can I say? I'm so, so sorry. Do you want to tell me what happened?'

Rose nodded. It would be good to see what it all looked like out loud. Maybe it wasn't so bad after all. Maybe it was just a bad row, the sort couples joked about afterwards. The sort of savage battles she and Ben had never had. She told Jane the whole simple story, knowing it wasn't simple, but needing to put her shape to it. Sharing it made it more real, but also a little easier to bear. Even the sense of shame was ebbing as she saw the distress in Jane's eyes.

'So it looks as though it's final; he said he'd been unhappy and he'd contact me when he got back. And that's all there is.'

'Didn't he want to talk about it?'

'He said that he'd been trying to talk to me for years. I don't know which hurt most – that or him saying that he didn't love me.'

'Got back from where?'

'Sorry?'

'You said that he'd be in touch when he got back. Got back from where?'

Rose looked around her slowly. All the details of Jane's kitchen were registering, irrelevantly, in her memory.

'I don't know. He didn't say. And, God Almighty, I didn't ask.'

Furious squabbling broke out next door. Jane leapt from her chair and reached the door-handle just as Kate, her youngest, was about to hurl herself into the kitchen, shrieking hysterically.

'Stop that screaming at once,' Jane demanded. 'Alison, please take Kate upstairs and help her into her pyjamas, and don't wake Grandma. Derek, I want to see you in the hall. James, go to bed – now. No argument, I said now.'

Rose smiled as the noises subsided. There were lowered voices in the hall. Jane's tone was firm. She came back into the kitchen and closed the door.

'Once Kate is out of the way they'll have no one to thwart, so it should be quieter for a bit. Now, where were we?'

'I don't know where my own husband has gone. Everything has happened so quickly that I haven't even been able to think.'

Jane nodded.

'Do you know where he keeps his passport?'

'Yes, it's in his desk, and I have a spare set of keys. I'll look when I get back.'

It suddenly became very important to know where Ben was. Even if he didn't want to come home, she needed to know where he was. If anything were to happen while he was away . . . What? What would he do? What could she do?

The Ben she once knew would have been there, just as he had been the time of Damien's meningitis. He had flown back from London, just to be home, even when the danger had passed.

But the Ben who left this morning with a bag? That

couldn't have been as spur of the moment as it had seemed. He had to have somewhere to go to, he must have done some advance planning. And yet he had told her nothing, didn't even give her a chance to understand the reasons for his going. That was pretty thin after twenty years.

Rose felt that this was all happening to somebody else. She began to feel detached from her body. The words 'deserted wife' blazed in front of her eyes. When they cleared, she saw that Jane had opened a bottle of wine and poured her a glass. She started to protest. 'Oh, not for me – the kids . . .'

'Drink it, or I'll use my Mammy voice on you. The kids are just grand. I've sent Derek for a video; Lisa and Brian can stay if they want – doubling up won't kill them for one night. Then I can bring them to school in the morning, and you can have a bit of breathing space. Take them home tomorrow when things are a bit clearer.'

Rose nodded, afraid of words.

'I'll talk to them in a minute. Can I ring Damien?'

'Of course.'

Rose put on her bright voice. Damien seemed pleased to have the run of the place for another couple of hours. Rose struggled with herself for a moment; then she decided that whatever he was at, for tonight it would have to be his own business.

'Cheers – or whatever is appropriate.'

'Cheers will do. Thanks, Jane. It really does help to tell somebody. What I can't figure out is why? Why now? Why didn't I know there was something *so* wrong?'

'That's for later. The most important thing now is to gather your forces. Get your friends around you, look after yourself and the kids. You've a lot of practical things to sort out, even if Ben has only gone for a few weeks.'

Rose looked at her in horror.

'Jesus, I've no money. Ben handles all the money; what if he's left me with nothing?'

Jane calmed her.

'That's not likely, Rose. Go to the bank in the morning. I'm sure you'll find it's OK.'

'My God, Jane, this morning at eight o'clock I had a happy family, and a husband I loved. Twelve hours later it's all gone and I'm wondering if Ben is such a bastard that he could leave us with nothing.'

Rose didn't say what else she was thinking. It couldn't happen to *her*. This sort of thing happened to other people, people in small houses with gangs of kids, damp running down the walls and ESB men coming to cut off the electricity. It didn't happen to solid, decent families where everybody knew the rules of the game and played by them faithfully for twenty years. This didn't happen to her.

Jane topped up her glass.

'Let's map out a plan of campaign for tomorrow. The worst thing you can do is do nothing. Whatever you find out, it's better than being in the dark.'

Rose took the notebook and pen that Jane handed her, and together they began to list the tasks that needed to be done before Rose could find out what was going to happen to the rest of her life.

And so evening came, the first day.

June 1972

Ellen's flares fit her perfectly. Her new platforms have ceased to pinch. She feels tall, self-assured, as though she has borrowed Ellen's personality.

Rose is waiting as Ben's car pulls up outside. Grace, only a few days away from her Inter. Cert., is keeping watch. She squeals so loudly that Rose yanks her by the collar away from the window.

'Shut up, Grace!' she says angrily. 'Do you want the whole road to hear you?'

She doesn't want Ben to come in, not yet.

She grabs her bag from the bottom step.

''Bye, all!'

And she is gone.

Ben gets out of the car and leans his elbows on the gleaming roof as she approaches. His shirt sleeves are rolled up, he has sunglasses on, his tie is casually askew.

Rose thinks she will die of love.

Clever, ambitious Ben. Twenty-two years of age, forty pounds a week, company car. He has it made. He knows he is going to go far. He also knows that he wants Rose.

On the second Friday in June, 1972, Ben Holden watches in satisfaction as his whole life spreads out before him.

There are no obstacles, only opportunities spread for the picking, like the city lights on the way home, winding away from Howth Summit towards the city centre.

Rose woke early. The house was very quiet without Brian and Lisa. Damien was still asleep. She'd call him shortly. She didn't know whether to tell him the reason for his father's departure. She didn't know *what* to tell him. She'd play it by ear.

She stepped into the shower. All the sluggishness of yesterday had disappeared. Twenty-three hours. One hour for every year she and Ben had spent together. The suffocating feeling in her chest was gone for the moment; she felt the urgency to find out.

She dressed, dried her hair and put on make-up. Her eyes were still puffy, but she looked normal enough for what she had to do. At half-past seven she called Damien for breakfast. She was buttering toast when he wandered into the kitchen in his pyjamas, yawning and scratching his head.

'Damien, you know your father doesn't like you at the breakfast table in your pyjamas. Go and get washed and dressed.'

It was out before she realised she'd said it.

'Yeah, but he's not here this morning, is he?' Damien grinned.

What the hell. It didn't seem worth arguing about.

'Brian and Lisa stayed over at Jane's last night. We stayed talking for ages and I didn't realise how late it had got. Was your dinner OK?'

Damien answered, his mouth full of Shredded Wheat. Another habit Ben hated. Rose said nothing.

'We're going to the swimming pool after school today. Can I have some money?'

Rose handed over a fiver, leaving herself enough coins for parking.

'I may need you to babysit tonight, Damien. So don't make any plans for after dinner.'

'Can John come around?'

Rose nodded.

'Yes, but no one else. Brian and Lisa didn't go to bed until all hours. I want them to have an early night or they'll be poisonous. When are you going to do your homework if John comes here tonight?'

'We'll do it together. Honest,' he said, seeing her look. 'We're working on a history project together anyway.'

'All right. Just don't cause me any hassle.'

Damien looked at her closely.

'Are you all right, Ma?'

'Yes. I've a couple of business things to sort out for your dad, so I'm going to be very busy for the next few days while he's away. I'm going to need your help.'

It was enough of the truth not to be a lie. If she could buy time until Friday, she mightn't need to say any more.

'Does that mean I can't go to the disco on Friday night?'

'I'm not discussing that now, Damien.'

'Thursday? Can I know by Thursday?'

Two days. Not to have to make a decision about it for two days.

'Yes,' Rose agreed.

Once he'd left for school, Rose began her search. Her whole body was speeding, energised. She had the strangest sensation of waking up after a long hypnotic sleep.

The passport was gone. Hers was still in the drawer, so was Damien's one from last year's holiday. But Ben's was missing. She unlocked the filing cabinet and took out the folder of Visa and American Express statements. Ben was meticulous. Nothing on the American Express indicated any business travel. She turned to the household account from Visa. Ben always paid up promptly. He did not believe in paying interest. This one had been paid in full last Friday, according to the cashier's stamp.

Then the name and the transaction date caught her eye. She held onto the desk as her legs gave way.

Hedigan's Travel. Sixteen hundred pounds. The seventh of March. And this was the fourth of April. He'd known for nearly a month exactly what he was going to do. And she was the April fool.

The tears came again, this time with rage. Only a very small part of Rose now held out hope that this might still be a mistake, that there was still a reasonable explanation. She rang Jane.

She was there in five minutes. Rose showed her the Visa bill.

'Do you know where he's gone?'

Rose shook her head. 'It doesn't say.'

'I know it doesn't say, but we – I – can ring Hedigan's and find out.'

'Would you?' Rose's voice was now a whisper; her hands had started to shake again.

Jane found the number quickly and dialled.

'Good morning. This is Jane Kennedy, Ben Holden's secretary. We booked some tickets with your agency on the seventh of last month, and I'm afraid Mr Holden forgot to give me the receipt for our books. I wonder could you forward me a copy? Yes, I'll hold.

'To Málaga. That's right. April the third to the seventeenth. Yes, for two, sixteen hundred pounds. Could you post it out to me, please, care of his home address? Thanks a million. Yes, Thursday will do fine. Thanks again.' Jane hung up. 'You heard.'

Rose nodded.

'I can't believe he could have done this. I'd better get to the bank straight away.'

'Do you want me to collect the kids again?'

Rose thought for a moment and shook her head.

'Thanks, Jane, but no. I think I should keep the routine going. But I wouldn't mind another glass of that wine after they've gone to bed.'

Jane hugged her.

'I'll be waiting. I'll throw my lot into bed early. Jim isn't due back until Thursday, so don't feel shy. Anyway, he'd be delighted to go out and meet Joe for a pint.'

Rose wondered at that for a moment. Ben had never had any friends. He insisted that home was where he wanted to be, after a hard day's work. He had business meetings or he entertained clients some evenings, but rarely. He so much enjoyed being at home that Rose gradually developed the habit of being there whenever he was.

She'd never minded. She was happy. She was sure of it.

August 1972

Rose and Ben are cycling. It is scorching hot. She loves cycling. She loves the challenge, the heat, the breeze, the exhilaration of the going. The getting there is always a bit of an anti-climax.

Ben is just in front of her. Even from the back, Rose sees how hot he looks. His white shirt is sticking to his back. He tends to be a little heavy, and usually resists Rose's efforts to get him to go with her. Today he has agreed, with quite good grace. But Rose knows by the grim set of his back that he is not pleased.

He indicates left and swings the bike roughly onto the entrance to Howth pier. She follows meekly. They have been together just a few months now and their rows have been inconsequential. Just spats really; nothing very serious. All forgotten very quickly. She feels that this one is going to be different.

He dismounts and lights a cigarette, coughing harshly as he does so. She hates the smell and sight of cigarettes, loathes nicotine-stained fingers. More than anything, Rose hates it that Ben smokes. She has not told him this, not yet.

'Don't,' he says, drawing on his cigarette slowly for added emphasis lest she miss the point, 'don't ever ask me to come cycling again.'

And that is it. In a way, Rose is relieved that that *is* it, that there isn't to be a scene in public. He doesn't seem angry or upset, nor does he want to talk. There doesn't seem to be anything to say.

'Are you ready?' he flicks away the cigarette butt, wheels the bike to the roadway and sets off at a punishing pace towards Clontarf.

Rose never does ask him again.

Tuesday, 4th April; 10.30 am.

Jack Morrissey was being very kind. He brought Rose into his office straight away, and offered her a cup of coffee. She accepted, realising as a headache began that she had had no breakfast.

She had rehearsed her speech in the shower, over and over. It was difficult to come to the point. Asserting yourself in front of bathroom tiles was one thing. Confronting a suit in official surroundings was another.

'Now, Mrs Holden, what can I do for you?'

Rose had the strangest feeling that he was speaking to someone else. With an effort, she began.

'Ben and I have been having some difficulties lately.'

No! This was not how she had practised it. She was to have been much more businesslike. It would have to do. She wished she could start again.

'We have decided to separate for a while until we decide what to do in everyone's best interests.'

Did that sound any better? She could see that Morrissey was getting ready to make sympathetic noises.

'As it happens, Ben went away on business rather urgently on Monday, so I've got the job of seeing where we stand financially.'

Weak, very weak. Rose could feel herself beginning to sweat. Her neck and forehead were prickly.

Jack Morrissey swung gently from side to side in his swivel chair, tapping a gold pencil against the desk in front of him.

'I can certainly get you a statement of your joint accounts,

Mrs Holden, but you will understand that there is some information which must remain confidential regarding your husband's business accounts.'

'But I'm a company director, Mr Morrissey. It's on the headed company notepaper, look, there's my name.'

Rose pulled open her handbag, spilling coins, papers, lipstick all over the floor.

She wanted desperately not to be there, not to behave like this.

He held up his hand.

'There's no need, Mrs Holden. All joint account statements will be prepared for you immediately; just hold on a moment.'

He left the office and Rose took a mouthful of lukewarm coffee. What did he mean by 'accounts'? There was a deposit account, a current account and a 'Finehold' company account, all in both their names. What did he mean by business accounts?

While she was waiting for the manager's return, Rose racked her brain for people who could help her through this. She didn't know what she needed just yet; her gut told her to steer clear of mutual friends. Would she need a solicitor? If so, where was she going to get one of those? For all she knew, she might have given her last fiver to Damien that morning.

Jack Morrissey returned, holding a sheaf of print-outs in his hand, a thick manila folder under his left arm.

'Now, Mrs Holden, that's the status on your deposit account,' and he handed her the first sheet. Rose folded it without looking at it.

'This is your joint current account, and this is the Finehold company account. I hope that everything is in order. Please don't hesitate to contact me if you have any further questions.'

Rose knew that she was being hurried along. She wanted

to go, lock herself in the office and pore over every scrap of paper she could lay her hands on. Please God there was enough to keep going even for the next two weeks. A perverse instinct made her delay as she folded the papers carefully into the front pocket of her handbag. She stood up only when she was ready. She held out her hand and smiled at Jack Morrissey, who was now looking uncomfortable. He kept touching the perfect knot of his tie. Rose was glad.

'Thanks very much, Jack, you've been very helpful.'

She opened the door herself and then looked back at him over her shoulder.

'I'll contact you towards the end of next week.'

She began to shake only as she entered the lift at the carpark.

She felt her blouse sticking to her back and her legs were wet with perspiration. She threw her jacket on the back seat and pulled her blouse out of her waistband. She opened the car window as she drove along the quays, grateful for the cool breeze. Her head was racing, full of impossibilities.

The last twenty years seemed utterly unreal, Ben a distant memory. Reality had started on Monday morning at eight o'clock. The total misery of the first twenty-four hours had changed into a will to survive, to come out on top of all this. That was even more important than what to tell the children. Stopped at traffic-lights, she reached for her bag to glance through the statements, but the lights changed almost at once and horns began blowing immediately.

Rose shoved the gear-lever into first, ignoring the grinding noise it made. Such things really didn't matter any more. She was amazed to find that the city traffic still moved, lurching along the streets as normal. People came and went about their daily business. Nobody knew anything of the individual calamities around them.

It was the same feeling as when her mother died, shortly after her engagement. And then Michael. She had felt deeply angry that everything just continued on, callously, as though nothing had changed. How dare milkmen deliver milk, postmen get on and off their bicycles, mothers deliver children to school, while she had just watched as coffin lids closed.

Dinners got cooked, trees burst into bud, people stopped calling and gradually, eventually, the normal lost its added dimension and pain found somewhere to live. Shepherd's pie on Tuesday, a friend had called it. Amid the appalling, the unthinkable, someone somewhere prepared the evening meal. Even though the world had just shifted on its axis.

She stepped out of her skirt as soon as she closed her front door. God, was she hot and sticky. She turned the shower on full, letting in as much cold as she dared. Gasping, she let the water course over her, standing there until her fingertips were prune-like, and the bitten edges showed up white and ragged.

She must eat something. She dried herself roughly, getting the circulation going again. Curiously, she stepped on the bathroom scales. Disbelieving, she stepped off, moving the scales to another position. She tried again. Five pounds. She thought her skirt felt looser. She laughed to herself at the irony of it. It was an ill wind, after all. If this kept up, she'd be right back to her wedding-day weight when Ben came back . . . She stopped herself.

'What a way for the mind to work at a time like this,' she said aloud, looking at her face in the mirror, patting the navy-blue blotches under her eyes. She made herself put on some make-up, although she thought it made her look worse. The kids would have to be collected in a few hours.

She wondered how many other mothers at the school hid such a wide gap between their public and their private faces with a dusting of toasted coral blusher, burnt-sapphire kohl-pencil and dusky cinnamon lipstick? The very names were miles away from this reality. Rose closed the bathroom-cabinet door, pulled her dressing-gown around her and went into the kitchen to see what she could stomach for lunch.

March 1974

Martha doesn't like the way Ben Holden has taken over. He seems to be everywhere, insinuating himself into their company. But she has to be careful. Rose likes him, and Rose has been her best friend since Low Babies. Martha has no boyfriend, not even one of 'soon to be' status. Her dislike might be seen as sour grapes. But she doesn't want to be a gooseberry either. It's funny the way uncomfortable feelings are like bitter fruit. She decides it is a good comparison.

Ben is certainly attentive to Rose. Martha senses a determination in him to have her. His manner is calm, polite, confident sometimes to the point of arrogance. Martha realises with regret that she and Rose are growing apart.

Using exams and pressure of work as an excuse, Martha gradually withdraws from Rose and Ben's company. The two of them still meet, maybe once every couple of weeks, fitting in with when Ben is busy. Martha has seen this so many times before that she grows to accept it as natural. Girlfriends squeezed out while boyfriends come first. Natural it may be; so is cancer. She doesn't have to like it.

On her twenty-first birthday, Rose and Ben get engaged. She meets Martha beforehand to tell her.

'I haven't told anyone else, Martha. I wanted you to be the first to know!'

Rose holds out her hand to show Martha her ring.

'I'm not wearing it yet, not until after the party, but I wanted you to see it.'

Martha is touched by her childlike joy; she suddenly feels very much older than Rose. Ashamed of whatever it is she is feeling, Martha hugs her friend right there, in the middle of the restaurant. She raises her glass of cheap red wine.

'To years and years of happiness, Rose. I wish both of you everything that's best.'

They are both a little emotional. Martha decides to put away her doubts. It is all decided. There is nothing she can say that won't sound wrong.

So she listens instead. Rose talks endlessly about Ben and their plans. She adores him, and Martha tries to listen generously to all the wonderful things he is.

Her friend's face is glowing, her eyes full of the future.

'Ben's very determined, and I know he'll succeed. He wants to go out on his own very soon, and I'll keep working at first. We've seen a house that will suit for the first few years. Then Ben wants to move back to Howth, if we can afford it.'

And what do you want, Martha wonders.

'And Martha, we'd really like you to be our bridesmaid.'

Rose has said this almost shyly. Martha wonders how much of her feelings Rose has picked up on. She feels instantly guilty. She makes a huge effort to be enthusiastic.

'I'd love to, Rose. I was hoping you hadn't forgotten!'

Rose relaxes at once. They talk weddings for the rest of the night.

When she gets back to the flat, Karen is still awake. Martha doesn't feel like sleeping. They talk until half-past two. Karen is great at getting things into perspective. Martha respects her judgement. By the time she sleeps, she has let go her feelings of guilt.

There is nothing more she can do for Rose. She admits to Karen that she detests Ben Holden. It is a huge relief. She thinks he is a bully of the worst kind, subtle and manipulative; she is afraid that Rose is heading for disaster. She doesn't even know how strongly she feels this until Karen encourages her to let it go, to stop feeling responsible.

'Karen Davis, you're going to make a wonderful doctor,' she says as she leans over to turn out the light.

'And your friend Rose will make a wonderful wife, by the sound of her. Let's get some sleep. We've a heavy day tomorrow. Let her go.'

And for several years, that's what Martha does.

Tuesday, 4th April; 2.30 pm.

The playground was teeming with kids. Lisa ran over towards her immediately, lifting her arms to be hugged. Rose bent down to her, holding her close, hugging her for the first time since Ben left. She'd missed her child. Brian, just about to finish sixth class, was much more cool. He sauntered over, having given five to at least three others in the playground, all faces that Rose recognised. They stood slightly apart from all the other groups, signalling their impending rise in status. But she could see that he was glad to see her.

'Right, you two, let's go.'

Rose opened the car doors for them. Normally she walked to meet them, but she was late today, and didn't want them to be kept waiting. Routine was particularly important just now.

'Did you have a good time at Jane's last night?'

Brian immediately burst into an incomprehensible explanation of one of Derek's new computer games, and Lisa tried to get a word in about Alison and Kate's new bedroom. Rose listened only for the tone, and was satisfied that they knew nothing, suspected nothing.

'What's for dinner?'

Jesus, food again. She hadn't even thought of doing any shopping. She did a quick mental calculation of the contents of the freezer. Damien had had lasagne last night; that meant there was a portion each left for these two, and a baked potato. Damien could have the small carton of left-over curry. She'd do him plenty of rice. She'd have a couple of scrambled eggs or something later.

She must put down shopping as a top priority for tomorrow morning after the kids went to school. There was no cereal, no meat, nothing for school lunches. The household show must be kept on the road.

They had dinner on a tray while Children's Television was on and Rose locked herself in the office once again. She pulled the pages out of her handbag and smoothed them.

There was one thousand pounds in the deposit account, eight hundred in the current account, and a two-hundred-and-seventy-thousand-pound overdraft on the Finehold account.

Rose looked again. Her heart stopped for a long second.

Ben had said nothing about such a large overdraft; she'd understood that the company was doing really well. Maybe this meant that it was doing really well. How would she know? She wished she knew a bit more about how the business was run.

Ben had always believed in a strict division of responsibilities. She had taken messages, provided lunches when colleagues called, picked up people at the airport, delivered them to train stations, driven them home after too many glasses of wine – all unimportant stuff really, the details that Ben shouldn't have to worry about. That and three children had kept her busy all these years. Now she began to wish that she had been less busy and more occupied.

She did some rough calculations. Up to two years ago, she had always kept household accounts, until Ben suddenly told her to stop, there was no need to, that was why he employed an accountant. So she stopped, taking money out of the bank for household expenses whenever it was necessary.

She was not extravagant; she always shopped carefully. She was grateful for her financial security; she wanted to do her bit to keep it that way. She was secretly proud of how well she managed money, but Ben waved away any talk of bargains or good value. He was politely uninterested, so she took over the children's financial education instead. She ran a strict policy of saving and spending which had its many exhausting ups and downs, particularly with Damien.

He could spend money in a way that amazed her. Jeans at Fifty Quid. (She couldn't help seeing this in capital letters – it was as much as she earned a week with overtime before she got married.) Then trainers – the sky was the limit. They had eventually compromised on her paying thirty pounds towards necessary replacements, and Damien made up the rest from his own savings. What the shortfall was, she really didn't want to know.

The mortgage was due on the twelfth. Then there was ESB, gas, Telecom, petrol, food and incidentals. She jotted down a rough figure for each. If she was very careful, she could manage for three weeks on what was in the current account. She decided to close the deposit account and open another in her own name. It said 'pay either' and she needed this as insurance. If she and Ben worked it all out, then that would be different. Right now, after twenty years, she needed something to call her own.

At least he had left them enough to get by on. He wasn't a total shit. Maybe he really did need some time on his own to work things out.

Then quite suddenly, Rose remembered. Sixteen hundred pounds. That must mean *two* tickets. Had Jane said so yesterday? If not, that's what she had heard. But she only now began to take it in, with a profound sense of shock. Another woman. Who *was* she? Rose pulled out the statements she had put away yesterday.

She began to trace the dates and places which were unfamiliar to her. She took a yellow highlighter, got a full year's statements into date order and began, methodically, to score through every entry that now screamed betrayal. There were approximately fifty transactions on the Visa that she could not recall. All were for hotels, restaurants, upmarket bars. She added it up roughly. Three thousand, two hundred and fifty pounds in one year. On a mistress. On her household account.

She grabbed the sheaf of American Express statements. Here was more than enough detail. Every single expenditure was itemised. She looked closely at dates, names.

These probably referred to clients, competitiors, whatever. She opened Ben's diary, where she herself had written down the dates of his business trips, contact persons, airport pick-up times.

She began the laborious task of matching dates and receipts. She broke off to feed the children and send them to bed early. Their humour was in inverse proportion to the good time they'd had the night before. She wasn't even mildly irritated with them, just firm and dismissive. They knew when to give up.

She went back into the office until half-past nine. John and Damien were working quietly at the kitchen table. She wondered how long it would last.

By that time she knew enough. She warned Damien to lock up and be in bed by eleven. She emptied one of Ben's most expensive leather briefcases and stuffed in all the papers she had been working on.

Then she took two of his best bottles of white wine and headed off down the road to Jane.

And so evening came, the second day.

March 1975

'There,' says Martha, handing Rose a tall glass, ice chinking against the sides. 'Something to steady the nerves.'

'Where did you get this? My father would never allow "the drink" across the threshold!'

Martha gives a huge wink, pulls up her bridesmaid's dress as far as her thigh, and points silently to her garter. Nestling among the ribbons and lace are two tiny bottles of Huzzar vodka – the kind you get on planes.

'I thought this would be the safest place,' Martha confides in a stage whisper. 'Your father thinks I'm a lovely girl. He handed over the 7-Up and ice like a lamb. I told him your throat was dry. Well, it's the truth, just not the whole truth.'

She raises her glass theatrically and Rose does likewise.

Rose remembers how long they go back. To primary school, together from Low Babies. In secondary school, thrown together once more, choosing the same subjects for Leaving Cert. Inseparable again. For Rose, Martha has been a constant; a close and satisfying friendship that has lasted even though they chose different paths after school. They had promised each other as children that they would be each other's bridesmaid. Martha is fulfilling that promise now.

'God, Martha, I'm really nervous. This is so final. I even dreamt last night that I couldn't get to the church. The car kept going round and round in circles, but there was no way in. Then suddenly we were driving along by the sea somewhere in brilliant sunshine. Everyone was on bikes, wearing shorts, and there I was in my wedding-dress. I told the driver to take me home, and then I woke up.'

'Dr Martha diagnoses a classic case of pre-wedding nerves. Knock that back and let me fix your headdress. You look absolutely gorgeous. I'd hug you except I'd crease your dress.' Martha kisses her forehead lightly and squeezes her hand. 'You'll be fine.'

Martha walks over to the bedroom window.

'No time for second thoughts, now,' she says lightly. 'The car is here.'

Rose feels peculiar. Not nervous any more, just indifferent, almost numb. She loves Ben, and hopes it will all work out. They have had no time together at all during the last six weeks. The preparations for today have taken up every bit of her time and energy. She has burst into tears more than once. The pressure has been extraordinary. And no mother to help her. Perhaps that is why she is feeling sad.

She takes a last look around the bedroom she has shared with Ellen and Grace. It looks shabby and untidy, but her heart is pulled towards the old earless teddy on the bed, her bed.

They are waiting. Everyone is waiting.

She leaves her old bedroom and walks to the top of the stairs. Her father is waiting for her below, smiling nervously. Rose bites her lip. She knows he must be thinking of her mother. When she reaches the bottom step, their faces are level. She puts both arms around his neck and hugs him close. Neither of them says anything.

She walks down the narrow garden path on her father's arm, feeling with each step that she is leaving something of herself behind.

Tuesday, 4th April; 10.00 pm.

Jane refilled Rose's glass more often than her own. Rose didn't seem to notice. She kept sipping abstractedly, leafing through bills and credit card statements with manic intensity. The moment she'd come in she'd pulled sheaves of papers out of a briefcase, and then suddenly stopped.

'God, Jane, I'm sorry. Here I am assuming you have nothing else to do – I'm really sorry, I don't know what I'm at.'

And she began stuffing the papers back in again.

'I invited you here tonight, you did not assume anything. I'm going for a corkscrew. You just pull all those papers out again.'

Jane returned with two glasses, a corkscrew, a child's copybook and a pencil.

'You fire ahead and let me know anything you need to make a note of. I'll jot it down, and you can make sense of it later.'

Rose nodded and Jane became consciously alert, listening and looking carefully, not wanting to miss anything that might be important. Rose's face was white. Shock was written all over her. She must have been through these pages before. She seemed to know them by heart. She kept repeating the same details, over and over. Jane saw that she was having a hard time accepting the obvious. Ben had a – what? lover? mistress? What was the word? And for some time now. The evidence was overwhelming.

This was not the right time to tell Rose about the night she and Jim had seen Ben and a woman together in the

Westbury Hotel. Jim had shrugged when she had pointed them out. He'd told her she had a bad mind. Maybe she did, but there was something in the way this woman had leaned towards Ben, something in the way he was listening to her that screamed sexual intimacy. She had good instincts; she was rarely wrong. This had been no business meeting. Jane kept her counsel.

'How come I haven't known? God, I must be really thick!'

Rose drained her glass angrily.

'Because you trusted him, Rose; you weren't looking for the signs, that's all. But for the moment, remember that he's the one having the affair, so why are you blaming yourself?'

'Because I feel that this is my fault.'

Jane tried to steer Rose away from the great big boulders of guilt she saw in her way. She helped her pick a cautious route between them. At the same time, she did not want to say too much.

She liked Rose. She knew that if she and Ben got back together again, she would most likely lose her as a friend. Rose would withdraw, embarrassed that she had revealed too much, defensive on her husband's return. Jane had seen it before. She wanted to help, and she wanted the friendship. She had to steer a middle course.

It was well after midnight when Rose got up to leave. At least her face was a little less white, due to the wine.

She thanked Jane, over and over. She refused to let Jane walk home with her, insisting that she was fine, the walk in the fresh air would do her good.

Nevertheless, Jane kept watch until Rose reached the corner, nearly halfway home. She turned and waved, clearly silhouetted under a streetlamp.

Jane waited until the phone gave three rings, and stopped. Satisfied, she cleared up the debris in the kitchen and went to bed.

March 1977

Dame Street is full of people. There is the excited buzz of the start of the weekend. Rose can see the build-up of traffic from her third-floor window. At least it isn't raining.

'Coming for a drink, Rose?'

June, the tireless organiser of office social life. Kindly, relentlessly friendly. She likes to take new girls under her wing and has tried to give Rose reason to be grateful to her. Rose likes neither her work nor her colleagues. She has nothing in common with them.

She, after all, is married. The discos, the parties, the pubs they all frequent, play no part in her life. Sometimes she envies them, and she does not like the feeling. She feels excluded by their Monday-morning gossip, their lunchtime confidences. After two years, she just wants to get out. She has what they all aspire to. How come they manage to make her feel so matronly, so dissatisfied? Rose is almost embarrassed in their company. Sometimes they stop talking when she enters the room.

To be honest, Ben hasn't helped.

They have been invited to several parties, to countless Friday-night sessions. Ben insists that it isn't his scene. He prefers the occasional excellent meal out to the company of strangers. He feels no need for conversation, for banter, for the raucous cleansing of pub-talk.

Rose enjoys herself on the couple of occasions when she does go along, more out of a sense of embarrassed duty than anything else. Gradually, the invitations stop coming, except for good old June. Rose feels tired this evening, and irritated by June's earnest efforts at goodwill. She also feels ashamed of herself.

'I'd love to, June,' she lies. 'But Ben's parents are taking us out for a meal. It's our second anniversary,' she confides, suddenly, to take the harm out of it. 'I've got to go straight home and change. Thanks anyway.'

June finally gives up.

'Enjoy yourself, then,' drifts back as she runs off, not wanting to be left behind by the others. Rose waits until she judges them all safely out of the building. It is ridiculous, this almost hiding. The little flutter around her heart reminds her that it might not be for too much longer. Two years, Ben has said. Two years and then they can start trying for a baby. Rose can hardly wait.

She wants to go out on her own with Ben, but his parents have been unusually persuasive. Rose wonders why. She isn't looking forward to it.

The bus fumbles along through the traffic and Rose makes it home in good time. A note from Ben shows he has been and gone. He'll be back to collect her, with his parents. Rose feels another prickle of irritation. Why couldn't he have waited for her?

He has made a sandwich, too. How can such a meticulous man create such domestic disaster? The long counter is littered with breadcrumbs, a lidless butter-dish, a knife welded to the surface with rapidly drying pâté. Milk dribbles its trail over to a coffee-mug and the biscuit barrel spills its plain contents. He's been searching for chocolate creams.

Rose tidies up, putting the delph into the sink, on top of the breakfast things which have not been washed yet. A dishwasher would be nice; then Ben's disorder wouldn't matter, would it? Maybe she'll start, quietly, to save for one.

Rose goes up to have her shower. She has two hours before Ben will come to collect her. Maybe she'll lie down for a while. Her feet are killing her.

In the bedroom, Rose takes the wet towels off the bed. Ben has had a shower. How come the towels always end up on her side? The unmade bed is now damp, uninviting. Rose runs a bath instead, and soaks luxuriously for an hour.

Warm, soothing water always repairs her humour. She never expected the everyday stuff to be so difficult. Are these just ordinary niggles, does everybody feel the same? Or does it signal some serious flaw in her marriage? Is it paranoid and unreasonable to feel so much taken for granted? Rose wishes her mother was still alive. She is beginning to feel that she has, in her mother's words, been sold a pup.

All these things Rose thinks on the evening of her second anniversary. There hasn't been a lot of fun lately. She wishes someone would tell her that these feelings of regret, sometimes intense, inescapable, are only natural. That every marriage has its period of adjustment, of transition.

She wishes Martha hadn't gone to Australia. But no, Martha would be the wrong person to ask.

Rose dries herself vigorously. She spreads some of the towels out to dry and puts the others in the linen basket. The bulging contents make her sigh. So much for the weekend. Shopping, ironing, and dinner with her in-laws.

Wednesday, 5th April; 6.00 am.

Wednesday. Day three. Maybe the world was created in seven days after all. A lot could happen in forty-eight hours.

Rose's head was muzzy. By the time she left Jane's last night she had been feeling no pain. The wine had loosened her anger at Ben. There had been a sense of cleansing; Jane was a good listener. Rose wondered how she'd managed without her as a friend for so long. God, she needed something to drink.

It was only six o'clock. She pulled back the duvet and put her feet to the floor slowly. If this was a hangover, how on earth did people function with a day's work to do. She was about to find out; she had a day's work to do herself.

There was no orange juice in the fridge. Shopping. She must go shopping. She filled a pint glass with water and hammered some ice-cubes from the tray. Nectar. She filled the glass a second time. Then she sat down to make a list.

All the old instincts of economy surfaced. She planned meals up to Sunday. She could go again on Monday while the kids were at school. Four or five days in advance was enough. She ticked off the essential items. Lots of chicken and mince. Casseroles to be made in advance. As little time as possible in the kitchen. There were too many urgent things to do.

Twenty past six. There was no way she'd get back to sleep now. She put on the kettle for a cup of coffee, and made herself a slice of toast. And there was still porridge. That would have to do them for this morning.

She opened her diary and wrote down the three things she wanted to achieve. One, shopping. Two, contact Barry Herbert, Ben's closest business colleague. He didn't believe in partners. Three, contact Jane and Jim's solicitor for advice.

In between, there were the school runs, preparing a meal, supervising homework and a bit of housework. Rose looked around her. On Monday morning this house had been immaculate, sparkling. She cleaned thoroughly, twice a week, upstairs and down. Every Friday, so that things were perfect for the weekend, and every Tuesday, once all Monday's ironing was done. Ben hated to see housework in progress; Rose felt she kept her part of the contract by being methodical and efficient, working quietly in the background.

Such housewifery now had to take a back seat. She'd clean the bathroom and the downstairs toilet, and wash the kitchen floor. Strictly minimal stuff. She needed to be free, to feel that she could keep on top of this mess.

Damien strolled into the kitchen, pyjamaed and unwashed. Rose didn't comment.

'You're up early again, Ma. Everything all right?'

His tone was too casual. Rose picked up the anxiety instantly. He was nearly eighteen, a man. He'd be out of school in a little over a year. At his age, she was starting to earn her own living.

'Sit down, Damien.' She patted the seat beside her. 'Your Dad and I are going through a bad patch at the moment. He's had to go away for a couple of weeks, right at the wrong time for both of us. When he comes back, we'll sort out what's going to happen. In the meantime, we have to be patient. This has nothing to do with you or Brian and Lisa. This is between your dad and me. We both love all of you very much.'

Rose stopped. She needed to take a deep breath. She presumed the last bit was true of Ben; she gave him the benefit of the doubt.

'Are you going to separate?'

'I honestly don't know, Damien. I'll tell you just as soon as I know what's happening.'

'You didn't want this, did you?'

'No, no I certainly hadn't ever imagined it. But perhaps it would have happened eventually, anyway. I really don't know any more, Damien.'

Rose did her best not to cry. It wasn't fair. He shouldn't have to deal with this at seventeen.

'How long is Dad gone for?'

'Two weeks, I think.'

'What can I do to help?'

'How do you mean?'

'Well, for a start, Brian and Lisa don't need to be left to school and collected by you. They're big enough. I can walk them to the gates and then get the bus on from there.'

Rose smiled to herself. She remembered suggesting this after Christmas and Damien had been horrified at the thought. His street image must have been a bit shaky so she'd dropped it. Now she enjoyed his conviction that this was his idea.

'And if you're not here in the afternoons, I'll get the two of them started on their homework.'

Rose's eyes filled at his eagerness to help, to take grown-up responsibility.

'And John says it isn't so bad.'

'What?'

'Having your parents separated.'

John next door. Bill and Suzanne. She'd never even thought how the unthinkable was becoming the commonplace all around her. Was it something in the water? Suzanne had probably felt just as she did when Bill left. And she, Rose, never knew, never took the trouble to find out.

'That would be great, Damien. I have a few appointments to arrange over the next week or so.'

'On one condition.' Damien held up his finger.

'What?'

He grinned.

'That I don't have to get washed and dressed before breakfast!'

Rose threw a tea-towel at him and went off to have her shower before she burst into tears. He was a really good kid. It was a long time since she had had such an intimate conversation with him. It amazed her how easily he seemed to adapt to the idea of a broken family. Had he seen it coming?

Under the steady stream of hot water, Rose began to remember the recent coldness between Damien and Ben. She'd forgotten about that over the last couple of days. Arguments over hair-length, earrings, schoolwork. The hostility between them had made her unhappy. Stuck in the middle, she'd tried countless times to be the peacemaker. But Ben had been unyielding. Damien had simply begun to avoid his father's presence, often leaving the room just as Ben entered.

Now, there seemed something almost smug in Damien's acceptance of his father's absence. It was as though he welcomed it, feeling justified that he had grown to detest everything his father stood for. Had he waited, hoping this might happen?

Rose began to feel really frightened of what was facing her.

Was she the only one who was Rip Van Winkle and April Fool all at once?

Well, she was awake now. Her senses were sharpened. She was going to need all her wits about her from now on.

November 1978

All Rose can do is gaze at the rectangular fishbowl at her bedside. She counts, again. Five fingers on each hand, five tiny fingernails. She can't stop looking at him. Her head feels dreamy, unsteady; she knows that if she stands up, she'll wobble. She giggles at the thought of even trying to stand. She's almost too sore to lie down.

She's had a pleasant floating sensation since the last injection. Now she can feel it beginning to wear off. She welcomes the return to reality, the ability to focus without difficulty on the little body beside her.

She wriggles into a sitting position, feeling the rubber sheet bunch and crinkle uncomfortably beneath her. A young nurse, all smiles and starch, comes into the ward.

'Are you all right, Mrs Holden?'

'I'm fine. Can you hand the baby to me?'

All Rose wants is to hold him. She is suddenly anxious that she will let him fall if she reaches from her awkward position. The nurse smiles again.

'Of course. What are you going to call him?'

Rose envies her her deftness. She is sure and swift in all her movements. The baby is picked up, his blanket fixed, his warm, soap-smelling body transferred to her arms in one easy scoop.

'Damien. We're going to call him Damien, after my husband's grandfather.'

Somehow, the nurse manages to fix the bed while she chats. Rose feels suddenly comfortable, alert.

At the same moment, Damien's eyes open. Deep, bright

blue, they look straight at her. Holding him close to her face, Rose talks to him softly. He can see her; she knows he can see her.

She changes him, feeds him, and is still holding him when Ben comes back for visiting hour.

Gradually, the room fills up. Ben's parents, Grace, Ellen. Rose is proud of herself. Ben stands as though on guard, both hands on the transparent cradle that holds the body of his tiny son.

There is laughter, gifts being passed around, Damien handed from one to the other like a parcel.

Oblivious, he sleeps through it all. Ridiculously, Rose is proud of his good behaviour, as though it reflects on her already. A good mother.

Rose is glad when they go. She is tired. She wants her husband and her son to herself.

Ben stays while she feeds Damien again; she's getting the hang of this. She watches as Ben changes his first nappy. She is completely happy.

Ben's eyes are luminous as he is leaving.

'He's great, he's just great, and so are you. I'm so proud of you both.'

Rose hardly sleeps at all that first night, but she doesn't care. Her fitful dreams are full of blue-eyed babies and happiness.

Her first thought the next morning as the babies are wheeled back into the ward is, this is the best thing I've ever done.

A new beginning. A new family.

She can't wait to go home.

Wednesday, 5th April; 8.45 am.

Brian and Lisa grumbled about the unfairness of life. Brian wanted to be left to school by car, and Lisa, Rose suspected, just wanted her. Rose promised to be there when they came home, mentally re-arranging her time.

She was outside the supermarket before it opened. She glanced at her list quickly in the car. Automatic pilot, really. She remembered how big a deal it was when she was first married, the strain of wondering what to buy, what to cook, how to vary meals. Ben had always left it up to her; he hated supermarkets.

Twenty years later. Still shopping. Was this the one enduring aspect of all human relationships? Was the buying and cooking of food the only constant? Its routine was comforting. At least it was familiar.

But there was something different today. It wasn't just that she was shopping more carefully, more economically. She was shopping from a different place. The solid ordinariness of women with buggies and prams and small children strapped into trolley-seats looked different. The well made-up women with rings and painted nails, even at nine o'clock in the morning, looked different. It began to appear a lot more fragile to Rose. She looked more closely at the faces around her. What had appeared always as a solid, respectable, middle-class wall of financial stability and gracious living now began to crack.

In Rose's imagination she saw the panic behind the well made-up faces and the bronzed, ringed hands. She smelt an air of desperation behind the mask of discreet lipstick and foundation. Surely you shouldn't need to be in a supermarket this early at that stage of your life, with all your probable children grown up. Was the supermarket a mooring-hook, somewhere to tie down to so that the days didn't drift one into the other without any distinguishing marks? Was going shopping a necessary addiction, to put shape to the day, to avoid the feeling that you had done nothing else with your life?

Rose felt a cold sweat prickle across the back of her neck. Was this what was waiting for her in ten years?

The younger women were different. Even the way they walked had purpose, showed the constraints of time. Rose could remember the speed and precision needed to deliver one child to school, another to playschool, get to the supermarket, home, unpack, back to collect the pre-school child, home, put the baby down for a sleep, get lunch, collect eldest from school, prepare evening meal, wash, bath, change, bedtime stories. She could almost read the timetable etched into the women's faces.

But she was no longer tied to such a rigid division of her time. All at once, with Ben's leaving her, she realised that her children were going, too, and that now things were all changing together. Soon, she wouldn't even be a mother in the old, needy way.

She felt sympathy for these young women, but not even a glimmer of nostalgia. She used to think that she'd have liked another baby after Lisa. She used to feel sentimental when she saw tiny faces peering out of lacy nests. Not any more. She didn't know how much of this had to do with Ben, or her, or what was happening now, but she'd had a change of heart. Or maybe it was just a sense of clarity, of finally realising even one thing that you wanted or didn't want after so many years of fuzzy thinking.

Picking items off the supermarket shelves, Rose felt a new sense of urgency about her own life. She was suddenly terrified of losing her grip on the next twenty years.

She picked up the special offer chicken pieces, calculating how many meals she'd get out of them. She now knew that the one thing she wanted was to live her own life, one finally shaped by herself. Ben or no Ben.

Pushing her way along the aisles, greeting familiar faces, Rose again wondered what was going on under the surface. Because her own world had turned around and inside out, it was difficult to believe that anyone else's was still normal.

She finished her shopping and went home. Her head was buzzing. It would be good to turn off the thoughts for an hour or so. It felt as though her mind was making up for years of inactivity, although she was never conscious of being dull or lazy.

She'd always tried to glance at the paper, at least, and the nine o'clock news was a ritual. She was aware of every controversy discussed by Gay Byrne, Joe Duffy and Pat Kenny. She had even thought of ringing Marian Finucane. She had been roused to laughter, to indignation, to sympathy. She was always well-informed.

This process going on inside her, though, had nothing to do with information. This was internal revolution, all her pillars crashing down. As she unpacked the shopping, she decided that no matter what happened in the future between her and Ben, she was going to live differently. She loved him dearly, she'd have him back tomorrow, almost without explanation. But it was not going to be the same.

Only then did she begin to cry. It took her very much by surprise. She hadn't cried in quite a few hours.

Out loud, to the kitchen walls, she said:

'What on earth am I going to do?'

November 1980

Ben gives her very little warning that Barry and Caroline are coming to dinner. Damien has the measles and she is exhausted. The normally placid two-year-old has turned into a little monster. He has measles everywhere, between his toes, in his hair, on his eyelids. His chest is infected and he has difficulty breathing. The doctor has called every day for the week, and Rose has felt really frightened. What if he goes deaf? What if his sight is affected?

The doctor has been calm, reassuring. Rose wishes Martha was still around; Australia is very far away. She feels angry at her friend for not being there. She is the only doctor Rose really trusts.

The illness takes ten days to run its course. Rose sleeps in the single bed in Damien's room, or rather, occupies it. She is amazed that the child can go for so long without sleep. Rose dozes fitfully during the day, taking to the bed whenever Damien does. She switches on the answering machine for a couple of hours each morning. Ben doesn't like the machine on during business hours; he says it creates an aura of inefficiency.

Rose doesn't tell him she is switching it on. She makes sure to be up well before he comes home for lunch. She returns all the calls and personally assures each client that Ben will contact them shortly after two o'clock. She feels a little guilty at this small deception, but she is in desperate need of rest. More and more she becomes convinced that this isn't just the aftermath of Damien's illness. This feels like the bone-crumbling weariness of early pregnancy.

Damien's recovery is now almost complete. The more he improves, the more exhausted and tearful Rose feels. Now that she doesn't have to watch him for every moment, to stand guard for twenty-four hours a day, her unnatural energy of the early days deserts her completely. All she wants is to sleep. She is looking forward to the weekend. Ben has promised to be there, to look after Damien for her. She thinks Friday night will never come.

When Ben comes home for dinner on Thursday evening, she is feeling better. She knows that most of the feeling of well-being comes from the delightful anticipation of Saturday. A day in bed, a long bath and the evening in her dressing-gown.

'You're looking a lot perkier,' Ben remarks. 'And Damien seems to be back to his old self,' he adds, putting his head into the sitting-room where Damien is surrounded by a multicoloured snowstorm of Duplo.

'Yes, I'm feeling more human. I slept well last night.'

Rose has decided not to tell Ben of her suspicions. She will wait until she is absolutely sure. She doesn't want another false alarm, another disappointment.

'Good. Another good sleep tonight and you'll be well set up. I've asked Barry and Caroline Herbert to supper on Saturday night. Nothing fancy, now, not a dinner or anything; it looks like he and I will be doing a lot of business together. I want to keep him sweet.'

Rose knows by his tone that it is pointless to argue.

She can hear his logical, sensible replies. Of course he'll take care of Damien on Saturday. She won't need to get up until evening time if that is what she wants. He'll get the shopping she needs. A simple supper. It won't take her long. They are just coming for a few drinks. They'll probably be gone by midnight.

Three hours isn't much out of a whole weekend, is it?

Rose is furious. It isn't the effort, it isn't the cooking, it isn't anything in particular. She just wants time. Time to create the sort of atmosphere, maybe, where she can tell Ben that she thinks they are going to have another baby. Time for his undivided attention. She doesn't want strangers in her home on Saturday night. Even the thought of it ruins the whole weekend. Apart from the cleaning and cooking that now have to happen before the weekend, she resents sharing Ben with other people.

'What sort of supper did you have in mind?' she asks.

Wednesday, 5th April; 11.00 am.

Rose pulled up outside Barry Herbert's office in the main street in Malahide. She'd tried phoning before she left the house, but both lines were engaged. Rose couldn't wait any longer, even long enough to dial again. She needed to do things, to know what was going on. She didn't want to be put off by anyone's secretary forcing her to make an appointment for later in the week. It had to be now; she didn't want this new sense of control to slip.

She was going to make Barry Herbert see her, even if only for a few minutes. She decided to sit in his reception area, leafing through magazines, until he found the time to see her.

It was a trick she remembered from Ben's early business days, when all his time was spent working from the office at home. Damien was four when they moved to a bigger, four-bedroomed house on the coast road. There was a large sitting-room downstairs which they converted into an office, with a smaller waiting-area off it, what had in fact been the house's original kitchen some forty years before. Rose could show clients into this little room without disturbing the privacy of their home. They were the first two rooms they had decorated shortly after moving in, and business was booming.

She remembered suited individuals sitting in that little room, determined to see Ben, or prepared to spend all day waiting. He inevitably would see them, if only to get rid of them. Their meetings rarely took longer than ten minutes, and Rose often thought that cold-calling must be the most thankless task in the world.

It was only eleven; she could afford to wait until two without even feeling pressured. Once she was there, she was achieving something. Sitting at home by the phone, waiting for something to happen to her, instead of making something happen, was not what she wanted.

The receptionist was very polite, as Rose knew she would be. She picked up *Time* and flicked through an article about Bill Clinton and the media's savaging of Hillary. She kept one eye on Barry's office door.

Barry came out to meet her almost at once. He shook hands and seemed a little flustered. Rose thought he was oddly formal. She must have got him at a bad moment.

'Come on in, Rose. Cliodhna, will you bring in – tea or coffee, Rose?'

'Coffee, please, Barry.' She was glad at the return to easy informality. He seemed to have recovered his balance.

His office was decorated in soothing tones of coral. The furniture was comfortable, discreetly expensive. Barry Herbert was doing well.

She noticed an overnight bag on the floor by the desk, its airline tag still attached. A copy of the *Financial Times* lay on the coffee-table, along with a pouch containing airline tickets. A bunch of keys lay beside a soft leather wallet, and Barry's suit jacket was thrown across the back of his chair.

'Apologies, Rose, I've just got back from the airport this minute. Sorry about the mess.'

Why did people always feel compelled to apologise for the mess caused by ordinary living? She could ask this question, she who until three days ago ran a kitchen as surgically precise as an operating theatre. Life's a mess, she wanted to say, go with the flow.

'That's OK, Barry.' She stopped herself from apologising, from saying, 'I won't keep you long' or 'I hope I'm not disturbing you, but . . .' She waited instead until he sat down and was facing her, giving her his full attention.

Cliodhna arrived with the coffee, and Rose hoped it was better than Jack Morrissey's.

'What can I do for you, Rose? Is everything OK?'

It was a formula question, not expecting a negative reply.

Rose took a sip of the hot, strong coffee. Better.

'I need some information, Barry. And no, everything is not OK. Ben walked out on me on Monday.'

Barry's face actually changed colour, from sallow to white to green. Rose found it quite interesting watching the physical changes produced by shock. His coffee cup stopped halfway to his mouth, in classic sitcom manner. He put it down carefully, looking at her over the tops of his fashionable glasses.

'He what?'

'He's left. I think it's pretty final; he says so. But I've no way of contacting him at the moment, and I'm worried about a few things. There are gaps I'd like to have filled. I don't want to compromise you in any way, Barry, but I need a little friendly assistance.'

It was as though it was someone else describing her life. She felt detached, completely separate from the person who had got up at the usual time on Monday. It was a feeling of isolation that was more than a little disturbing. Rose was appalled and delighted at her ability to sound so unconcerned, so matter-of-fact.

Didn't I do that well? I'm getting better at this.

'When did he leave?'

Rose looked at him. Wasn't his shock just a little bit over the top? What did it matter to him when Ben had left? Unless . . . he'd walked out in the middle of some business deal and left Barry high and dry? That might account for the man's peculiar colour.

'Monday. Monday morning, early,' Rose added helpfully.

Barry made a steeple out of the tips of his fingers.

'Rose, you've just solved a problem I didn't know I had until this morning, ten minutes ago.'

He picked up an envelope and extracted a single sheet of writing paper. Even upside down, Rose recognised Caroline's large, confident handwriting. She was reminded of Christmas cards.

'Unless I've got it totally wrong, your husband and my wife are right now lying on some beach together in the south of Spain.'

Something began to buzz in Rose's ears. There was a sensation of light and lightness, of images and sounds. Flashes of memory superimposed themselves, one over the other. And there was the almost physical sound of things clicking into place, like a well-oiled door-handle.

'I do believe you're right,' she said softly.

November 1980

Rose ends up cooking a full dinner. Ben is grateful when she suggests it. He is helpful, takes charge of Damien, does the shopping.

The funny thing is, Rose likes Caroline Herbert immediately. She has been prepared to hate her. She no longer feels angry with Ben, he has been so kind all day; but she still wants to hate Caroline.

She isn't at all as Rose has imagined. She is small and fine-boned, dark-haired, dressed in soft peach silk. Rose feels large and clumsy beside her, then warms to her easy manner. They sit down on the sofa and Caroline touches the photograph of Damien on the coffee-table.

'What a lovely little boy! How old is he?'

They talk children until the last feelings of strain and resentment dissipate. In spite of herself, Rose begins to enjoy the evening.

The dinner is a complete success.

She watches Ben, sipping her wine very slowly and carefully. Perhaps this night will be perfect, after all.

After dessert, Rose smiles at Ben across the table, and he surprises her by squeezing her hand, in full view of Barry and Caroline. He seems to be making a public statement of love. Caroline understands the gesture and smiles at Rose.

Bliss. Damien is sleeping peacefully, the measles crisis safely past. Ben loves her. She thinks about the new baby. She will tell him later. The atmosphere is perfect.

Caroline is saying, 'Oh, Barry, for Christ's sake, don't be so pompous!'

Rose hasn't heard Barry speak. She is shocked.

She would never challenge Ben in public like that. But Barry is taking it in good part, and even Ben is laughing. They are enjoying the joke that marriages aren't always made in heaven. They seem happy enough.

She notes that Caroline and Barry seem quite content with each other's foibles. She is glad that she and Ben ask more of one another, at least in public.

Rose is fascinated by Barry and Caroline's relationship. They are so familiar with one another. There is a blurring of the lines; it isn't clear who leads and who follows. This disturbs Rose; she likes order. She can see that Ben admires Caroline; she is the professional to her fingertips. More so than Barry. Rose is surprised to find that he is a softie.

Rose admires Caroline, too. She is briefly upset that Ben, who so definitely believes in a mother being at home with her children, seems so taken by Caroline's endless ability to organise, to delegate, to run Barry's business and their family so efficiently. But Rose is able to feel generous towards her tonight. Ben has just openly expressed his longing for another son.

Rose knows that he means child, but son is what Ben knows, what is most familiar to him, through Damien.

His cheeks are a little flushed.

'Yes,' Ben is saying, 'he's a great little fellow.'

He looks directly at Rose.

'We'd love another son. Here's hoping.'

And he raises his wine-glass to his wife. Laughing, they all toast each other.

Rose suddenly wants them both to go. She wants to rid herself of any niggling feelings of rivalry, ridiculous as they are. She wants to tell Ben about the baby.

'Would you like more coffee?'

Rose hopes that they will accept the polite signal that it is time to go. Ben offers brandy, urging them to stay a little longer. But the spell has been broken. Caroline murmurs about babysitters, and Barry pats his suit pockets, finally locating his car key.

Caroline looks at him coolly.

'Do you want me to drive?'

Barry insists that he is fine, and Caroline shrugs behind his back. Rose enjoys that.

Once they leave, Rose urges Ben to have a brandy; she even suggests leaving all the dishes and the mess until the morning. Ben is surprised; it is unlike her even to suggest it. He doesn't like a morning mess, normally. But tonight, he is in high good humour.

Ben replays the evening, as he usually does. Rose is content to sit and listen, now a little ashamed of her earlier ungraciousness, thankful that everything has gone as Ben had hoped. She waits for a suitable pause.

'Damien is so much better tonight,' she remarks.

Ben nods. 'Yeah, I went into him there after seeing Caroline and Barry out, and he's sleeping soundly. He doesn't have a temperature any more. I tucked him in.'

Rose chooses her words carefully. Ben tends to miss out on subtleties.

'Well, I'm very glad he can return to his old routine. I'm going to need to take things easy for the next couple of months.'

Ben looks at her, not understanding fully, afraid to think what he is thinking.

'Are you sure? Is everything OK?' he puts down his glass and crosses the room quickly. Rose nods happily.

'Rose, that's fantastic . . . I'm so happy.'

He puts his arms around her and rocks her to and fro, stroking her hair. She hugs him back, fiercely.

'Let's go to bed now,' she whispers, hugging him close. She still remembers that night as the highest point of her marriage.

Wednesday, 5th April; 1.00 pm.

Rose left Barry's office and walked unsteadily down the stairs, heels clattering on the polished wood. She held on to the banisters in case her knees crumpled. Hot and sticky again, she wanted to get home quickly and turn on the shower. It was becoming her refuge, the only place she could think. The children respected the bathroom as a private place; it was the one room in the house that wasn't saturated in memories. The water soothed her; she imagined that it helped her thoughts to grow, to take form.

It was a room that suited her new sense of nakedness and vulnerability. Under the healing flow of water there was no pretence, no carefully arranged clothing to hide behind. There was nothing except the covering of her skin. She could cry a lot there, too, great heaving, silent weeping that was washed away. She felt cleansed of the sense of failure that was growing within her like a weed.

She had an hour before Brian and Lisa came home for lunch. She remembered her mother's words in times of crisis – damned and blessed routine. Barry Herbert had shocked her, but not much. In a way, it was a relief finally to know for sure. Rose wondered how much her gut had known that her head had ignored. Soaping herself for the second time, she thought that it was no coincidence that Barry had been first on her list. He, poor man, was devastated. He had had no instinct to warn him. He had cried bitterly and Rose had tried to comfort him. She had never before seen anyone who so thoroughly fell to pieces.

The irony was not lost on her as she handed him tissues

from her bag, answered his phone and told Cliodhna he was not to be disturbed. She was consoling the man whose wife had run off with her husband. For the first time in three days, in fact for the first time in an awful lot longer, Rose felt a real urge to laugh. What was the phrase Jane used often – GUBU, that was it. Grotesque, unbelievable, bizarre and unprecedented. Rose was unable to be distressed for herself while she watched Barry weep. It wasn't that she didn't believe his suffering to be genuine. She knew only too well that it was. But she had, perhaps only temporarily, lost the ability to feel anything except a strong sense of the absurd. She had welcomed the sense of detachment and strength which flooded her as she walked over towards the window, giving Barry time to absorb what had just happened to him.

Outside, people hurried along with shopping bags, calling to each other, dodging traffic, all rushing around on impossibly urgent business. Rose wondered what the point of it all was.

Barry lifted the phone and spoke sharply into it. Rose didn't catch what he said, but the tone was enough. She turned towards him to see his face completely transformed by anger. She wondered at the strength of his feeling. Maybe anger would come for her later. For the moment she was too intent on survival, tooth and claw.

Barry said many angry things against Caroline. Rose was surprised. She blamed Caroline of course, but Ben was her husband, after all. She felt that Barry was being very disloyal. But if he blamed Caroline and she blamed Caroline, then where was Ben's part in all this? Of all the stories she had ever heard of broken marriages, affairs and trial separations, Rose reflected that all parties involved referred in the most vindictive terms to the woman.

Men were regarded as the passive victims of predatory females. *I blame her.* This was the phrase Rose had heard over and over again, and in the past she had agreed in her heart. Now she didn't know. It couldn't be that Ben was just a passive vessel waiting to be filled to the brim with dangerous sexuality, could it? She couldn't shake the vision of Caroline in soft peach silk, all those years ago. Not anyone's idea of the average scarlet woman.

She let Barry's anger run its course. He made as though to apologise, but a brief movement of her hand stopped him.

'Please don't, Barry. I'm sorry for both of us, that's all I can say.'

He nodded, his colour still high, shirt crumpled, tie askew. In fact, at that moment, she was a lot sorrier for him.

'Are you OK? I mean have you enough . . . for the kids . . . ?'

He trailed off, embarrassed that he had made such a potentially insulting suggestion. Rose saw mortification written all over his face, and wondered how he ever did any business. Maybe there were enough people out there who valued his old-fashioned honesty. She hoped so; Barry was in for some rough times ahead.

'I'm fine, Barry, but I'd like to keep in touch.'

He nodded eagerly.

'Yes, yes, please . . . do. Maybe we'll be able to help each other out. Let's do that.'

Barry kissed Rose on the cheek as she left. She wondered how long it would be before Barry began to see her as a too painful reminder of what had happened, perhaps to blame her as well for the awfulness of Caroline's desertion of him and their family. Their family! God, she'd never even thought of their kids. She didn't envy Barry his job, telling them. She had the same job to do, maybe soon, with Brian and Lisa; but it was one step at a time.

Softly, softly. Sufficient unto the day.

Right now, it was home and shower.

Once again, Rose applied the face that helped her to meet the world. Brian and Lisa would be home in half an hour.

She'd have their lunch ready for them when they came in. Maybe it was time to test their emotional temperature. To tell or not to tell. Tell what? That their Dad was having a fling for himself in the south of Spain, enjoying sun, sea, sand and sangria? Not to mention. Or that they all might not be living together any more? She herself didn't know what the truth was.

If Ben came back . . . Rose suddenly straightened up from where she'd been pulling a saucepan out of the press under the sink. To hell with what Ben might or might not want. What about her? She opened a can of tomato soup, the kids' favourite. She rarely let them eat it; she made her own. They usually ate it without comment, like polite but unimpressed guests. So today, lunch was courtesy of Mr Campbell; that and toast and cheese would fill the gap until dinner.

She had trouble holding on to her train of thought. Did she really need to wait and find out what Ben intended to do before she made any choices for herself? Surely not. The old routine was gone, shattered in less than three days. Three incredibly slow and painful days. But three days in which her mind and self were functioning in a way she could not remember ever knowing before. She stirred the dark red thick mixture and thought about killing.

She knew that husbands and wives everywhere frequently used blunt and sharpened instruments on each other. One woman had whispered at a recent coffee-morning of how she'd lunged at her husband with a pair of scissors. She had broken the skin on his chest and the dark, sticky trickle had frightened them both into reconciliation.

'They weren't my sharp ones; the dressmaking ones were downstairs,' she'd said.

'You mean they weren't sharp enough!' interjected a woman Rose vaguely knew.

Rose had been startled by the gust of raucous laughter which swept the kitchen. Other tales followed. Stiletto heels, shoulder bags, ashtrays all used as weapons of marital warfare. The surprising thing was, Rose had thought, that more serious injuries had not been inflicted. Their laughter had been infectious. Jane had wiped the tears from her eyes with the teacloth, and Rose had laughed more at her than anything else. She had been shocked at their careless violence; but after the laughter had subsided there was a palpable feeling of release in the air. Rose couldn't put her finger on it; it was like the feeling she had had as a child coming out of confession. She hadn't thought of that morning again until now; it had made her uncomfortable. Although she had laughed along with the others, her laughter had been cautious, polite, a little shocked.

She hadn't ever thought about family violence before that, not as it related to her. It was an Issue, a Social Problem that got discussed on the airwaves. It was one of those things that had always made her shake her head in disbelief. She used to feel so grateful that none of these awful things ever visited her family. She would protect them, of course, if it ever came to it, but it never would. Such things always made her feel especially tender towards Ben.

She remembered going home after that coffee-morning and preparing a really special meal for all of them for that evening. She'd felt grateful. Life was good.

Now as she stirred the bubbling soup she was reminded of the boiling eggs on the morning that Ben had left. If he came back, would she feel angry enough to stab him with the nail scissors, to stamp on his bare foot with her stiletto heels? Maybe these things weren't so clear-cut after all.

She poured out the steaming soup into bowls as she heard Brian and Lisa argue their way up the drive.

After lunch, Rose looked around her, planning the corners that could be cut in the housework. She sent Brian and Lisa to do their homework in separate rooms. She was suddenly tired of their bickering. She was aware that they were watching her. She didn't want to deal with that, yet.

Giving the pictures a cursory dust-over, she struggled suddenly against an overwhelming exhaustion, wave after wave of fatigue. Without even thinking of the children she made her way blindly towards her bedroom. Black, shifting pinpoints of light and darkness danced in front of her eyes. She realised quite clearly that she was going to faint.

The weather is perfect for a funeral. Heavy grey clouds hang over Balgriffin cemetery; fine, wet rain blesses the mourners. Rose holds Damien's hand tightly; she can no longer see the younger children. Damien looks very adult in one of Ben's suits. Rose is dressed in black. It has always suited her.

Somewhere a voice drones on about Ben's generous contribution to his community. Rose feels that she is looking down on herself from some point high above her head. Everything is clear, too clear. There is a brittle quality to the scene below her as if it will shatter into tiny pieces at any moment.

She feels the panic gathering in her chest; she fights against the suffocating tightness which is coiling its way downwards into her stomach. What will she do when it snakes its way down to her feet? Will she be able to stand? Or will she slide muddily into Ben's grave, dragging Damien with her?

Damien, who looks so grown-up, so kind, so much like Ben used to look before the greyness came. Rose struggles to remain upright, but she is sliding, sliding away from everyone. She cannot grasp any of the hands that are reaching out to her. Fingertips brush tantalisingly against her slick black gloves. What a long fall this is, she thinks.

With one of those sickening jumps that often happened just as she was about to slide into sleep, Rose woke.

The curtains were pulled, the clock showed six-thirty. Rose lay there for a moment, wondering what had happened. It took a while for the horror of the dream to subside. Her heart was pounding and her limbs felt leaden. She could not remember making it to the bed, but she was covered with the duvet and her shoes were off. She must have got there safely before she fainted. Rose turned into the pillows and allowed the tears to flow silently, dissolving the steel band across her chest and the back of her neck. This time, she felt better when she had finished. She allowed herself to feel optimistic as another rush of energy took the place of her inertia.

Go with it. This is obviously how it is going to be. I have made it through since Monday, I am doing OK.

Rose pushed the dream away; that was one to be saved for Jane and another bottle of wine. She brushed her hair, not even bothering to repair her face, and went into the kitchen to meet her children.

Lisa's eyes were red. She was poking miserably at sausages and beans; chip bags from the local takeaway littered the table. There was a dangerous silence in the room. Lisa's eyes sliced through her; Damien was grim-faced; Brian was stuck into a computer magazine. Rose sized up the situation in a couple of seconds. Damien had kept Lisa from disturbing her. Rose felt a rush of bitterness that the three of them were being forced to grow up so quickly. By the time she reached the table, she knew how to handle it.

'Well, I'm impressed! I really needed that snooze — you're all great for not disturbing me. I feel like a new woman.'

Rose bent down and gave Lisa a hug, ignoring the child's resistance.

'Come on, Brian, put the magazine away until after dinner. No reading at the table.'

She smoothed the hair at the top of his head; it was permanently spiky.

'Did you keep any goodies for me?'

She passed behind Damien's chair and went to fill the kettle. On her way, she rested her hands lightly on his shoulders and squeezed gently. To her surprise, he reached up and held her hand briefly.

'Well, did you? I'm starving! Lisa, let me heat that up for you. It can't be nice cold.'

She took Lisa's plate and put it into the microwave.

'I'll go down and get you chips, Ma. I'll go on my bike so I'll only be a minute.'

Brian grabbed a handful of coins from the middle of the table, the back door slammed and he was gone. Rose hated chips, but right now, there was nothing she'd be more delighted to eat.

Lisa looked at her hopefully; Rose was careful to keep her face neutral.

'Now, who's going to help me water and feed all the plants after dinner? They're looking a bit sorry for themselves.'

It was Lisa's favourite job. She nodded eagerly, mouth full of chips and ketchup, eyes beginning to brighten. Rose mentally arranged the rest of the night. Plants, a cuddle and a long bedtime story for Lisa; a careful look at Brian's school computer project, perhaps a later bedtime so that she could reassure him that everything was OK. And then Damien.

The plants weren't the only things that needed tending around here. She could do with some of it herself.

And finally evening came; the third day.

February 1981

Rose is suddenly wide awake. Her heart is thumping. She can feel the solid warm mass of Ben's body beside her. Something is not right.

A low ache is beginning. It spreads relentlessly downward, widening, gripping her back and making her gasp with the savageness of its assault.

'Oh God no please no don't let it happen now, please . . .'

Ben jumps into wakefulness. She has gripped his arm tightly, sharing the pain.

'Rose, what is it? What's wrong? Quick, tell me.'

He switches on the light and turns to look into Rose's face.

The white mask of anguish frightens him. Two deep brown eyes, everything else paper-white, blue-veined.

'Rose, talk to me. Háve you pain?'

Rose nods, whimpering over and over to a God she can no longer believe in. A cruel, heartless God who can do this to her and her baby. It is too soon. It is much too soon.

The pain reaches her knees. She closes her eyes, deciding to sleep until it all goes away. Strangely, she can still see Ben. She is looking down on him from a position above herself. The pain is somewhere distant from her now, no longer located inside her body. Has Ben taken it away?

Thoughts run into each other. Sensible thoughts about tomorrow's dinner and Damien's swimming lesson. Funny thoughts about floating and her mother. Somewhere in all of this, it strikes her that she is going to die.

The thought doesn't frighten her. But she has something to say to Ben. She must make him listen.

Ben is not listening to his silent wife. He pulls back the duvet, ready to lift her.

Rose hears him cry out.

'Jesus Christ Almighty!'

All the blood is keeping her warm. She will be happy sleeping like this; it is good.

But they aren't letting her sleep. Strong hands, lots of hands, lifting her onto a cold hard surface. She doesn't want to go. She cries out to them to leave her, but it is only a sigh.

They are carrying her somewhere. Her hands are cold.

Ben is speaking to her; someone is rubbing her hands. Just as his voice is reaching her, another sensation begins to grow and grow at the base of her throat.

Is this how the baby is going to be born? Is her little child no more than a scream? Rose opens her eyes in panic. Ben is sitting beside her, holding her hand, rocking wildly from side to side.

Why is she sailing? She suddenly recognises the feeling pushing up, up, taking over. Rose clutches wildly at Ben.

She wonders why he is crying.

Then she vomits, again and again, weeping, bleeding, losing herself, being drained away through every pore.

Exhausted, she lies back. She is suddenly aware of a high-pitched whine, just like Damien's favourite toy makes. His bee-baw car.

Rose's eyes snap open as she remembers something important. But it keeps slipping away from her.

Ben is smoothing her hair from her forehead; there is a look of tenderness on his face. Rose knows that all is lost.

'We're nearly there, love, nearly there. Hang on just a few more minutes.'

Radio crackling in the background. Someone behind her answering:

'Two minutes.'

She closes her eyes again. She does not want to see Ben's face. Does not want to know what she sees there.

They are wheeling her somewhere. She must have dozed off.

Someone fumbles painfully at the crook of her arm. A young man in a white coat, stethoscope around his neck.

'You're doing fine, Rose. Sorry for the poking around. Your vein is just a little difficult to locate.'

He smiles at her, talking, soothing.

Someone else is gently unwrapping her, pulling away layer after layer of what feels like towels, blankets.

Her ears sharpen. She hears someone across the room. She hears 'foetal heartbeat'. There is sudden activity all around her.

'I've lost the baby, haven't I? Is the baby dead?'

The nurse places her hand on Rose's forehead.

'The heartbeat is a little slow.'

'What does that mean? Please, please tell me. Please find out.'

The doctor is back beside her. He puts his hand on her arm.

'I'm sorry, Rose. We can't get a heartbeat. You've lost a lot of blood. It would be difficult for the baby to survive.'

Rose begins to shake all over, uncontrollably. A nurse appears at her left side, face full of kindness.

'Let me put these blankets around you. You're cold.'

'Where's my husband?'

'He's just outside. He'll be with you in a tic, just as soon as Dr Harrington has finished. We have to give you some more blood, Rose. You've lost quite a bit, but I can see your colour coming back already.'

The nurse is massaging her left hand. Kindness, always kindness.

Only six weeks to go. What a cruel God.

'We'll give you something to help the pain, Rose. Your labour is starting.'

Rose looks at him in horror.

'Can't you just take it away? Do I have to do it all for nothing?'

Then she begins to feel drowsy again. A warm sensation creeps up her right arm.

Blessed blackness.

Thursday, 6th April; 6.30 am.

Thursday morning was beautiful. Rose woke after a very thin sleep, but was instantly alert. Half-six. She got up immediately. She was already learning that lying in bed in the mornings was not good for her. If she didn't get up immediately, waves of depression washed over her. She hadn't time to be anxious. She needed to be up and doing.

She knew she had a call to make to the solicitor. She didn't want to. It seemed a very final sort of thing to do. Logically, it was right to make sure she was protected, to find out what her options were if Ben didn't come back. But her heart found it hard to operate at that level. She kept putting it off.

She was going to spend the morning cooking. All meals for the rest of the week were going to be in the freezer by lunchtime. She needed to feel in control of that part of her life. And Jane had invited her for lunch, so she had something to look forward to.

Last night had been good, too. Lisa had gone to bed a much happier little girl. Rose had said nothing to her about Ben; for the moment, softly, softly.

Brian had asked when his Dad was coming home. Rose said honestly that she didn't know, but that she thought it would be on the seventeenth. He seemed satisfied with that. He explained his computer project to her in great detail, and she pretended not to notice how late it was. The look of triumph on his face when she pretended to realise that it was half-ten was enough to satisfy her that he, too, was OK for now.

Damien sat up with her until two o'clock. From midnight on, she battled against the urge to open another bottle of wine. She had never been a drinker before, now she looked forward to a couple of glasses each night. It helped to ease her into the darkness. It crossed her mind that this was probably the ideal way to develop a problem. To hell with it – she'd deal with that one later on.

Her mother's favourite phrase kept repeating itself to her. Sufficient unto the day is the evil thereof. And she had had more than sufficient. After a battle lasting almost an hour, when it became obvious that Damien was not going to go to bed just yet, she gave in. Damien was wound up. She had never known him so talkative. This time, when she got the bottle and the corkscrew, she also got two glasses.

She could see that he was pleased. But warning bells were going off in her head. She wanted to be honest with him.

'Damien, I don't want you to feel you've got to take your dad's place while he's gone.'

Gone seemed to her to be the most neutral, the safest word to use. He shrugged.

'I don't,' he said. 'But I'm old enough to know that something is going on. And there are things I can do to help.'

Rose had the uneasy feeling again that Damien was glad that Ben was gone. It made her sad.

'I don't want you to shield me, or to keep the kids out of my way. I am grateful for this afternoon, because I didn't so much sleep as pass out. But things are going on in your own life, and you've got to go with them.'

He suddenly grinned.

'Does that mean I can go to the disco on Friday?'

'Yes, it means you can go to the disco on Friday; I'll even pay for you to go to the disco on Friday!'

They had laughed and chatted then in a warm, relaxed way and Rose realised that there would be no turning back. Whatever happened, she had another adult in the house, and she wasn't quite sure how much she liked that.

She shook her head when he put out his glass for a refill, and they argued good-naturedly for a bit. Sighing and shaking her head in pretend despair, she covered the end of his glass with wine, just.

At two o'clock, all the day's weariness seemed to hit her at once. She pushed the cork back into the bottle and told Damien to go to bed. She put the bottle into the press in the sitting-room and, as an afterthought, locked it and put the key into her dressing-gown pocket. No point in tempting fate.

This morning, she felt remarkably refreshed after so little sleep. She was also another two pounds lighter. In the shower, she actually chuckled as she thought about what to tell Jane at lunch about her discovery. A foolproof way to lose weight. Pay someone to have an affair with your husband.

Guaranteed to lose a stone in a fortnight. Your husband or your money back.

Thursday, 6th April; 12.00 noon.

Rose was just putting the finishing touches to the quiche when the phone rang. She wiped her hands quickly and lifted the receiver. There was the tinniness of a long-distance call even before she said, 'Hello?'

Her stomach sank and her heart began to beat faster. Her mouth felt dry; it was difficult to form the word.

'Hello?' she said again.

'Rose?' A woman's voice.

Caroline? Had Ben had an accident? Was he dead? Rose began to feel afraid.

'Yes, this is Rose.'

She gripped the telephone cable, holding on for dear life.

'Rose, it's Martha.'

She almost cried with relief and disappointment.

'Martha! Where are you?'

'In Sydney, you great eejit. Where else!'

The delay was annoying. They both started to speak at the same time, and their voices collided on the line.

'You go first!' Rose cried.

'I'm coming home for six weeks. Don't book any summer holidays for July! I'm dying to see you!'

Almost twenty years. Only one visit home, ten years ago, when her father died. An only child, Martha always felt she had no family once her father was gone. Contact had been very close for the first few years; then, with little in common to feed it, their letters had tailed off. And now she was almost here, just when Rose needed her most.

She couldn't tell her now, not on the phone. She'd write. That was her treat to herself for tonight. She'd write to Martha. She'd arrange it all on the blue airmail pages and see what it added up to. It would help her make sense of everything.

Perspective. That was always a great word of Martha's. She'd get some perspective.

'That's wonderful! It'll be great to see you! Are you still at the same address?'

Martha's voice wavered. Rose couldn't catch it.

'Are you still at the same hospital?'

Rose was shouting now. She was desperate to hold onto the contact.

'I'll write to you at the hospital, OK?'

'That's fine! I can hear you perfectly, but you're obviously having problems hearing me. The hospital will do fine. Department of Paediatrics. Do it soon!'

'Tonight, I'll write tonight, I promise!'

The rest was indecipherable. Rose put the phone down and sobbed.

Her wedding day. Martha as bridesmaid. The vodka and 7-Up. Rose cried and cried until she was empty.

Then she sat down listlessly in the sitting-room until it was time to go to Jane's.

Thursday, 6th April; 1.00 pm.

Jane pulled a face as soon as she opened the front door. She gestured towards the kitchen, and raised her eyes to heaven. Rose guessed that someone had dropped in uninvited. She shook her head to Jane that it didn't matter. They said hello, loudly and cheerfully. Jane led the way into an unusually tidy kitchen.

'Rose, this is Colette, my sister-in-law. Colette, meet my pal, Rose.'

Rose was pleased. First Martha, now Jane introducing her as her friend. Rose could feel herself working up towards something like feeling happy.

'Pleased to meet you, Colette.'

Rose shook hands. She handed the quiche to Jane who whooped with delight.

'You little pet! Mmm – it's still warm; hot off the presses!'

Rose watched as Colette showed more than polite interest. Jane egged her on.

'Look at this, Colette – bet you'd give your right arm for a few of these!'

'It looks delicious. Come on, don't keep me in suspense.'

Rose sat down as Jane cut three generous portions and put the glass bowl full of salad onto the kitchen table. Colette helped herself. Rose couldn't decide whether the woman was very hungry or just very rude.

'Perfect.'

She spoke bluntly to Rose.

'Have you ever thought of doing this for money?'

Rose looked from her to Jane and back again.

'No,' she said finally. 'No, I haven't.'

But wheels had begun to buzz inside her head. She knew that Colette's was no idle enquiry.

'Colette runs a small restaurant in Greystones with her partner. You arrived just as she was telling me about problems with her suppliers.'

Jane's face gave nothing away.

Rose waited for Colette to continue.

'I'm on the lookout for someone to supply me with quiches, homemade brown bread, scones, that sort of thing. Do you think you'd like to make me samples of a few things? Then if we're both happy to go ahead, I'd give you a weekly order. Do you think you might be interested?'

'Yes, I would. I'd be very interested. When would you like me to deliver?'

This was something that Rose, suddenly, badly, wanted to do. She need consult nobody; for the moment, there was no one else and their plans to fit in with. It would keep her busy, and maybe there would be more work where this came from.

'How about tomorrow morning?'

Colette gave her one of the restaurant's cards. Rose read it quickly. La Bonne Bouche, Greystones, Co. Wicklow. A bit of a drive. She'd have to plan her day very tightly. She could see that six o'clock was about to become her daily rising time. She was filled with a sense of purpose. Such a small thing to do; her excitement was out of proportion.

She smiled at Jane with real gratitude. She began to eat her lunch in a new, critical frame of mind, already adjusting ingredients and costing each item. God alone knew, it was something she was good at; she'd served a long enough apprenticeship.

She left to be home when Brian and Lisa got in from

school. Colette and Jane were still chatting; she'd catch up with Jane later. Right now, she had things to do.

When she got home, there was a strange car in the driveway. Rose approached the door cautiously. It was Lisa, white-faced. Her teacher got out and greeted Rose apologetically.

'I'm very sorry, Mrs Holden. We did ring about an hour ago, but there was no answer. Lisa insisted you'd be home soon, and nothing else would do but to come and wait for you.'

Ann Walsh moved closer to Rose and lowered her voice.

'She has been sick, but she's also worrying about something. She was so anxious to come home that we felt it was best to sit here and wait for you.'

'Thank you, thank you very much. Did she say what she was worried about?'

Ann hesitated for a moment.

'She seemed concerned that you were ill. She was frightened that you didn't answer the door, especially as your car was here. I told her you'd probably gone for a walk, it was such a beautiful day. But she seems uneasy.'

'Thanks,' said Rose again. 'I know what's wrong. I'll look after her.'

She opened the passenger door of the car and put her arms out to Lisa.

'Come on, sweetheart. Let's make you better.'

Lisa dissolved. She clung to Rose and sobbed. Rose nodded to Ann that everything was OK and she half-hugged, half-carried Lisa to the front door. She brought her straight to her bedroom, and they lay down together on the double bed. Rose pulled the duvet over both of them, and cradled her little girl until the sobbing eased.

Now it was time to tell.

Thursday, 6th April; 3.55 pm.

Rose closed the bedroom door very quietly. Lisa was asleep, finally. She must have slept herself, it was nearly four o'clock.

She had a stab of panic until she realised. Thursday; Brian's basketball practice. She pushed the kitchen door to and filled the kettle. Both boys would be home within half an hour. She had to find a way of telling Brian, without it appearing that she had been lying the night before.

Lisa had overheard John and Damien talking on the way to school. So lately kids themselves, they had forgotten that children hear everything, particularly what they're not supposed to hear.

John had asked Damien was his dad coming back.

Rose could see how he would have answered. A shrug; 'Don't think so; haven't heard a word.' Lisa had put that together with what she called the 'unfriendly feeling' in the house, and all last night's good work had been for nothing. She was scared. Sometime during the morning she became convinced that Rose would go away too, and she had to come home and stop her.

Rose did her best to explain.

'Sometimes grown-ups make a bit of a mess of things, and it's better that they live apart for a while. But I'm not going anywhere, Lisa; wherever you are, that's where I'll be. I promise I'm not going anywhere.'

'Who's it better for? The grown-ups?'

Out of the mouths of babes.

'Well, yes, but for children too. It's not good to grow

up with people who aren't getting along together; it makes you unhappy.'

'Were you and Daddy not getting along?'

Rose found it difficult to answer.

'No, sweetheart, we weren't. But whatever happens, we'll both make sure that all of you are together and looked after and as happy as we can help you to be.'

'Can I have hot chocolate?'

Rose kissed her.

'You most certainly can. In fact, we both will, and I'll bring it back to bed.'

But before Rose had left the room, Lisa was asleep.

Rose was thankful for children's ability to switch off when they had enough information; she had no doubt that the questions would be asked again and again. She would keep giving the same answers, plain and simple, until finally the questions became a matter of form. No longer looking for information, simply wanting the same reassuring words to be repeated like a mantra.

Rose made herself a cup of instant coffee. She was worried about Brian's apparent lack of concern, his retreat into the safety of computer world. She'd have to tell him more or less what she'd told Lisa. He was more difficult to read. It would be hard to know that he felt reassured.

And she'd have to warn Damien to watch what he said in front of them. Jesus, this was all very complicated. Rose dragged her hands through her hair, trying to ease the tension in her forehead. All this chaos and none of them knew about the other woman!

She was deeply grateful to Martha for her phone call. She desperately needed a few hours of absolute solitude; that letter was rapidly becoming a bright light in her darkness.

Early night for everyone, and tomorrow she could . . . Christ! The quiches! She forced herself to slow down.

'I am not going to mess this up.'

She said this aloud as she threw her coffee dregs down the sink. She was going to do exactly as she'd planned; Lisa could have the day off school and help her. The journey to Greystones and back would be an opportunity to chat. They could even have their lunch together in Colette's restaurant.

Thank God tomorrow was Friday. Two full days to gather her forces, and then it would be a week. Seven days without Ben. The end of the first week. Benless.

Brian and Damien arrived home together, starving. Rose put the oven on and turned the flame on low under the vegetables.

And so evening came, the fourth day.

February 1981

It is very bright when Rose wakes. Ben leans over her. He takes her hand in both of his.

'Welcome back.' He kisses both her cheeks. 'I'm sorry love, I'm so sorry.'

But she'd known, really. Known the moment she woke up that awful night, hundreds of years ago.

'What day is it?' she asks suddenly.

'Thursday.'

'Then when did it happen?'

He strokes her hair.

'Last night, love. Well, really this morning, at two am.'

'Tell me what happened. I can't remember.'

Gently, sadly, Ben fills in all the missing pieces.

'Where is he? Where have they taken him?'

Ben wipes his eyes with the back of his hand.

'I don't know. The doctor will be around shortly.'

Rose doesn't care. She begins to cry. Bit by bit she fits together the details of the worst night of her life.

Grief gathers and spills, gathers and spills, over and over.

Rose will spend the rest of her life crying.

Friday, 7th April; 5.50 am.

On Friday it rained. Rose hated driving in the rain. When she woke and saw the heavy greyness she felt immediately cantankerous. In the shower at ten to six, she reflected that it was the first normal emotion she had felt all week. Everything else had been extremes; despair and euphoria, hope and responsibility, fear and more fear. It was actually nice to feel something as normal as bad-tempered; maybe this was a good sign. Maybe the world was shifting back, slightly, towards where it had been less than a week ago. Maybe this was the new normal.

The letter to Martha had done her good. When she had finished pouring out all the details of the past four days, she had covered thirteen sheets of thin paper. She had written small, neatly, as though saving paper was saving her own personal rainforest. She felt the need to be careful with everything, sparing of everything, to ward off future need. Her words seemed to spill out without form, but they created the fullest picture yet of the teeming monsters within her head. Once they were on paper, they were born, released from her. She spared herself nothing, from her wedding-day to her babies, to her dead baby, to her bruised and battered love for Ben. She wrote to Martha of all the contradictions she hadn't even known she felt.

She wanted him home; she wanted to kill him; she wanted him home to get a chance to kill him; she needed him to put her world back on centre again.

When she'd finished, she did a balance sheet. Writing to Martha made her conscious that she was forty-two. All that week she'd been accosted by people who'd achieved something by the time they were forty-two. Not necessarily people she knew personally. Just people. She'd felt a sense of panic when she saw people's ages under their photographs in the paper, if they were anywhere close to her own. The thought kept rising, like a monster from the deep, that it was too late for her. She had achieved nothing; her time was gone; she was now the older generation. Nothing separated her from octogenarians except the quantity of years. Her kids saw everybody of her age or older as simply – old. There was no distinction. And Martha, Senior Registrar in Paediatrics.

All she had was a couple of smoked salmon quiches. Which reminded her, Brian wouldn't eat his last night. He'd been irritable after his basketball practice, and Rose urged him to eat, seeing the child's exhausted face. He had blown up, shouting angrily at her and slamming the kitchen door on his way out.

'Does he know?' Rose asked Damien.

'He asked me was there something going on; I said I didn't know. Then he called me a liar. He said he'd heard us talking the night before last. I said nothing. He was getting really angry, but I didn't have time to warn you. I'm sorry.'

Damien's eyes filled with tears. Rose tried to touch him, but he moved away abruptly. She let him go.

'It's not your fault, Damien. There's no perfect way or time to tell. I've had to tell Lisa today, so it's time for Brian, too. Don't worry about it; this had to happen.'

Rose felt quite calm, filled with a sense of the inevitable.

Brian was much quieter than Lisa had been. She told him the same things, used the same formula. He sat away from her, rigid. She was careful not to move into his space. He sat on his bed, she took the little wicker chair by the window.

When she'd finished, Brian asked stonily, 'Can I watch television now?'

She felt cut to the quick. Her child's white face sliced like a scalpel at her heart. She knew how much he looked up to Ben, how he adored him. Rose felt tears begin to threaten. She didn't know which was worse: Damien gloating over his father's bad behaviour, or Brian's stony anger at herself. She kept her voice steady.

'Yes. I'll keep your dinner in case you want it later. I'll be in the kitchen if you need me.'

Rose knew that he needed time to absorb what she had told him. Back in the kitchen, there was a heavy silence. Damien's food was untouched; she had no appetite. Lisa was still asleep and Brian was unlikely to want any of her food.

The absurd image of an ice-skating championship swirled before her eyes. She imagined judges with their cards, awarding marks for performance. In this arena, her prize quiche had just fallen flat on its arse. She was beginning to dread the very word 'quiche'. This morning, she had to list, and buy, and make three of the godforsaken things, and drive to Greystones in the pissing rain and drive back again.

She took several deep breaths. Softly, softly, catchee monkey. Things were too brittle around here to have the luxury of being grumpy.

Brian was up and dressed when she came out of the bathroom. He was not an early riser. He had gone to bed, silent, the night before. She greeted him quietly, no false brightness, no hugs, no Mammy stuff. They circled each other for a while, leaving huge distances between them as they got their own breakfasts. He was careful not to come near her; she was careful not to touch him.

They sat. He spooned his porridge around his bowl, mixing in the sticky pool of honey. She watched as his small face literally caved in and he began to cry. Thankgod,

thankgod, thankgod; the word circled her mind and she waited. She felt her own eyes fill as her child raised his huge-eyed grief towards her, offering her his willingness to be comforted. She rocked him and held him and he did not resist. She whispered what comfort she could give.

Once she sensed that he had had enough, she wiped his face, smiling at him, making him smile back.

'Tell you what, I'm keeping Lisa at home today. I've got a few things to do later on. How would you feel about a day off?'

He brightened considerably.

'You mean it?'

'What the hell. I think we could all do with a day together. Wouldn't mind a bit of help, though.'

He was eager now.

'Sure, whatever you want. Can I play the computer first?'

She nodded.

'But finish your breakfast, there's a good lad. You OK?'

'Yeah. It's cool.'

The ultimate accolade. Cool. OK for now. Sufficient unto the day.

She told Damien, but offered him no such choice. She waited for the inevitable cry of it's not fair. But it didn't come.

'Nah, it's all right. John's playing today against Joseph's, and I'm going along to support. Is it still all right about the disco?'

Rose felt as though she'd spent the last twenty-four hours in high-level UN negotiations.

'Yes, it's fine, but half-past twelve's the limit.'

One look at her face told him to quit while he was ahead.

'Right,' he said and buttered his fourth slice of toast.

February 1981

If anyone else tells Rose she has an angel in heaven she will thump them. She does not want anything as insubstantial as that. She wants a screaming, flailing, sleepy, hungry, wide-awake, three o'clock in the morning *baby*. What possible use is an angel to her. She will scream if anyone else tells her to have another, as though babies, *people*, are replaceable.

There is a tremendous silence when she comes home.

Her father is really most unwell and cannot see her, he says. Grace keeps a careful distance. It is what Rose would have expected, if she had ever thought about it. Nevertheless, it disappoints and angers her.

Ellen is the only one to say simply to Rose: 'I'm sorry.'

Ben's parents are formal with her, more guarded than normal. Rose thinks she sees something once or twice in her mother-in-law's face that gives her hope, but they are never left alone together.

For the first few days, Rose wonders if she is going mad. Has she given birth to a child at all? Why do they want her to believe she has made a monster?

She is glad she fought them, glad she held on to Michael for as long as they let her.

Holding his cold little body close to her was not monstrous at all. She warmed both of them with a sweet feeling of peace, holding him in her arms. She stays angry and abusive to the nurses until they leave her alone.

Then, when she is ready, she lets him go.

She wishes she had a photograph, a lock of hair, anything

to prove that he has been. They are all in such a hurry to forget him. Even Ben wills himself to forget.

She will not forget him. She will not forget herself.

She is Rose. She will not let this destroy her.

But day by day, the distance grows between what Ben wants from her and what she is becoming.

And so, very soon, she starts to walk.

Friday, 7th April; 8.50 am.

Once again, Rose was outside the supermarket before it opened. She had a strict list of ingredients; this was business. Home was OK until Monday. That would be another shopping trip. This one was separate.

In one of Lisa's discarded copies, she had ruled columns to note the time the shopping took, the cost of the ingredients, the preparation and cooking time, travel time and petrol. If it worked out, she'd do proper accounts later.

When the doors opened, she felt nervous. There was a completely different feel to this sort of shopping — shopping for a job that paid money. She took her time, weighing, choosing, calculating. She had decided to make three different quiches, ham and courgette, smoked salmon and cream, and vegetarian. Her breads she had thought out carefully, searching through long-shelved cookery books at two o'clock in the morning, after she had finished writing to Martha. Brown rolls, soda bread, almond buns and Russian Easter Bread; her first batch of samples.

But she must have fresh yeast. She searched the cold cabinets, then up and down the shelves, feeling the first stirrings of panic.

'Excuse me, do you sell fresh yeast?'

The uniformed young man looked up from his brush and stared at her blankly.

She showed him the small blue tin in her hand.

'This is dried yeast,' she explained, almost hearing the clock ticking inside her head. 'I'm looking for fresh yeast. Could you find out for me, please?'

He and his brush hurried down the aisle. Rose glanced again at her watch. She worried that he'd forget. He was back in a few minutes, empty-handed. Rose felt as though the skin on her forehead was stretching.

'We don't sell fresh yeast, but the bakery will give you some if you like. How much do you want?'

She felt the tightness in her face begin to ease.

'Four ounces would be wonderful. Thank you.'

Her hand shook a little as she replaced the blue tin on the shelf. She had to get this right. The young boy hurried off and back again, suddenly purposeful, important-looking. Rose felt sorry for him. He was probably only a little younger than Damien. She thanked him and pressed a pound coin into his hand.

Rose was back home, unpacked, and up to her elbows in flour before ten o'clock.

She found the whole process therapeutic. She kneaded the brown rolls thoroughly, slapping and punching the spongy mass again and again on the kitchen counter. Her earlier crankiness ebbed away and she began to enjoy what she was doing.

As she kneaded, she planned for baguettes, home-made doughnuts, rye loaves. She'd do samples of them all, and supply Colette with whatever she wanted. Maybe if Colette didn't want her, someone else would. This, at least, was something she could do.

She'd never get her picture in the paper, she was still forty-two, but maybe, maybe, she would yet make a living with an ordinary, down-to-earth, humble, brown roll.

The journey to Greystones was surprisingly pleasant. The grey pall had lifted as soon as they left Dublin behind. The sky began to brighten. Lisa and Brian were relaxed and seemed happy; the atmosphere in the car was lively, even a bit hysterical at times. Rose was happy to have told them the truth. Any more talk was out of the question. Tapes were being played in strict rotation and the decibel count was high.

'It's my turn,' Brian was saying. 'I haven't even had side one of Nirvana yet.'

Rose welcomed the chance to have her own thoughts, to reflect on the new truths as she understood them. There were so many.

Ben's truth, her truth, the kids' truths. It was hard to hold on to what was real. If now was real, then what had the last twenty years been? Had Ben been living a lie all that time?

She tried to sort out how it was for her, now. She was beginning to see the possibility of a life for herself, without Ben. She didn't welcome it, but she could see that it was there. Scary but at the same time, exhilarating.

The fifth day. It might as well have been five million years. Time was nothing; the emotional distance was immense. She'd had more preparation for her trip to Wicklow than her journey through the void of Ben's leaving. Rose had difficulty fitting it all inside her head. Distracted for a moment, she almost missed her turning.

Brian and Lisa shouted at her, snapping her back to reality.

'Mam! There's the sign for Greystones! You have to turn off here!'

She slowed down, changed gears smoothly and made her way directly to the Bonne Bouche. She had to concentrate. She hadn't time to agonise.

She was exactly on time, and Colette came out straight away to greet her.

'Rose. Good to see you. You made it on time.'

Rose felt a prickle of irritation. She found Colette's tone condescending.

They carried in the trays of food together. Colette's partner, Annie, came forward to shake hands.

'Rose! Delighted to meet you! Any trouble finding us?'

Rose took to her immediately. Her face was friendly and open.

'No trouble at all, thanks.'

Annie looked directly at Brian and Lisa. Colette hadn't even noticed them.

'Annie, this is Lisa, and this is Brian. They're my helpers for today.'

Annie shook hands with them.

'I'm sure both of you could do with a Coke and something to eat. Come with me.'

Rose could hear her making normal conversation with them, urging them to have buns and scones, pointing out the nicest ones. She was conscious of making Colette wait.

'Well, shall we have a look at these?'

Rose could hear the anxiety in Colette's voice.

There were a few elderly women there, lingering over coffee and scones.

'Early mornings and lunchtimes are the crazy times,' Colette told her. 'Things are quiet now.'

She picked up her tray.

'I'll just go around with some of these.'

She motioned Rose towards a table. Before Rose even had a chance to sit down, Colette was gone.

She made her way around the tables, offering her customers pieces of the breads and buns which Rose had brought.

Rose watched as Annie refilled the kids' plates. She smiled over at Rose and came to join her. She glanced at the empty table. Rose saw a flicker of annoyance in her eyes.

'Would you like coffee, Rose?'

'No, thanks, Annie, I'm fine.'

'I've deliberately saved myself for your quiche! Would you like to stay for lunch?'

Rose lied that she had to get back, wanting to get this over with.

Annie didn't press her.

Colette came back to the table, beaming.

'These are wonderful, Rose. The almond filling is delicious.'

As she took another large bite, Rose just felt tired. She was glad she didn't have to like Colette.

She did like the restaurant, though. It was warm and colourful, with exposed brick walls, bright red tablecloths, real napkins. Maybe, maybe something like this was for her, somewhere in a distant, calmer future.

She glanced at the menu. The dishes were simple, all making the most of easily available ingredients. Boeuf Stroganoff, Coq au Vin, Spanish-style fish. Salads and fresh vegetables with everything.

Rose was getting nervous. She was hoping they wouldn't take too long to make up their minds. She priced each dish on the menu as she waited, calculating time and profit.

She jumped when Annie finally spoke to her.

'We don't need to keep you in suspense, Rose. Everything is delicious. Are you sure that you could manage to supply us with the quantities we need?'

Rose assured both of them that she could. Annie said, 'Welcome aboard!' and the next hour went in detailed discussions of quantities, types, times of delivery. Rose outlined rough cost guidelines, doubling the amount spent on ingredients as her rule of thumb. She promised a more detailed costing at the end of the first week. They seemed satisfied and solemnly shook hands with her.

Rose wondered why she didn't feel more upbeat. Last night, while preparing the yeast dough, she had been planning on selling her car and investing in a van. Great, ambitious schemes had seen her through the night. Now, everything felt rather flat. She should have been delighted that her skills were in demand. But really, she couldn't have cared less. All this work now seemed a means to a very uncertain end.

On the way home, Rose worried that she had got herself into something she couldn't manage. What if she had to stop when Ben came home? Life after the seventeenth of April was not going to be the same, no matter what happened. She suddenly felt terrified. She had promised something she might not be able to deliver. And what if she made no money at it?

Rose was very, very tired when they got home. Brian and Lisa were quiet in the back, sleepy. In the mirror, Rose noticed Lisa's thumb creeping up towards her mouth several times, a habit the little girl had almost broken, months back.

The house seemed hostile, bare, even though Damien had been in and had turned on the heating. He was out, in John's house. It had started to rain again.

No one was hungry yet; they were too eager to watch TV. Rose let them, leaving instructions that she was to be called at half-past seven.

She pulled the duvet over her head and sank instantly into a heavy, dreamless sleep.

April 1981

Rose takes the same walk every morning. It is therapy, something to do. It gives her body something to feel other than emptiness.

She leaves the house each morning, pushing Damien in his buggy.

It is a ritual. She makes herself leave the house at half-past nine on the dot. She walks briskly towards the wooden bridge at Dollymount. By the time she reaches there, her legs are loose, their morning stiffness eased.

There, at the prom, the real walk begins. The doctor has advised some brisk exercise every day. It will help her overcome the natural depression at the loss of her baby.

He says.

Little Michael.

It also puts a shape to her mornings. Afternoons are easier, somehow. Facing the routine every morning is the worst.

She meets, or rather sees, the same people every time.

The woman with the Walkman, the man with two greyhounds. She wonders what devils they are exorcising.

Once past the bridge, Rose begins to pick up speed. The wind is against her, always, on the way to Clontarf. That feels good. She pushes hard against it. On the way back, it rewards her determination and helps her home.

After the first week, she gets a plastic hood for Damien's buggy. The child hasn't been able to catch his breath with the strength of the wind and the speed of his mother's anger. The hood protects him from both. Sometimes he turns around to laugh at her in delight as she walks faster and faster. She always laughs back. She is glad he doesn't sit facing her.

Past the Victorian houses on the front, past the clumps of palm trees, surviving despite the punishing gales. Past Vernon Avenue, on and on towards the end, or the start, of the prom. Depending on where you are coming from.

She never tires of the sameness of it. Its familiarity, its boundaries, give her comfort. The same landmarks every day; the same piss-smelling shelters; the same freezing seats; the same rusting stairways to the sea. She loves each and every one of them.

She times herself. She pushes herself to shave ten seconds off the outward walk each day. If she does, it will be a good day. Like stepping over the cracks in the pavement when she was a child. All good things will follow if she keeps to the rules.

Mostly, on the way out, she cries. She relives every moment of little Michael's birth, his tiny body. Like a giant movie screen, the night plays itself out in front of her eyes, day after day.

If the day is fine, she wears dark glasses so that she can cry behind them. If it is bad, she cries into the driving rain, pushing forward relentlessly, willing the pain to go away.

Sometimes it does. Sometimes, the walk is calm, effortless. She still walks quickly, but feels that her energy will go on for ever.

These days she calls her islands. Places where there is peace. But only while the waves of grief draw breath, to renew themselves with greater ferocity the next time.

Gradually, the distances between the islands grow less. The great bright light in front of her eyes shifts a little to the side. Its beam becomes narrowed, more focused. It begins to move away from the centre of her forehead. She can feel its heat in the crown of her head. The movie stills grow dimmer. Behind her eyelids becomes her own again.

Just before the arches of the railway bridge, her walk ends. She sits on the sea wall, and Damien has a drink from his Tommy Tippee mug and a Liga. Rose drinks long and deep from a bottle of water, kept in the fridge each night.

As she sits and plays with Damien, she feels her legs start to tremble from the effort. Her knees seem to disappear.

Plasticine legs, she says to Damien. Old marla legs. She holds his hand tightly as he walks along the little wall by the sea. He pauses to examine the holes, filled with green sea-slime. He bends over these, one hand on his knee, like a little old man. He chatters to her incessantly. When he walks again, he pulls against Rose, leaning over to look down at the sky-dappled sea.

He pulls against her with surprising strength. She lets him lean away from her, keeping her grip firm. She likes the way he pulls away, the way he is so sure of her. Only when he is safely on the ground again does she let his hand go.

Gradually, the thumping of her heart subsides. Very soon, she begins to feel cold. She places the water bottle in the net carrier strung across the handles of the buggy. She snuggles Damien up in his blanket and heads for home.

She does this every day for six months after Michael. The vividness of his little face begins to fade. Sadness begins to take the place of anguish. She is proud that she doesn't need, doesn't want, any pills.

Sometimes, on the way home, when Michael is at peace, a different darkness begins to gather inside Rose's chest. This feeling has nothing to do with him.

Once, having fallen asleep in the chair mid-afternoon, she dreams that there is a rat growing inside her. It gnaws and gnaws at the inside of her chest. When she wakes, it is still there.

Heading towards home, sometimes the rat wakes up. It gnaws and gnaws and sometimes its head pushes against the lump at the base of her throat.

Rose doesn't know what hole it has crawled out of. All she knows is that it is here to stay.

She tries to give it a name, to make it familiar. She gets used to its heavy presence, growing darker and darker as she comes nearer home.

And so, day after day, she learns to live with it.

Friday, 7th April; 7.30 pm.

'Wake up, Mam, please!'

Rose struggled back to consciousness. Something was wrong. Damien was shaking her.

'Mam, please wake up!'

There was panic in his voice.

Suddenly aware of her bedroom, her son, the time of evening, Rose became fully alert.

'Come on, wake up!'

'What is it? What's wrong? Quick, tell me!'

She searched for dressing-gown and slippers, but realised that she was fully dressed. Who was hurt? Would she be able to drive to Temple Street, or should she call an ambulance? What new calamity had arrived?

'Nothing, Ma, it's OK; only I couldn't wake you.'

Damien's face was white, his eyes huge, his lips trembling. Rose knew instantly what he had thought. She felt completely calm, even in the face of such distress.

He had even thought to close the bedroom door. Had he locked it, too? This was one she could handle straight from the hip. No ambiguity, no guilt.

She opened the curtains so he could see her face clearly. It was a beautiful evening; the sea was calm, glinting; the rain had finally stopped and the sky was a real springtime blue. She returned to the bed and sat down, facing him.

'Damien, the very, very last thing on my mind is killing myself.'

Damien looked away, already beginning to be embarrassed. She continued to look at him steadily, not averting her gaze for even a moment.

'I don't blame you for being afraid. This has been a very distressing house to live in all week.'

As she said it, she realised how true that was. The very walls seemed to radiate loss and sadness. The whole house, once so sure of its order, now seemed lost without its principal player. Was this what some people meant when they felt a house was haunted? If they left this house now, abruptly, would this incomplete grief be felt by the next people to live there?

While everything had changed radically for her, Rose realised that they had changed in a very focused, concentrated way for Damien. Before Ben left, all Damien's energy had gone into hating him. He had wanted to be as different as possible from his father. Sometimes, he couldn't bear to sit beside him. Looking at Damien's unhappy face, Rose suddenly realised that he felt guilty for playing a part in driving his father away.

The thought depressed her. Everyone at fault except Ben. It would explain Damien's anxiety to be helpful, his willingness to do more than his share.

'None of this is your fault, Damien,' Rose said quietly. 'This has nothing to do with you. It is only about your father and me.'

She waited, but he would not look at her.

'I know you two weren't getting on, but that's normal at your age. Young people need to kick against their parents, to make themselves different.'

'I hate him.'

'I know you do. Maybe one day that will change, maybe it won't. The important thing is,' and here Rose made him turn to face her.

'The important thing is that I have far too much to live for to ever think of killing myself.'

Rose didn't flinch from his embarrassment; she didn't acknowledge it. She spoke to him plainly, adult to adult.

Maybe it was just as well he didn't hero-worship his father. At least his anger gave him strength. He was growing up fast.

'I have my own life, Damien, I have the three of you, and I have a job to do. I'm not going to give up all of that, ever.'

He nodded, examining his hands. Then he stood up quietly. He seemed about to say something. He changed his mind and walked abruptly from the room.

Rose let him go. For the moment, there was nothing more to be said.

At nine o'clock he bounced in looking for money. Rose had got up and showered and changed at once. They all had dinner together. She and Damien had a glass of wine, and each of the three children toasted her success with the Bonne Bouche. Rose felt as though she had moved on to a new place. She had told the truth, as her children would understand it, and she was at peace with herself. For the first time since Monday, she felt that the dogs were no longer snapping at her heels. Dinner was eaten and appreciated. The two younger children were not bickering, for once. They even offered to help with the washing-up. Rose felt as though she had reached an oasis; she was in no hurry to move on.

John and Philip also came in to say hello. Damien stood waiting.

'How much do you want? Sorry, I mean, how much do you need?'

Rose teased him gently. John and Philip were both looking on, grinning. Rose was aware of flirting with her eldest child in front of his friends. They were enjoying it, Damien was enjoying it as she handed him a pound coin. She was aware of the need to be seen as a cool mother. Just for tonight. A mother in touch, in control. One who would never do anything as stupid as kill herself.

She pretended horror as he asked for more. Satisfied eventually, the three went off, laughing. Rose prayed to her own god that Damien would forget about her for tonight, would cease to worry about her, would become seventeen once again.

She had no doubt about this as the three friends walked down the curving driveway. She stood at the window, watching them as they punched one another, tripping up one or the other, displaying affection for one another in the only way adolescents knew how.

She could see by the way they walked that they were looking forward. Damien didn't even try to glance back. Watching as the three of them approached the gate, Rose suddenly saw them as a stranger would. It was as though her eyes had focused on another reality, another level of existence. These were three young men, long-legged, loose-limbed, self-assured. Philip was the most manly-looking of the three. Broad-shouldered, sleek-haired, large, competent-looking hands. Suddenly, they rounded the corner and were lost from sight.

Now what? The house was quiet. Rose toyed with the idea of planning her next delivery to the Bonne Bouche, and dismissed it. She wanted to be still for a while, to enjoy this new sense of peace that surrounded her. The walls that had closed in on her all week receded, allowing her to breathe. The corners were no longer filled with dark shapes. Although it was getting dark outside, the kitchen was still bathed in a comfortable westerly glow. Rose pulled a chair over to her and put her feet up on it. Another habit Ben frowned at. She hadn't done it in ages.

She tried to figure out what was suddenly so different. Her whole perception of time had altered drastically; it had been pulled in every direction, so that it appeared, all at once, elongated and denser. She realised with a shock that she hadn't thought of Ben all day. She was surrounded by the circumstances of his leaving, of course, but she hadn't actually thought of *him*, the man, her husband.

And she suddenly knew what was different. For now, for tonight, he was no longer missing. She felt complete. She stretched luxuriously.

A phone call, a weeping child, a sudden memory could shatter it. She was going to make the most of it. She corked the bottle of wine and put it back into the fridge. Last Sunday's papers were still on the shelf under the microwave.

Rose put on the kettle and opened the news section of the *Tribune*. Sufficient unto the day.

And so, quietly, dimly, the evening came.

The fifth day.

Saturday, 8th April; 6.00 am.

This was the first Saturday Rose could remember – in how many years? – that she and Ben had not spent together. It suddenly struck her that she had delightfully, lazily, nothing to do. She most certainly was not getting up at six am. She was going to take two days off; do nothing. On Sunday night, she'd plan for the week. She could do anything she liked. The sense of peace had not deserted her; on the contrary, it felt solid, less fragile than the day before.

She was seeing everything very clearly. The past few days seemed etched in glass. Her surroundings seemed to her fresher, delineated as though she was seeing them for the first time. When she closed her eyes, she could visualise what waited for her next week. As the two lazy days stretched in front of her mind's eye, it became more difficult to focus on Ben's face, to imagine exactly what he looked like. She could open her eyes and look at the photograph on the bedside table. But she chose not to. She slept.

It was Lisa who woke her at midday. Rose felt groggy and immediately regretted having fallen asleep again. But she managed a smile as Lisa stood there, holding a cup of coffee very carefully. Rose noted that the damage had already been done. The toast was soggy in the saucer. She sat up and pretended great delight. Lisa went on and on . . .

'And so, can I go?'

Rose made an effort to focus.

'Go where?'

'Ma-aa-am! You're not listening! To Ciara's birthday party!'

'Sorry, love – give me a minute to wake up.'

Lisa put her hands on her hips impatiently.

'At what time?' was the only intelligent response she could manage.

Three o'clock. Yes, she could go. Time for a shower, lunch, buy a birthday present, drive to Portmarnock. Yes, that was all possible. Damien was going over to Philip's and Brian was going down again to Derek.

Another oasis of peace and solitude. She would use the time to decide what to say to the solicitor on Monday.

She would take stock this afternoon.

Then she could enjoy being lazy.

Saturday, 8th April, 3.55 pm.

Rose was back home before four. She felt suddenly frightened as she pushed the front door to behind her. She waited, holding her breath. She went slowly down the hall, opening the doors of rooms one after the other. The afternoon sun warmed the back rooms and the kitchen; the light was bright and clean. Relief flooded through her as she visited one room, then the next, then the next. In each one there was the same sense of light and space she had begun to feel yesterday; there was no longer the overwhelming sense of something hacked off and bleeding, hurting and haunting in each room that she visited. The house was her home again, no longer a hostile witness to cruel events. Even the plants were looking happier, healthier since she and Lisa had cared for them, and for each other.

Looking out at the garden, Rose knew immediately how she wanted to spend the rest of the day. The grass was patchy and tired after the winter; her rose-trees needed tending. There were bunches and bunches of cheerful daffodils to be gathered before they were past their best. She wanted to fill her lovely blue stone vases with dozens of them. Rose changed into old trousers and a heavy sweater and stepped out into the bright, chilly afternoon.

Three hours later, the grass was cut and edged, the shrubs tidied and the daffodils captured. Rose's face glowed. She had really enjoyed the exertion, had pushed herself to keep going without a break. Doing a job that was usually Ben's added to the sense of satisfaction as she finished. The smell of the cut grass was intoxicating; Rose felt something approaching euphoria. It was a small triumph, but she felt the joy of being in control of something outside herself.

Another week of neglect and the garden would have been unrecognisable, choked and ugly. Take your eyes off it and look what happens. The thought suddenly depressed her.

Rose replaced the mower in the garden shed and tied the black sack, ready for the binmen on Tuesday. She took off her old shoes at the back door and made straight for the kitchen.

The three kids would all be home soon; eight was the latest, another half hour. Another little bit of peace to consider what next week might bring. The silence was comforting, soothing. Rose took out her diary and began to allocate tasks to the different days. She knew that she must keep busy. The Bonne Bouche would keep her hands occupied, but she needed to think through the implications of Ben's leaving, and his return. To Ireland, at least, if not to her. Monday was a definite to call the solicitor; if only to be able to say to Jane, 'Yes, I did it.'

She still felt an enormous reluctance to do anything so final. She'd much prefer to talk to Ben first. But what if he didn't want to talk? What if he had gone off only after he had made all the arrangements to suit him? Would she have no say at all?

Suddenly very frightened, Rose put a great big ring around David O'Brien's name and number, and wrote 9.00 am beside it. She would force herself to do this first, before the shopping or the ironing or anything else that threatened to make itself appear more urgent. She had a week in which to arm herself with knowledge. She would keep every morning free for gathering information. If that meant very early baking mornings and very late housewife nights, so be it.

Rose made herself a sandwich and had just poured a cup of tea when she heard Lisa's voice calling 'Goodbye!' Quickly, she got up and reached the front door in time to wave to

Ciara's mother, en route to delivering at least another three hyperactive little girls to their homes. Rose hugged Lisa, delighted to see her face red and her eyes shining. Another emotional temperature tested and taken.

'Did you have a great time? Come in and tell me all about it.'

Clutching a goody bag and talking at the top of her voice, Lisa followed her mother into the kitchen. Rose put her diary into her handbag and encouraged Lisa's tales of videos and an adventure playground, of millions of presents and a birthday cake in the shape of a ballerina.

And so evening came the sixth day.

September 1984

The truth is that Rose has signed up for pottery classes in a fit of temper. Two small boys, torrential late September rain and being taken for granted have all driven her to claim one evening a week as her own.

No babysitter needed, Ben assures her. I'll be home at six o'clock.

She feels she can put up with anything, once she gets out tonight. She believes that the children catch something of her mood. Or perhaps she just feels more loving because she feels less trapped. Lately, Ben's work has become an obsession. He has become heady with his own success, wanting his finger in more and more pies. He insists it is all for her, all for his sons.

But she doubts him. He likes the power of business, the wheeling and dealing, the lunches in expensive restaurants. Sometimes, she thinks he is drunk with admiration of himself. She has become a little tired of being a wife-in-waiting. She wants other people's company.

As the evening approaches, Rose begins to feel genuinely excited. She has never done anything artistic in her life. Perhaps she might even be good at it. She loves her plants, plunging her hands wrist-deep into good, rich compost. Now she is looking forward to feeling the other clay seep through her fingers. She imagines its coldness, its smoothness. She wants to transform something; pots seem a good place to start.

From the moment Rose wakes up, she begins to build her day around her escape. Seven to ten; three lovely hours.

She will need to leave at half-six, drive fifteen minutes to the class, find her way around, be relaxed beforehand. A little bit of her is nervous, as though she is going back to school.

Rose works a mental timetable back from half-six. Brian will be fed, changed and ready for bed by then. Ben can have dinner, play with him until half seven or so and then tuck him in. At least Brian is sleeping through the night, finally. It has been a difficult four months, a difficult pregnancy. Rose lived in terror for the nine months, convinced that every twinge spelt disaster.

She and Damien will have their dinner together at five. She will prepare the evening meal once Damien is off to school and Brian is down for his morning sleep. From eleven to one she will work like a tornado: preparing food, washing and drying the endless baskets of baby clothes, cleaning out the fire, tidying up.

Then back to collect Damien, home, homework supervision and taking calls for Ben. It can be done, as long as she's organised.

It will be done.

She wishes Ben would call, so that she can remind him. He remembered this morning, though. Surely that is enough.

Rose is kinder to the boys this Wednesday. Brian, a restless baby, is in a happy mood. Damien, all grown up and in Senior Infants, does his homework importantly at the kitchen table. Rose, solemn and patient, watches as he laboriously traces his letters.

After dinner, Rose leaves the two boys watching cartoons; Brian in his bouncy chair, Damien beside him, in charge.

She has a quick shower and changes. She even agonises over what to wear. Catching sight of her unusually pale face in the mirror, Rose stops and takes a deep breath.

'Get a grip.'

The fear abates slightly as she puts on her most comfortable jeans and a bright red sweater. Look confident even if you don't feel it.

By six she is ready. A little make-up helps to hide the fear.

She turns off the TV after the news headlines and sits Damien on her knee. He sucks his thumb and runs the satin edge of his blanket through his fingers as she reads him two *Thomas the Tank Engine* stories. He is drowsy already. School always exhausts him. He sits contentedly beside her as she reaches for Brian. He is not always an easy baby to cuddle, unlike Damien. But tonight he is good-humoured.

Rose keeps him in her arms as she goes to the front of the house to keep an eye out for Ben. The oven is on low, vegetables cooked. Ben hates reheats. He'd better hurry up.

Rose isn't worried yet. It is only a quarter past six. Even if he's delayed, she can still make it in time if she leaves at a quarter to seven. It is unlike Ben. She can usually set her watch by him.

Over the next hour, Rose swings from real anger to fear. Something must have happened. Has he had an accident? She tries desperately to remember where he said he was going. Has he said? Rose can no longer remember.

She puts the baby to bed. Damien gets into his pyjamas and plays Lego, sitting cross-legged and silent on the sitting-room floor. He often picks up on Rose's moods.

At eight, Rose puts him to bed, reading him a final story, trying to make up for her anger. She hopes the child knows the anger is not for him.

What is going on? Is her night out so unimportant to Ben that he has actually forgotten? She wishes he would call.

Rose feels rightly caught. She can't leave the children to go and pick-up a babysitter, even if one were available at this late hour. It is now dark. She can hear the rain driving against the back of the house. Maybe there's been a terrible accident.

Ben arrives just as she is trying to decide, again, whether she is just furious or worried. He comes into the front room, pulling at his tie.

'Hi, love. Sorry I'm late.'

Rose is too angry to reply.

Ben doesn't seem to notice.

'One of Barry's contacts came through. I met him late this afternoon, and we're in business! It looks as though there's about six grand in it for me!'

Something in Rose's face makes him pause.

'Rose?'

'Could you not have telephoned?'

But Ben is jubilant.

'He was flying back to London tonight, Rose. I couldn't just leave him! And the contract is going to bring in a right few bob. What's the matter?'

Ben's tone changes abruptly.

Rose can smell whiskey from where she sits. Has there not been time, during the informalities, to excuse himself for a moment? To look for a toilet, perhaps, and use the phone on the way? To reassure her about his lateness, even if he'd forgotten all about her pottery class?

Even before she speaks, Rose knows that all right-thinking people will regard her as wrong, spoilt, childish. Ben, priding himself on being an excellent provider, has been doing just that. Providing for his family.

It is only a night-class. In pottery. Is he to abandon income so that his wife can feel the ooze and grit of wet clay between her fingers? Isn't that an unreasonable demand?

'I've been waiting to go to my night-class. I couldn't even get a babysitter because I didn't know what was happening. Couldn't you have got in touch somehow?'

To her own ears, it sounds like whingeing. The real question is, why is her time always so less valuable than his? Her needs always less important? But that is a question that cannot be asked, not now.

'I don't believe this, Rose. We're talking here about our family's security, and you're bitching about a night-class in pottery? You'd want to get your priorities right. I'm working my guts out so that you can . . .'

'You're working your guts out? What about me? Do you think I'm sitting here all day doing fuck all while you're out supporting me?'

Ben literally takes a step back. He hates it when Rose swears. She seldom does so, saving strong language for strong feelings. This is one of the right times.

'You're being unreasonable. This could not be helped. You can go to your class next week. For goodness' sake, this is only September. It goes on until Christmas. Grow up.'

Ben leaves the room, slamming the door behind him. He stamps angrily up the stairs.

Rose gets her coat and keys and goes for a long, satisfyingly furious walk in the rain. By the time she comes home, she wants to forgive and be forgiven. It is a long life.

But Ben is asleep.

The following Wednesday, the contract is signed. Rose is invited to dinner. She accepts, of course.

The Wednesday after that, Ben goes to London, and Brian has croup.

By the end of October, Rose has given up.

Sunday, 9th April; 9.30 am.

Sunday was a day of complete rest. The weather was foul. Great dark billowing clouds, stinging showers and from midday, huge and frequent hailstones. Rose made no mention of Mass. She really did not want to face all those familiar happy family faces. Next Sunday was Easter; maybe they'd all go then. It seemed a bit ridiculous to maintain a Sunday routine that had now become meaningless. They could go in the evening if it felt right.

For now, they had breakfast together and Brian and Lisa went off to have a shower. Rose had listened to each of them moaning, bickering about who was to go first, complaining about being made to pick up their clothes and wet towels. Rose shouted at each of them once and, as usual, they then complained to each other.

She felt that the morning was like a normality test. They did what was expected, she responded as expected and that was the end of it. Even Brian's usual protest about not needing a shower, he'd been swimming on Friday, was half-hearted. It was as though each of them was carefully recreating what they knew to be a normal Sunday. Their experience told them that this was what happened first, followed by something else.

'But I don't want to see *The Lion King*. I saw it already, on Keith's birthday.'

Rose could hear the aggression in Brian's voice. She hated it when he bullied Lisa. She waited to see if the little girl would hold her ground.

'I don't care. It's my turn to choose. Mam said so.'

There was no whinge. Lisa, expecting things to be fair, stood firm. My turn. A week-old promise remembered. Rose caught a glimpse of her standing in the hall, fists by her side, face defiantly raised towards her brother. She could almost taste the tension coming from them. Ben was emphatically the missing piece from their jig-saw. First Mass, then ceremonious Sunday dinner, then an outing had given shape to Brian and Lisa's Sundays for years. Damien had long since opted out to do his own thing.

Rose resented what she felt as their needs. She didn't want to bring them to the pictures. She didn't want to bring them anywhere. Immediately, she felt guilty. Poor kids. It wasn't their fault. She'd make the effort. She opened the entertainment section of yesterday's papers and had a look at what the local cinemas had to offer.

Dinner was ready, just a matter of flicking a switch. She didn't want to spend time in the kitchen. Damien arrived in from the local shop with the Sunday papers and extra milk. Rose felt a wave of affection for him. Dripping wet, he sloshed his way across the kitchen. Rose closed the door behind her.

'Are you meeting the others this afternoon, Damien?'

'Yeah. At two. I've to phone Philip now. Are you going to UCI?'

'I was hoping not to. I really don't want to go anywhere this afternoon.'

Rose's request hung heavily between them. Damien began to look uncomfortable.

'We're all going to *Pulp Fiction*, Ma. It's been arranged for ages.'

Damien shrugged his way out of the massive rain jacket, Rose tugging at the cuffs. There was a long silence. When Rose looked at him again, she saw guilt written all over his face.

'It's OK,' Damien said finally. 'I'll bring Brian and Lisa to the pictures.'

Rose couldn't speak for a moment. Her heart was very full. She did not want him to feel like that. She made a decision.

'No, Damien. On second thoughts, the three of us are going nowhere. Brian and Lisa are going to have to amuse themselves for one day. But thanks for the offer.'

She watched as Damien's face flooded with relief.

'Well, if you're really sure . . .'

'I'm really sure.'

'Can I use the telephone? Just one quick call?'

Rose nodded. 'Tell them I insist!'

'Thanks, Ma! You're the best!'

Jeaned and jelled ten minutes later, Damien raced towards the gate just as John and Philip reached it. Each of them was hooded and huddled into slick waterproof jackets. The three musketeers. Rose watched as they made a mad dash across the road to catch the bus; laughed as the bus suddenly drenched the ends of their legs, and wondered what wet jeans would do to their image.

When she went back into the sitting-room, Lisa had discovered some painting pencils long hidden in the bottom of her toybox. She was colouring enthusiastically. She was even lending some to Brian who was putting the finishing touches to his computer project. He looked up at Rose as she came in.

'We're staying at home, today, you guys. We'll have a treat next weekend, for Easter.'

Lisa stopped colouring for a minute. Both children looked at Rose. She waited, but neither of them said anything. Then Brian, a little anxious, asked, 'Do you want a game of Monopoly, Ma?'

Rose looked longingly at the Sunday papers, her chair beside the fire. She smiled at him.

'How about later, Brian?'

He nodded, reassured. 'OK, about four o'clock?'

Rose smiled at him again. 'Four's perfect.'

'Can I play, too?' from Lisa.

''Spose so.'

Rose put her feet up and opened the Magazine section of her paper. She wondered briefly what Ben and Caroline were up to now. She decided not to think about it. She was going to enjoy her own Sunday afternoon for the first time in twenty years.

And so on the seventh day, she rested.

Sunday, 9th April; 12.30 pm.

Ben tilted the umbrella further to ward off the midday glare. A week of perfect blue skies, perfect temperatures, warm nights. He was happy.

It was strange to be with Caroline, without the added frisson of possible discovery. It had made both of them uneasy with the other for the first two days.

At dinner on their second night, Caroline told Ben that she had noticed a change in their relationship. She was matter-of-fact, cool. She didn't appear to be anxious; she was simply stating a fact.

Ben was startled, unused to such directness.

He had felt it too. He was a little disappointed that the first couple of days had not been the crazy, passionate affair he had hoped. He had wanted to recreate their early days together. Stolen afternoons, furtive Fridays. That sort of thing.

Caroline saying it first threw him off balance. It made it difficult for him to reassure her, both of them, that this was a natural response.

She was talking of it as though two other people were involved. Her detachment unnerved him.

He was utterly attentive; filling her glass, holding her hand across the table, buying her a red rose from a flower-seller who looked as though she had just stepped out of a tourist brochure. Caroline smiled at him more as evening darkened into night. She seemed to become looser-limbed, brighter-eyed.

He was relieved that she was becoming again the Caroline he knew.

But the following morning she was up before him, dressed,

sitting on the little balcony, her face towards the sun, a book in her lap.

Ben felt the sting of sexual disappointment.

But she was warm and loving all day, taking his hand, kissing him in public. They got a little drunk at lunchtime and Caroline giggled as he dragged her through the narrow streets back to their hotel. But she stopped laughing once he closed the door.

They undressed each other urgently. Ben could feel all of Caroline's coolness and detachment melting away.

She was passionate and demanding, he was overjoyed and tender. It was better than the best of secret meetings.

Afterwards, she seemed perfectly content, at ease with him. He was aware of watching her like a hawk, terrified of losing her.

It was working. He knew it was working. Her reserve was almost gone; he wanted her to know how much he needed her.

He wanted to tell her that he had left Rose. A passionate burning of boats; a ritual coming-of-age. He had nothing to go back to. He wanted nothing to go back to.

He wanted her to be with him.

He decided to tell her that night, their first full Sunday together, ever. For him, it was final. He felt it was for her too, now that the initial strangeness had melted into newness again.

He watched her across the table, fusing that evening with the countless others when he had faced her like this. He felt that there was no division between their selves; boundaries dissolved when he was with her; he felt at one with the rest of the world.

He watched as she tucked her hair behind her ears, a gesture she repeated constantly. The pleasure of watching her do this was an almost physical pain. He loved where her hair just brushed the side of her jaw, falling silkily forwards as she bent her head.

Her earrings glittered. Jewellery he had bought her; discreet and expensive. Caroline was the sort of woman who bought exquisite earrings for herself; his gift would never give rise to any comment.

He wanted passionately to buy her the sort of jewellery she could wear that would proclaim her as his, publicly, finally.

He reached across the table, intimate in candlelight. Her hand was cold from touching the icy sides of her glass.

'Caroline, we need to talk.'

She looked up quickly, smoothing her hair behind her ear again with her free hand.

'Yes.'

It was a statement, not a question. So she had obviously been thinking too that it was time to decide.

Given courage by what he saw as her agreement, he plunged ahead, drowning in love for her.

'I love you, Caroline. This whole week has shown me that, more than ever.'

Caroline began to sit up straighter.

'I know we agreed not to do anything final until the two weeks were up, but I couldn't wait.'

Ben's voice was filled with emotion. He didn't notice Caroline's expression.

'I've left Rose. I didn't tell you until now because I didn't want you to feel pressurised by anything I had done. But it's final; I've told her.'

Caroline's face seemed to register with Ben, finally.

'Caroline, listen to me. I love you, and I've left Rose. But even if we hadn't got to this stage, it wasn't a marriage any more. I'd have left her anyway.'

Caroline was beginning to stand up. He could see in her face what he had realised the second he'd said it; he was a liar.

Caroline began to walk unsteadily out of the restaurant. The waiter, arriving to take their order, looked puzzled.

Ben leapt to his feet, rushed to follow her. The waiter blocked his way, politely.

Panic-stricken, Ben shoved a thousand peseta note at him for their drinks, and pushed his way through a noisy party just arriving.

When Ben got outside, there was no sign of Caroline.

Part Two

Monday, 10th April; 12.30 pm.

Rose tested the new locks, back and front. The front door felt a bit stiff. Rose didn't care. She felt happier with the extra security locks installed. Just as the locksmith left, Damien arrived home from school. He dismounted and locked his bike deftly. Rose looked at him in surprise.

'Damien, I didn't expect you home for lunch!'

'I told you. We're going to the Writers' Museum this afternoon. That's why I took my bike.'

So he had told her. It was coming back to her now. She was glad the locksmith had left. Her mind was fuzzy, unfocused for the last few days.

'What's all this?' Damien fingered the chain inside the front door.

'I wanted a bit of extra security. There have been a lot of break-ins around here recently. I feel I need a bit of extra insurance at night.'

Damien nodded. Rose knew by his face that he didn't believe her. She offered no other explanation. Sufficient unto the day.

He asked his usual question when there was just the two of them.

'Any word?'

Rose shook her head. 'There's some spaghetti bolognese left from last night. Do you want to heat it up in the microwave?'

When in doubt, offer food. Damien was permanently hungry. It was a good distraction.

Rose was damned if Ben was going to walk back in here

next Monday, or whenever, as though nothing had happened. She had been dreaming of his return, hearing his car pull up and his key in the lock. The first time, she had woken up enormously angry. The dream had immobilised her. She had been paralysed in that awful dreamlike way where no action was possible. She was not going to wait, passive, until he returned.

He would enter her home on her terms. He was due back in less than a week. She wasn't going to be taken by surprise. She handed Damien a set of keys.

'Don't lose these. I don't want to go through this hassle again.'

He nodded, mouth full.

'Will you be home at the usual?' Rose asked, wiping down the counter top.

'Yeah. Should be.'

'Will you collect Brian and Lisa from Jane's? Her mother-in-law will be babysitting, so try and get there as near to four as you can. OK?'

He nodded again. He didn't even ask where she was going.

Rose said carefully, 'I should be back around six, but I could be a bit later. There's a casserole for dinner. Just cook some rice and feed yourselves. Tell the other two I said to get on with their homework.'

'Right. Aren't you going to eat?'

'Leave me some of the casserole. I'll look after myself when I come in.'

'Right. I'm off.'

He passed Jane as he ran up the driveway. She called out something to him and he waved in reply. Rose opened the door while she collected her coat and bag from the hall cupboard.

'Ready?' called Jane.

She took one look at Rose's face.

'You don't have to do it, you know.'

'I know. But I want to. I know it's stupid, but I really want to do it.'

'You can change your mind at any stage, you know that. I'm just the driver.'

Rose locked the door behind her. She dropped the keys into her handbag.

'Let's go.'

30th March, 1993

30th March, 1993

Rose sets to work as soon as Ben has left.

It is the best day for it; Ben won't be home until late. Rose is worried that Barry Herbert is causing him so much grief. She hopes he'll sort it out today. He is really in very bad form.

She makes an effort to put Ben and his troubles to the back of her mind. She is glad to be busy, though she hates this job.

Rose takes every ornament off every surface in the room. She takes down pictures and spreads old newspapers from the hall door right through to the back of the house. She takes down the curtains from both big windows. It is time they were cleaned. Even through the rubber gloves she can feel the grime from a year of fires – and Ben's smoking.

This is a day that always depresses her. The house is dirty-looking and bare. If O'Farrell and Sons arrive early to sweep the chimney, then she will have everything back to normal before Ben comes home. He hates the disruption.

Rose throws a sheet over the television and tapes newspaper over the stereo. She takes down the books and magazines off the shelves. Out of this chaos she will create order; she begins to feel a sense of satisfaction.

Everybody on the road knows that O'Farrell and Sons are excellent; they do a thoroughly good job. They also leave a trail of destruction behind them after every cleaning. Thank God it is only once a year.

By midday she is ready. The kitchen table is piled high with things to be washed. Every surface is covered with books and papers, waiting to be sorted. Rose fills the sink with hot soapy water; the front doorbell rings.

Good. They'll be gone by lunchtime. She'll be back to normal by six. Dinner is in the oven. All the children safely in school. All is right with the world.

O'Farrell and Sons tramp through the hall, dragging their brushes and equipment. Rose nervously watches their progress. The wallpaper is expensive.

They reach the sitting-room without incident. Laconic as ever, they refuse tea. Rose withdraws, praying they won't spill anything.

Years ago, she tried to persuade Ben to let the central heating do the work. Abandon fires altogether. But he liked the look of it, he said. It gave the room a focus, he said.

And so the ritual continues.

Rose cleans out the ashes every morning, sets the fire for evening, washes the fireplace and mantelpiece thoroughly and vacuum-cleans everywhere. She gets it over with early.

Starting today, the entire spring-cleaning will last for a week. She is no longer disappointed that no one else seems to notice when it is done. At least she knows everything is bright and shining.

As she plunges her arms into the soapy water, she wonders will she still be doing this in twenty years' time. Life has begun to be very predictable. Still, she has a lot to be grateful for. She knows that.

While O'Farrell and Sons rattle away inside, Rose fills and refills the sink, using a toothbrush to clean the awkward bits of china.

She wishes she could go to a pub for lunch. She has a mad instinct to phone Ben at Barry's office. A mad, unpredictable desire for a pub lunch with her husband.

She looks at the clock. It's too late. By the time O'Farrell and Sons are finished, Lisa will be coming home from school.

And she, Rose, will need to shower and change before going anywhere.

A nice idea, but not today.

Maybe another time.

Monday, 10th April; 1.15 pm.

Jane made her laugh all the way to the airport. Stories about her brother and his unsuitable wife, about her mother-in-law's absent-mindedness, about her own part-time job in the local coffee-shop. Their peculiarities made Rose feel better about what she was doing. Jane's sense of humour was infectious. Rose was beginning to rediscover hers.

'Well?'

They had paused outside the terminal building.

'What does madam require? Home, or the long-stay carpark?'

'Definitely the long-stay carpark!'

'Quick, let's go before you change your mind!'

It took them about fifteen minutes to locate Ben's silver BMW.

'Keys, please.' Jane held out her hand.

Giggling, Rose pressed the alarm button and handed the keys to Jane. The locks sprang up obediently.

'You're sure he'll remember where he parked it?'

'Absolutely. He never forgets.'

'OK, let's go.'

Jane eased the car out of its parking space. Ben had reversed in, perfectly placed between the white lines.

'Where to?'

'As far away as possible. Go right over to the other side of the carpark and look for a space. Then drive into it. He hates reversing out of parking spaces.'

It was such a little thing. Rose imagined Ben's frustration, then perhaps his panic as he thought the unthinkable – his pride and joy being stolen, maybe even wrapped around a lamppost somewhere.

Revenge was sweet. They were both as high as kites as they drove around the carpark, squealing with delight as Rose spotted a space at the opposite end of the huge lot. Jane parked with care, sliding in between a sleek Mercedes and an arrogant Jaguar.

Rose opened the boot, to see if there were any signs of – what? Ben's mistress? His plans? There was nothing, except his red and black silk tie. A Valentino she had bought him for some birthday or other. Apart from that, the car was unnaturally clean.

He had even had time to do that before he left. The more Rose thought about it, the more time and planning became obvious. This had been no spur-of-the-moment, passionate gesture. Everything had been arranged.

And she had been the last to know.

It made this little gesture easier to enjoy. It justified the changing of the locks. It was good preparation for the meeting with David O'Brien tomorrow.

Then there was Easter. And then there was the seventeenth. She'd be ready.

Jane was waiting. The alarm beeped discreetly. Rose put the keys into her handbag, and linked her arm through Jane's. She hadn't done that since Martha.

Feeling lighthearted, she made her way back towards the car.

'I can see the headlines now: "Man arrested for suspicious behaviour in airport carpark."'

Jane laughed. 'With Caroline and cases in tow!'

'Can you imagine it? Trying to convince the security man that his car has been stolen?'

'And then finding it safely parked exactly where he said it wasn't!'

'Can't you just see his face?'

Rose didn't want to go home just yet. She needed Jane's humour, her solidity, her friendship.

'Head for Malahide,' she said suddenly. Jane looked sideways at her, quickly. She had caught the urgency, wasn't sure where it was coming from.

Rose was smiling at her broadly.

'I am treating you to lunch. No –' She held up her hand to wave away any protest. 'I insist.'

Jane grinned. 'I wasn't going to object. I just want to know where we're heading for so's I'll know where to park. I'm starving!'

For the first time in well over a week, Rose felt hungry. There was no pressure. She had all afternoon. The kids were safe, the Bonne Bouche well in hand.

And Ben. He was a million miles away, getting further all the time.

30th March, 1993

Ben is getting really impatient.

'For Christ's sake, Barry, apply a bit of pressure. You're acting like a nursemaid.'

Caroline watches as the two men lock horns. She hopes Ben realises that Barry can be very stubborn when he feels that what he's doing is right.

His colour is high and his mouth a straight line.

This is no longer negotiation. Barry has made up his mind, and nothing will shift him.

'The man has withdrawn for perfectly valid reasons, Ben. I'm in no position to bully him, nor would I want to.'

Ben smooths his tie.

'Look, Barry, this sort of deal comes along once only. Four hundred thousand among four of us for that property is chickenshit. Even as it stands, without renovation or extra commercial tenants, it's worth half a million. We could sit on it for a year, do nothing, and still make a killing. Georgian property is *big* – we can't let this go.'

Barry shakes his head.

'I know all of that. I also know Mike. He feels he has too much exposure at the moment, and he's not going to commit to a deal that he can't see through. I've offered him less than a twenty-five per cent stake if he wants it. I figured the rest of us could probably manage twenty-eight and a third each. I've told him he could have fifteen initially, with an option to buy into a further ten per cent in a year or so if things were easier. But he needs out.

'We've been all through it, Ben, it's just not on. Twenty-five to twenty-eight is really my limit – I certainly don't want to go into a three-way deal just now; I'm too committed. Let it go, Ben. There'll be others.'

'Can't we find another partner?'

Barry shakes his head again.

'We've done all that research. Not now – it's just the wrong time for too many people. There's no one else I'd feel comfortable with who would go the distance until this building really pays off. We could be talking ten years for maximum return.'

'What about Peter?'

'No, he's a quick-kill merchant. No use for something like this. This takes patience. We need people who take the long view, people we can trust.'

'Like Mike?' asks Ben bitterly.

Barry gives him a long look.

'Exactly like Mike. He pulled out before any of us had committed, for very sound business reasons. Better that than jump ship in six months and force us all to sell in less than ideal market conditions.'

Barry raises his hand just as Ben is about to speak again.

'It's over, Ben. They were holding the price until two o'clock today. They gave us forty-eight hours, now it's over. It may even go for less than four. But the point is, *it doesn't matter*. It's too late for us. This one is gone. There'll be others.'

Barry begins putting papers in his briefcase.

Caroline watches Ben's face. He is beaten. And he is angry. She can see that Ben is prepared to risk anything; Barry is not. That is only one of the differences between them.

'Now I'm going to the bank to tell them the deal's off, and why. We'll leave them happy and they'll see us right the next time. There will be a next time, Ben. This is just one we lose.'

He turns to Caroline.

'After that, I'm going home.'

Ben is standing up and is looking out the window, hands deep in his pockets.

'I'll carry on here. There's a lot of paperwork that needs to be tidied up. I'll be home at the usual.' Caroline tries to keep her voice neutral.

Barry looks at her. 'Won't it keep until tomorrow?'

Caroline shakes her head.

'Look at the phone log. This Merrion Square fiasco has taken up every minute this week. The bread and butter has to be looked after now.'

Caroline is aware of the impact she has made. 'Fiasco' shows a clear shift of allegiance. Barry's deal, Barry's failure.

Ben's back becomes noticeably straighter. Caroline wonders very briefly if she knows what she is doing.

Barry leaves. Neither man acknowledges the other.

Ben turns away from the window when the door closes. All signs of temper are gone. He is looking pleased.

'Well, that's that. I'm going for lunch. And I could do with a drink.'

And then, almost as an afterthought: 'Would you like to join me, Caroline?'

The tone is just right, friendly, casual. But the tension has not left with Barry.

It has changed into something else, between them.

Caroline knows she has a decision to make. She arranges papers carefully on her desk.

She smiles at Ben.

'I'll just get my coat.'

Rose gets the vacuum-cleaner out straight away. O'Farrell and Sons have done their usual. She is glad that that is over for another year.

She cleans and dusts, replacing books and ornaments, filling a black plastic sack with rubbish in the process. She stops only to get the kids' lunch and get homework in motion. Brian in his room, Lisa at the kitchen table. It works best that way.

By five o'clock, the room is spotless. Rose bundles the curtains into a bag and puts them in the car to take to the cleaners tomorrow.

She gets the stepladder from the attic and the clean, bright summer curtains from the top of her wardrobe.

Her shoulders are aching by the time she has them hung. But she is pleased, really pleased with her day's work.

She fills the bath with hot water, throwing in handfuls of salts. She checks the timer on the oven, and signs two homework journals, inspecting all copies a little less thoroughly than usual.

She throws her dirty clothes into the basket in the bathroom. She chooses a black skirt and her pink silk blouse from the wardrobe. Perhaps she can entice Ben out for a drink tonight. They haven't had a night out to themselves in ages. When he comes home, she'll be ready.

Rose sinks into the steaming water, ducking her head right under, warming her face and scalp.

She lies back, enjoying the aches as her body relaxes.

The pub has started to acquire a dreamy quality. Caroline's perceptions are sharpened as she and Ben speak. Everything else has begun to fade into a dim background.

She has hardly touched her food, neither has he.

Ben barely recognises himself. A middle-aged man, no Adonis, restless and dissatisfied for years, suddenly transformed into a dynamic, risk-taking visionary.

No longer a businessman making an excellent living from luck and hard work, slogging away in a spare room, but an entrepreneur, poised for greatness, the sky's the limit.

He tells Caroline plans he doesn't even know he had. He grows to fill her impression of him. He has a rush of confidence, a sense of possibilities he hasn't had in years.

Caroline can even forgive the fact that Ben smokes. She decides she likes the mixture of tobacco and aftershave. She wants him to kiss her. They are sitting so close already that any little movement on her part will give the signal, and he can believe it is his idea.

She smooths her skirt, her hand just brushing against his thigh.

He catches her hand then, raising it to his lips. Any other time, any other couple, and Caroline would have laughed at the corniness of it.

Now it seems an impossibly romantic thing to do. His hand is surprisingly dry and warm. His grasp is firm, wrists strong and hairy. He is altogether more substantial and solid than his tubby waistline has led her to believe.

She begins to wonder what he is like naked. Barry's body is spare and wiry, often clammy to the touch.

Ben, she suspects, would be different.

When he kisses her, she feels an erotic charge that is only ten per cent gin.

He kisses her again, caressing her face, her hands, her neck, anywhere he can find skin.

Tuesday, 11th April; 6.00 am.

Another Tuesday. Another six o'clock start. Rose wondered if she had ever lived any other way. Going to the airport yesterday, playing that silly trick on Ben had made her feel good. But now, in the silent kitchen, she felt surrounded by all the trappings of her failure.

She wondered what Ben was doing. She still felt a pang when she thought of the two of them together. She remembered Ellen's sour words from long ago:

'I just hope he's worth it.'

She moved in and out of anger. Right now, there was just emptiness.

She kneaded and pushed and shaped the dough with the heels of her hands. This helped.

This morning she was thinking how very little room there now was for God in her life. No amount of letters from the Pope saying how special she was, how special all women were, would convince her that the cards weren't stacked against her.

She supposed she had never been really religious, not in the sense Ben was. And after Michael, she became even less so. It was a ritual, one she went through for the children. She would never voice her doubts to them.

But Ben felt differently. Sunday was always sacred to him; he prayed every night. A good Catholic.

She wondered how he managed to feel that, and still do what he did.

Today, her strongest feeling was that she had been cheated out of twenty years. She'd played by the rules and someone had changed the game. Twenty years' hard work in house and home had earned her nothing.

God could offer her no comfort for that.

Rose put the trays of loaves in the oven. Cup of tea, and then the interminable photocopying. She decided she would do as David O'Brien told her, but it was yet one more finality, one more nail in the coffin.

He had been businesslike on the phone yesterday, a man in a hurry. Rose had been disappointed; she had needed someone to be kind to her.

'Every memo,' he had said, 'every letter, every invoice, bank statement, share certificate – make copies of everything. Then we can see where we stand.'

At least the 'we' had been comforting. Someone else on her side.

Rose didn't feel she had quite so much energy, quite so much optimism as last week.

She pulled out her notebook again. She was terrified of not having things to do.

Slowly, thoughtfully, in the empty kitchen, she invented the tasks for the week that would help her feel once more that she was beginning again.

10th April, 1993

Ben replaces the receiver very gently. His hands are sweaty. He takes his handkerchief out of his pocket and wipes his palms. He pushes back his swivel chair and walks to the window.

He can hardly believe his luck. She will see him again. He has been afraid that she would pull back, would say it was all a dreadful mistake. In the middle of the night, lying beside Rose, Ben has felt frightened. What is he risking?

By the morning, he no longer cares. He wants Caroline. They will be careful. He will make sure no one finds out, at least until they are ready. He has no doubt they are meant to be together.

Standing there at the window, he watches Rose. She is hanging out clothes. She is struggling with a large white sheet. The sheet from their bed. The wind whips it away from her for a moment. Then, in a savage gust, it wraps itself around her. Rose struggles to free herself from its stinging wetness.

The scene disturbs Ben for a reason he does not understand. For a moment, he is moved to go and help her. Then he feels annoyed. Why can't she just use the tumble-dryer? He wonders if she ever gets bored being so dutiful.

Abruptly, he turns away from the window and closes his briefcase. The little domestic scene has made him angry.

He picks up the briefcase and walks out the back door towards his car.

Rose hears the door slam.

Her heart sinks. That is the second time he has left without saying goodbye. By the time she runs to the end of the driveway, the BMW is pulling out into the light afternoon traffic. He is gone. She wonders what it is that is going so wrong.

Ben, catching a glimpse of her in his rearview mirror, presses his foot on the accelerator.

A middle-aged woman with a peg-bag around her neck.

Ben presses the button on the CD player and it closes smoothly.

Gershwin. *Rhapsody in Blue.*

He turns the volume up slightly and heads towards Malahide.

Wednesday, 12th April; 8.00 am.

Middle of week two. Rose found it hard to believe that she had survived this far. A week and a half. A lifetime and a half. All yesterday's defeats were gone this morning. Her energy was limitless again.

It was a good feeling today, to be making her own money. Easter was a time for treats. She calculated what her paypacket would be. She wanted to give Damien a few extra quid for the special disco on Saturday night. And she wanted to take Brian and Lisa to see a film and have a hamburger afterwards.

Arrayed before her on her kitchen table and counter tops were four dozen hot-cross buns, ready to go into the oven. Then there were two dozen brown and two dozen white rolls. Plus half a dozen Vienna rolls – her first order for those. They were tedious and time-consuming, but she wasn't going to look a gift-horse in the mouth. Then the specialist Easter stuff, and finally the doughnuts, which were ready to be deep-fried.

Rose made herself a quick coffee and jotted down in her notebook the estimated baking-time for each batch of dough. With a bit of luck, everything would be wrapped and ready to go by ten o'clock. Without it, maybe eleven. Joe was due to call with the van at eleven-thirty. Either way, she should make it.

She was beginning to need this time in the early mornings. There was something very satisfying about working with bread. Sometimes she used the food-processor for speed, but more often she plunged her hands up to the elbow in the fermenting masses. Kneading, pushing, rolling, shaping;

she loved the sense of completion. It was work she never wanted to hurry; she enjoyed the smells and textures, the yeasty richness underneath the heel of her hand. For the first time in her life, Rose knew what it was to take pride in your work.

It sometimes saddened her that what she used to do for love, she now did for money.

But that, she reflected, was the way of the world. Homage to home and housewife was just so much cant. Money was the measure of success and significance; it was weighed as surely as the flours and sugars she weighed for her bread. Money was the yeast, raising Ben to wealth and respectability.

She was there because he brought her along. When it mattered most, all her work for love, for family, for breadwinner, was worth fuck all.

Leaving, he had taken what was theirs, not just his.

Rose got really angry at this at some point every morning. But gradually, the anger lasted less and less time; her plans for herself became more elaborate, and anger was just part of the ritual.

The timer buzzed shrilly. Rose took out a tray of beautifully rounded, puffy Easter loaves, oozing goodness.

As she put the next two trays of rolls into the oven, Rose swore to herself that she would never let it happen again.

February 1994

A dark, heavy February day. Rose hates February; the sky is low, claustrophobic, blotting out colour. Everything around her is a uniform grey.

It has been raining, of course, since early morning. The taxi has failed to turn up, so she leaves Ben to the airport at six o'clock. She is relieved he is going. He has been very difficult to live with lately. Or maybe she is the difficult one. She hardly knows any longer.

If anyone asks her how she feels, she will say, 'Weary.' Her energy these days deserts her more readily, more frequently.

She is already looking forward to going to bed early. A take-away, a bath, bed. The simple pleasures.

Ben has been increasingly restless since Christmas. Or perhaps even since before Christmas; he is by turns energised and lethargic. There is a brittle quality to him, as though things aren't quite holding together. He is also drinking more than Rose thinks is good for him.

Last night she had suggested, very hesitantly, that they go out together before his week in London. To her surprise, he agreed instantly. It is the first positive response she has got from him, on any level, for several months. He is slipping, sliding away from her. When she thinks of it, Rose becomes terrified.

Maybe now she will reach him, ease her way through the barbed wire all around him.

When they get to the pub after a long, silent walk, Ben turns immediately to the bar. Rose goes off in search of seats.

There is something at the base of her throat, beginning to strangle her. She smiles at some neighbours and her face feels frozen over. She thinks of the childhood taunt: if the wind changes, your face'll stay like that.

Ben is making his way back from the bar. Rose watches the set of his jaw, the stiffness of his gait. He often grinds his teeth in his sleep. He looks as if he is grinding them now.

He sits down heavily beside her.

'Wish I didn't have to do this trip.'

Rose's heart leaps. Is he coming back to her? Is he telling her he loves her, would prefer to stay with her?

'The timing is all wrong. Barry Herbert hasn't done his homework. These guys aren't ready to sign a contract. I can feel it in my bones.'

He takes a large sip of whiskey. Rose notices it is a double.

'What's going on, Ben?' she asks quietly.

Immediately, the stone at the base of her throat shifts a little. She can breathe again.

He turns to her quickly. Rose thinks he looks suddenly paler.

'What do you mean?'

'You've been so preoccupied. We don't seem to have had any time together in months. I'm worried about you.'

It is a formula that usually works. Ben does not like to be confronted, to be reminded of any shortcomings, real or imaginary.

Rose thinks she sees relief flash across his face. Does she imagine it? Did he think she was going to make a scene in public? Does he not know her yet?

Ben takes her hand and squeezes it.

'I'm sorry, love. This business deal has me a bit worked up. Barry is far too laid-back for my liking, and I'm afraid I'm walking into a mess.'

'Will he be with you on this trip?'

Ben waves to someone at the bar. He takes his time before looking directly at her again. He takes another deep sip of whiskey.

'No. He's tied up here. Look, this is nothing for you to worry about. I'll sort it out and we'll get back to normal. Another drink?'

Rose nods. Defeat engulfs her like a February cloud. When Ben returns, he is more upbeat, the paleness has vanished.

She makes a huge effort to match his mood. Their talk becomes easier, she is almost joyful walking home. The distance between them seems to have closed a little. Perhaps they will make love tonight.

Ben checks on the children while Rose undresses. Back in the bedroom, Ben kisses her briefly.

'I'm going to take a shower. I've got to get up at five. Could you throw a few things into the case for me? Don't wait up, I've got papers to sort.'

Numbly, Rose nods. A part of her wants to scream Do It Yourself.

She folds seven shirts, four ties and two cashmere sweaters. Then she carefully puts the case on the floor at Ben's side of the bed, turns out the light and falls asleep.

Five o'clock comes, without the taxi.

She drops Ben at the airport, still puzzled at his extreme nervousness. She begins to be angry at Barry Herbert. Once Ben is gone, Rose begins to regret that she has felt so negative. Then she is relieved that she is on her own. A week. Space.

The five o'clock start begins to tell on her in the late afternoon. School runs, shopping, swimming runs, a brief visit to her father, the weekly mountain of washing and drying. Take me away from all this, she thinks at nine o'clock.

Lying in the bath, Rose begins to think back. There

is something elusive about Ben, something she cannot put her finger on. Mid-life crisis? Maybe that's what it is.

She resolves to try harder when he comes back from London.

Keep your hat in the hall.

Her mother's saying. The way she had lived her own life. Busy with children, housework, whatever – Rose's mother went out with her father at, literally, the drop of a hat.

Rose's father was not one for pubs, nor was her mother. But on many, many evenings that Rose can remember from her childhood, her father would fold his evening paper, look across the fireplace at her mother, knitting or sewing contentedly in her armchair, and say:

'What about a walk before we turn in?'

The knitting or mending would be put down instantly. Ellen would be told she was in charge, and Rose was to go to bed soon. Kevin and Grace, in Rose's mind, were always in bed anyway. They do not figure in her memories.

Off they would go, arm in arm, straight down the long avenue that led to the sea.

Ellen and Rose would occupy their places near the fire, make tea, and keep eating until bedtime.

Winter memories.

Rose smiles as she soaps her legs.

Maybe what had worked for her mother and father for over twenty years had something to teach her. Maybe there is something she isn't doing right.

With a great rush of happiness, Rose decides she will ask Ben if that is so. If there was any way of contacting him tonight, she'd ring him right away.

It is only then, bathing in love, that Rose realises Ben has left her no number where she can contact him.

That is unusual.

Rose sighs, but not unhappily. Her opportunity will come again. She'll think about it all tomorrow, when she is not so tired.

Thursday, 13th April; 11.30 am.

Joe arrived promptly at eleven-thirty. He was a retired army man, an obsessively correct timekeeper. Rose found this a great comfort. Something solid and unshifting in a world where the goalposts were constantly moving. He accepted her offer of a cup of tea and an almond bun with grave politeness, as though he were bestowing a considerable favour. Rose could see where his daughter, Annie, got her efficiency from. He was delightful company, courteous and old-worldly. Rose enjoyed the contradiction of his pride in his daughter's success and his lament that he lived in a world where women had to earn their own living.

He knew nothing about her circumstances, Rose was sure.

'And as for these men who walk out on their responsibilities – in my opinion they should be horsewhipped. Horsewhipping'd be too good for 'em.'

Rose knew it was not as simple as that now, if it ever was. Wisely, she said little. She had grown to know his hobby-horses, could number and name them.

When he'd gone, muttering hugely about a world he no longer understood, packing large baker's trays into the back of his snug little van, Rose really missed him. He had filled the kitchen with his certainties, had created a warm comforting glow of righteousness in the midst of chaos. And he had made Rose think. She had held on to her own certainties, unquestioningly, for twenty years. What gave her the right to smile, knowingly, at Joe's indignation that his world had let him down?

Her world had let her down, too. She hadn't seen the signs either. Signs that she and Ben were diverging.

Knowledge was rising within her now, nourished by Ben's absence and her own wakefulness.

She felt open to everything; she could cope with anything. Knowing she had made mistakes, had been wrong, had willingly if unconsciously participated in the death of her marriage suddenly made her strong. She could face it.

But there was one thing she would never own. And that was the manner of Ben's leaving. No matter what had happened, or not happened. No matter what had been said, or left unsaid. To behave like that was wrong.

Knowing where to direct her anger gave her a tremendous sense of strength. Now she was beginning to feel the things she really wanted to say to Ben. Whole sentences achieved a clarity she had not known before.

The kids had an early finish today for Easter; she only had two hours to herself. She didn't mind that at all. She'd be glad to see them home early, to plan for a really special Easter.

Rose pulled a page out of her Bonne Bouche notebook and poured the last cup of tea from the pot.

One by one, she began to plan all the things she wanted to say to Ben.

And if he never came back, they were things she wanted to say anyway.

31st March, 1995

'Rose – I'm off. I've to meet Barry Herbert and Jack Morrissey.'

The truth, just not the whole truth.

'I'll be home late, don't worry about dinner.'

Rose appears at the top of the stairs.

She looks pale; there are dark circles under her eyes, and she wears no make-up. Ben feels impatience grow as she stands there.

'How late?' is all she says.

He shrugs.

'Probably ten or eleven. But don't wait up.'

Rose wonders how much more of this she can take.

She is conscious of Brian and Lisa on the landing, suddenly watching her.

'I won't. I'm tired.'

He nods, relieved.

'Right, then. I'm off.'

'Bye, Dad,' calls Brian.

'Bye, Dad,' calls Lisa.

'Bye, kids, be good.'

And once again, Rose looks as the door closes behind her husband.

Wednesday, 12th April

After Ben's revelation, Caroline thought she was going to be sick. Only when he started to speak did she realise the last place she wanted to spend her life was with him. She was shocked into recognising the strength of her feelings. She ran madly away from the restaurant. She hailed a taxi and gave the name of a hotel she had noticed earlier, mainly because of the garish sombrero which formed part of its hideous entrance.

'Hotel Don Pancho, *por favor.*'

That was the sum total of her Spanish. Less than five minutes later, she was in Reception.

They gave her a room on the third floor, looking out over the lights of the city. She kept the room in darkness and pulled up the outside blind. Caroline sank into the wicker chair at the end of her bed and breathed in all the smells of Spanish night air. A soothing mix of strong cigarette smoke, garlic and cologne.

If Ben had really told Rose that he was leaving, then Barry had to know.

He wasn't a fool. He'd never forgive her. For the first time in almost three years, Caroline realised how much that mattered to her.

She had loved Ben, in a way. But more than love, she had allowed herself to be carried away by the strength of his passion for her, and her own desire to be loved. She had responded to his need for her, fulfilling a need of her own.

But she did not love him as she loved Barry. That

was a life shared, bruised and battered sometimes, but real.

She thought of Aoife and Eoin. At eighteen and fifteen, they didn't seem to need her much any more. Tonight she realised how very desperately she needed them. All the lies, the deceptions and evasions – she felt the strength of her guilt as a physical pain, a tightness in her chest.

She wanted to go home. Once the thought was formed, the numbness within her began to dissolve. She started to cry. She had to get home.

She only hoped she wasn't too late.

Thursday, 13th April; 10.30 pm.

Rose moved restlessly from the kitchen to the sitting-room, touching things, rearranging cushions, sorting papers. The children were asleep, Jane was out. She needed to reassure herself that ordinary things were still real, still solid. That nothing else had suddenly shifted away from her.

Ellen would be up. Rose wanted to talk to her very much. She had been very kind after Michael, offering her kindness abruptly, almost harshly, the way she'd offered her new jeans and jacket all those years ago.

She'd ring Ellen. It was a while since she'd called the London number. She had to look it up: the prefix had changed.

The phone was answered immediately.

'Ellen? It's Rose.'

'Rose! Long time no hear!'

Her tone was friendly. Rose was encouraged. There was a click and a long hiss down the line as Ellen lit a cigarette and exhaled extravagantly.

'How are you all?'

'Fine,' Rose lied, waiting for her moment. 'How are you and Richard?'

'Oh, Richard is indulging in another one of his long absences. I'm waiting here at home like the dutiful wife I am.'

Rose wanted to hang up. She did not want to hear another rant against Richard, and she certainly didn't want to tell about Ben, now.

She tried to keep her voice even.

'When is he due back?'

'Not for another month. I didn't want him to go. But you know men. They suit themselves. How's Ben's business going?'

This was the nearest Ellen ever got to asking about Ben.

'Oh, you know. Up and down. It's a complicated world. It all seems to have been so much simpler in the old days!'

It was an innocent comment. An effort to defuse, to smooth over the cracks in her sister's voice, to avoid being drawn. She was unprepared for the assault which was immediate.

'You're always going on with that crap! You have this romantic notion about Mother and Father and how wonderful it all was! You're still a child, Rose.'

Rose felt the familiar patterns shape themselves. She would not be angry this time.

'She was told not to have any more children after you were born. She nearly lost you – and almost died herself. But Father wouldn't listen. She had two more and was dying before she was thirty! How about that for romance?'

Rose felt bone-weary. How could it happen that they had two such completely different sets of memories? Where she had seen devotion, Ellen had seen only hardship. Where she had seen companionship, generosity, Ellen had seen selfishness, coercion. How come their memories diverged so much?

'Mother told *me* what it was like. But you were never to know, *precious* Rose.'

Rose heard the unmistakable sound of ice chinking against glass. Her heart sank.

'Ellen, I didn't ring to fight. Can't we just accept that both sets of memories have some truth to them, and let it go at that? Please?'

'You really had no idea, you know. She sheltered and protected you always.'

Rose could sense that Ellen's anger was nearly spent, for now. Her tone was becoming sentimental. She changed tack abruptly.

'Was there any special reason you called? Anything new in the world?'

'No,' said Rose. 'Nothing new. I just wanted to keep in touch. It's a while since we spoke. Are you coming home for Christmas this year?'

'Dunno.'

Rose heard the ice chinking again.

'Depends,' she added darkly.

Rose decided not to ask on what.

'I'd better go, Ellen. Talk to you soon.'

'Yeah. Goodnight. Love to the kids.'

'Thanks. Goodnight.'

Rose hung up. Perhaps she had been protected, sheltered. Perhaps the eldest always got a raw deal. Now thoroughly depressed, Rose switched off the lights and got ready for bed.

She'd have to be very careful with Damien.

She wanted his memories to be different.

Friday, 14th April; 9.30 am.

On Friday morning, early, the phone rang.

Rose felt her stomach tighten, even before she answered it.

'Hello?'

'Rose – it's Barry. I need to talk to you. Can I come round?'

The kitchen was full of bowls, all the work surfaces were covered in flour. Rose noticed bits of candied peel on the kitchen floor. It didn't matter.

'Of course.'

'See you in twenty minutes.'

The kitchen suddenly felt distant, part of another reality, as Rose moved towards the sink to fill the kettle.

She sat down to wait. The knot in her stomach began to loosen. One way or the other, the waiting was nearly over.

Barry arrived exactly twenty minutes later.

When Rose opened the front door, she was surprised at the change in him. He was thinner and paler, but it wasn't just that. He was surrounded by a cloud of energy that she recognised instantly. It was anger.

'Caroline doesn't know I'm here. She won't know unless you choose to tell her.'

Even the way he moved was different. Decisive, sure-footed. Rose closed the kitchen door behind him.

'She got back yesterday. The affair is over.'

Rose's heart leapt with hope.

'And Ben?'

'She came home alone.'

'Caroline left Ben?'

For a moment, Rose allowed a savage, spiteful satisfaction to grow within her; that'll show him. The bastard.

'Yes. She didn't even tell him she was going. She just upped and left.'

Rose sensed a gap.

'What are you telling me?'

He hesitated.

'Barry, after the last eleven days, I can stand anything. Tell me.'

'This is her side of the story. There's always another.'

Rose nodded, unable to speak.

'Caroline says she didn't tell me she was leaving me because she honestly didn't believe it would come to that.'

Barry took the mug of coffee Rose offered him. He wrapped both hands around it.

'She says she'd made Ben promise to make no decision until the two weeks were up. She only found out after the first week that he'd left you. I think that really shocked her, the finality of it. Basically, she panicked and ran.'

'So Ben doesn't know where she is?'

'No.'

Rose tried to picture it. Ben, desolate, sunburnt, hating the heat. High and dry. Mooning after Caroline. At that moment she hated him. She was glad. Her anger was shifting from Caroline, from the other woman, to where it belonged. To a selfish, stupid, arrogant man; her husband.

'Thank you for this, Barry. Can I ask you something?'

'Sure, fire ahead.'

'Are you both going to be all right, you and Caroline?'

He shook his head, a gesture of uncertainty, not quite denial.

'I don't know. Caroline is different. All the reserve is gone. I've never seen her quite so emotional. But it could be just window-dressing ... I'm not prepared to put up with any more crap.'

As he was leaving, he handed Rose a slip of paper.

'That's the flight number. It gets in at half-nine on Monday morning.'

Rose nodded her thanks.

At the front door he turned to her and said, 'I don't normally give advice, Rose, and God knows I'm no expert ... but can I tell you something I've just learned?'

She nodded.

'Please!'

'Don't be too understanding when Ben comes home. Don't let him exploit your good nature; make it tough on him.'

'I will ... don't worry.'

Rose thought about nothing else but those final words for the rest of the day. Her own sense of guilt since Ben had left had been priming her to be reasonable and quiet, and to listen to Ben's explanations with as much understanding as she could summon. At least at first. But Barry's energy had forced her to see that there was another way, a way in which her hurt and humiliation would be acknowledged. If she had not a clear way of behaving mapped out in her own mind, she could see that Ben would slip into her uncertainties, filling all the gaps with subtle insinuations about how she was really, ultimately, to blame.

She thought she knew how she was going to handle him.

But what if he didn't come home at all? He might just run away for good. He might disappear without contact, without explanation. She really hoped he would not do that.

She wanted to see him. She needed him to know how she felt.

This time, she would wait for him.

But only this time.

Monday, 3rd April; 8.00 am.

Ben is annoyed when he gets to the kitchen to find that the kids aren't there. Rose has sent them back upstairs to brush their teeth.

He'll have to say something now.

'Rose, we have to talk.'

Her lack of response angers him. She is almost – *inert*. Isn't he even worth fighting for, in her eyes? All she does is wipe the spills of water from around the hob.

He hears her speaking.

'This is final, isn't it?'

He can't help himself. His anger, his impatience, her inertia all conspire together.

'I think so,' he hears himself say. 'I don't love you any more.'

It is done. He feels guilty that he's broken his promise to Caroline, furious that Rose has made him do it.

Abruptly, he pushes open the back door, letting it swing shut slowly behind him. The silence is strange.

He walks to his newly polished BMW and releases the central locking.

The car's smoothness pleases him; its swift response is satisfying after Rose. He decides against the morning news. Some classical music will be more soothing.

He chooses Dvorak's *New World Symphony*, pleased at the appropriateness of the title. He eases his silver BMW down the driveway towards the snarl of morning traffic. His hands grip the wheel clammily. Waiting for a space to pull into, he glances in the mirror several times. He has imagined this moment often. Rose, running distractedly towards the car, hair flying, Lisa in her arms. No, Lisa is much too big to be carried.

Rose and the children standing at the window, pale, uncomprehending.

Rose on her own at the window, weeping.

He misses his chance to sneak out into the morning traffic; a passing motorist blows his horn impatiently. Ben focuses on the road again. He looks in the mirror one last time before pulling away.

Nothing.

No hysterics. He should be relieved, but Rose's flatness about everything infuriates him. He feels uneasy about leaving them like this, but he needs this time to be free, with Caroline. As he heads towards the airport, he begins to feel the exhilaration of real freedom. Solitude, peace, tension uncoiling like the traffic. For over two years he has imagined this escape, ever since he really noticed Caroline. Caroline as distinct from Barry and Caroline. His gut knots when he thinks of her. This is new to him, even after more than two years. He's never felt it with Rose. He is glad he feels it now.

He is going to meet his lover. They are going to be together, they are going to decide.

Leaving Rose is like leaving madness behind. Caroline is real, earthy, gritty; a new sanity. Although Ben has never slept properly since they became lovers, he is never tired. He wakes up thinking of her, goes to bed filled with her.

Ben indicates left as he pulls off the roundabout and into the airport complex. He is hours early for his midday flight. He needs to be there, waiting for her. He drives into the long-stay carpark, cursing as his hand doesn't quite reach the ticket-machine. He opens the car door and struggles to reach the ticket without taking off his seat-belt. A young man in a leather jacket and jeans, with his arm around his girlfriend, watches Ben with amusement and whispers something into the woman's ear. She laughs and kisses the side of his face, their dark sunglasses touching each other.

Ben feels suddenly angry, conscious of his suit and tie, suddenly awkward. He drives off. In the mirror, he sees the couple watching the BMW's fast and elegant departure. The young man shrugs his shoulders; the woman is laughing.

Suddenly mollified, Ben reverses cleanly into the parking space. He checks to make sure the interior is still immaculate. He lifts his suitcase out of the boot, throws his tie in and wraps his cream cashmere sweater around his shoulders.

The alarm sounds politely, locks salute into place.

Ben puts the keys in his pocket and walks towards the terminal building. Then he sits down to wait.

Rose cannot move.

The schoolyard is emptying, mothers pushing buggies are hurrying away. They are calling to one another, waving, smiling.

She watches as a man in a suit rushes into the yard, holding a little boy by the hand. He bends down, tilting the young face towards him. They hug. The man waits until the child has reached the school door. They wave.

It is all so ordinary.

Rose tries again to turn the key in the ignition. Her hands seem to have turned to water. On the third attempt, she succeeds. The noise of the engine is somehow comforting.

Very carefully, she pulls out from the kerb. She turns the car and drives away slowly. The feet on the pedals don't seem to belong to her. Rose knows she has to be careful. This time of the morning is dangerous, even on ordinary days.

She wants to be home. Safe, surrounded by her own four walls.

Part Three

Part Three

Monday, 17th April; 5.30 am.

Two weeks. Two whole weeks had passed. Rose woke with
the thought at precisely five-thirty am on Easter Monday.
Today was the day. She got up immediately. Ben's plane
was due in at nine-thirty.

The telephone rang at half-past ten, exactly.

Rose picked it up. She was ready.

'Hello?'

'Rose? It's Ben.'

She allowed a long silence to grow. She judged its length
perfectly. Ben was nervous when he spoke again.

'Rose, I need to see you. We have to talk.'

Now where had she heard that before?

'Do we? I thought you'd said all you wanted to say the
day you left. You didn't want to listen to me then.'

She stopped for a moment, not wanting to slam the door
completely. She'd leave it open just a crack.

'I accept that. I really need to see you, to explain. I'm
still not sure how I feel, Rose, I don't know what's going
to happen, but I do want to see you.'

Rose could feel the power shifting already. The assumption that everything depended on his feelings, on his needs,
angered her deeply.

'I don't know if I want to see you just now, Ben; I need
some time to think. I had no idea you'd be calling today.
Perhaps you could ring me on Wednesday or Thursday; I've
a lot of things planned for the kids' holidays.'

It was her first blatant lie in over twenty years. It felt
good. She could taste his surprise across the phone line.

'I'd really like to see the kids, too, Rose.'

Rose hesitated. The one thing she had sworn was that she would not use the kids as a bargaining tool.

'I'm sure they'd like to see you, too. I'll rearrange things a bit.'

But she wasn't going to give too much away.

'Why don't you ring me tomorrow afternoon, sometime after four?'

'OK. If you want to contact me, I'll be at my mother's.'

His mother's. Rose almost didn't believe it. She felt a knife-edge of contempt.

'I will not want to contact you at your mother's. I'll expect to hear from you after four tomorrow. Goodbye, Ben.'

She sat at the kitchen table for a long time. Now that the waiting was over, she felt very, very tired. There were so many different feelings churning around.

Bed. She would go to bed. She felt hollow, brittle. The fact that Ben's mother was now involved was a real humiliation.

Rose knew that Ben had no friends, no one in whom he could confide. But to run back to mother? The man had never grown up; he was still a little boy, grabbing all he could get and running home howling when he couldn't keep what he wanted. He had at least two weeks' growing up to do, the same two weeks she had just put in.

It was disappointing. She had hoped for more.

To hell with going to bed.

She pulled her blue ledger out of the drawer and planned her shopping and baking for the coming week.

She became completely absorbed; the next time she looked at the clock, it was one. Time for lunch.

It was becoming something of a ritual. She took out one of the few remaining bottles of Ben's good wine, wrapped it in a brown paper bag and went off down the road to Jane.

The following afternoon, Rose warned the children not to answer the phone; she was expecting an important call. Lisa nodded, eyes on the TV screen. Brian said nothing; he just looked at Rose, blankly. She could still feel his eyes on her back as she turned to leave the room.

Damien followed her into the kitchen, and she told him his dad was home.

'How is he?'

'I don't know. He wants to see you all.'

Damien was poking at the floor with the toe of his runners.

'Is he coming home?'

The casual question, the eyes locked on the floor, the hair falling over the still-soft cheek. Rose thought her heart was going to break. Tears, threatening since yesterday's phone call, welled up, almost spilled over.

Damien looked up sharply.

'It's OK, Ma. Really, it is.'

She nodded, biting hard on her lower lip.

'Damien, I want you to give him a chance, give us all a chance to put this right.'

He nodded.

'This doesn't mean that I have to get my hair cut before I see him, does it?'

Rose laughed.

'No, it doesn't! Just lay off the campaign for the earring for a bit!'

It was at that point that the phone rang. One minute past four.

'Hello?'

Rose answered, aware that she and Ben were both playing games, like some kind of black courtship ritual, neither wanting to appear really interested.

'Yes, Ben, tomorrow morning will be fine. Eleven; I'll have the kettle on.'

Brian and Lisa walked in, looking at her uncertainly.

'Is Dad coming home?' Brian asked.

Rose looked at his white face. He had become sullen again over the last few days.

'He's coming to see us all tomorrow. He's really looking forward to seeing you guys, so make sure you're back by eleven, if you go out to play.'

'In that?' said Lisa.

Rose looked out at the sudden rain.

'Maybe it'll be better tomorrow. If not, you can have Kate and Alison here to play.'

Routine was so necessary. Rose's tiredness began to return.

She'd busied herself all day, baking, cleaning, anything. Her mind kept racing ahead. It was like a contest. The prize was now sleep.

'What's for dinner?'

Prize-giving deferred.

'Chicken curry, and it's ready now, so don't anyone leave the kitchen. After dinner, I want you all to do your jobs quickly and get into pyjamas early.'

She raised her hands to stem the cries of protest.

'You can watch your film until nine, as I promised. Then it's bed. I'm whacked. No arguments or I'm likely to bite. There are three big bowls of popcorn on the counter for later . . . Damien, are you going out?'

He shook his head, mouth full of curry.

'Anyone coming in?'

He shook his head vigorously again.

'Right, so that's settled. A quiet night in the Holden household.'

She felt anything but quiet herself. As she scraped the last bits of rice onto Damien's plate, Rose felt terrified.

No matter what happened, tomorrow was going to be the most important day of the rest of her life.

Wednesday, 19th April; 6.00 am.

Damien padded softly downstairs to the kitchen. Rose was sitting at the table in her dressing-gown, her notebook open in front of her. A piece of half-eaten toast and a mug had been pushed to one side. She looked up sharply as the door creaked.

'Go back to bed, Damien. It's only six o'clock.'

Rose was absorbed; her tone was not welcoming. Suddenly she smiled.

'I'm fine. Getting up early is a habit now. I'll probably get sleepy in an hour or so, and go back to bed. Will you call me at ten?'

Damien nodded eagerly.

'No problem.'

He really didn't want to get up just yet, and she did seem OK. He would set his alarm for five to ten and call her. He was glad to have something to do.

Rose watched him go. How much to push him away, how much to allow him to assume adult responsibility? And how much influence did she really have, anyway? He seemed to have grown so much in the last fortnight, physically as well as every other way.

Ever since Ben's return, Rose had been watching her children very closely. Lisa was still very much a little girl, apparently undisturbed by the emotional turmoil all around her. Damien she could figure, day by day, but she was terrified at the prospect of conflict between him and Ben.

It was Brian who was the real worry. He had become a very restless child, full of jerky movements. His awkwardness irritated his brother and sister. He was unable to sit still; he mooched constantly on the sofa and thrashed about in bed at night. Rose had several times replaced his duvet and eased his body back towards the centre of his bed. She was no psychologist, but adolescence and the loss of an adored father were obviously taking their toll. She and Ben were going to have to work something out fast, for his sake.

She went back to her notebook. She needed escape from the pounding thoughts that had kept her company since four o'clock.

It was now seven. The waiting was nearly over. Rose's eyes began to close. She climbed the stairs quietly, deciding to ignore the scuffling sounds coming from Damien's room.

Gratefully, she snuggled under the duvet and instantly slept.

Rose got up immediately Damien called her. She was surprised and gratified at his appearance. He was dressed in a pair of dark cotton jeans and a rather formal white shirt. He had brushed his long hair very carefully and tied it neatly in a ponytail. He had cleaned his fingernails and polished his shoes. To her this said: Things did not fall apart, Father, while you were away. Rose is a good mother and we are responsible, caring children. We minded one another.

To Damien she simply said, 'You look really well. Your hair suits you like that.'

When she passed his casually open door, she saw that he had tidied his bedroom. It was immaculate. No clothes on the floor, bed made, curtains tied back. She felt proud. It was a vote of confidence in all of them.

At breakfast, Brian pretended unconcern. He managed to knock over the milk carton and stand on Lisa's toe. She screamed so shrilly that Rose scalded herself with the kettle and had to stop herself from shouting angrily at both of them.

They ate in a tense silence. Rose thought: This is ridiculous. Aloud she said:

'This is going to be a difficult morning for all of us if we don't say what we're thinking. Your dad is going to be here soon, and we have to find a way to talk to one another.'

She stopped for a moment, wondering where to go to next.

'When he comes, and after you've all said hello, I'd like to spend an hour or so here in the kitchen with him, just the two of us.'

Brian looked at her, full of hate.

'Are we not allowed to talk to him?'

Oh, Christ, thought Rose. Here we go.

'Of course you're allowed. Would you like to talk to Dad first?'

Thus challenged, he retreated.

'No,' he said. 'I haven't anything to say.'

Oh yes you have, thought Rose, and I hope you can say it to him, and not take it out on me.

'There'll be plenty of time over the next few weeks. We just need to get some things cleared up first.'

It sounded so matter of fact, so simple. The assumption that every problem had a solution. The solicitor, David O'Brien, had been firm and logical. To him, a separation was a process, and if she decided to become his client formally, there were certain things she must accept; according to him, she deserved and was entitled to fair treatment. But that was no help dealing with the minefields around marital disharmony. This was no process with a beginning, a middle and an end. This was twenty years of her life, *all* of her adult emotional life, and the reason she now had three children. There had been, through the years, dozens of different Bens, dozens of different Roses. They were by turns kind, loving, humorous, gentle, generous, bad-tempered, selfish, lazy, sad and cruel.

She now had to focus on a Ben she had never known –

Ben the unfaithful, Ben the betrayer, Ben the deserter. How could she discuss, negotiate, agree, bargain with a man she had never met?

It was almost eleven. It was raining, of course. Brian and Lisa went off to watch television, she limping in an aggrieved fashion, he subdued. Damien went to his room.

At precisely eleven o'clock, the silver BMW snaked up the driveway. Rose had to fight back the laughter that surged as she remembered the airport carpark. He parked exactly in his accustomed place and patted his pockets to find his key.

Rose didn't know whether he rang the bell and put his key in the lock simultaneously – a sort of advance warning system – or whether he rang the bell after he discovered his key didn't fit. Either way, the second ring was definitely irritable.

She waited as long as she could, and opened the door. She had the pleasure of seeing surprise on his face as he took in her slimmer figure in jeans and a simple silk shirt that hadn't fitted her for years. She doubted if he even remembered it. She had chosen it deliberately. Caroline's fabric, Caroline's colour. Peach silk. It gave her great pleasure to wear it.

'Hello, Ben.'

She stood, framed in the doorway for a fraction longer than was necessary. She stepped back slowly, every gesture saying: my territory, my space to which, at least for now, I admit you reluctantly.

He was caught off guard. The new locks, the changed wife, the now disputed territory of home made him uncertain. All of this passed in no more than a couple of seconds, but he knew, and Rose knew, that she was, so far, mistress of this situation.

'Hello, Rose; you look well.'

She acknowledged the compliment with a small smile. Her silence told him what they both knew. She could not return the compliment. He looked awful. He had that red, half-boiled look that fair skins get when they are stupid in the sun. His forehead and scalp were positively glowing. His hair was definitely thinner.

Rose thought that she might come to feel love for him again and then this would not matter. But for now she saw and was glad that he looked a most unattractive man.

She remembered, oh, so many holidays in the past when the children were small. In the days before high-factor suncreams. She would be really careful of the children, keeping them covered, putting them to play under the beach umbrellas, making them wear wide-brimmed straw hats. She remembered with horror incidents from her own childhood when her shoulders and the backs of her legs screamed in agony as the skin tightened, blistered, split and eventually peeled. It was a normal part of summer. She would plead with Ben during the first few days of the holiday every year, to be careful, to take it easy, to sit out in small doses. The response was always the same. Crossly, impatiently, he would say: 'Stop worrying, Rose, I'll be fine.'

But she didn't and he wasn't. He would suffer agonies for the first week, retiring to bed and darkness while she shushed the children and took them out of the apartment as much as possible. By the second week he'd have learned to be sensible, and Rose would have learned, again, not to expect acknowledgement or apology for a miserable first week.

'I'll be fine.' It was like a mantra. Any way you said it, any emphasis you gave it, it amounted to a thoroughly selfish way of looking at life.

All these thoughts passed with astonishing swiftness through Rose's mind as she watched her husband greet his children.

'Daddy!'

Lisa came running for a big hug and Ben swept her off her feet.

'Hiya, kiddo!'

He pulled a large parcel from the leather holdall at his feet.

He had always been hopeless at buying presents. Were these chosen by Caroline before her moonlight flit, or perhaps by Ben's mother . . .

Stop it! Rose spoke to herself severely. She could feel the onset of bitterness in every thought. She wasn't even giving him a chance.

Brian stuck his hand out stiffly to his father. Ben seemed surprised, and shook it carefully, not closing the physical distance which Brian had opened up between them. The child mumbled his thanks for his parcel, and stumbled out of the kitchen, knocking his elbow painfully against the door as he went. Rose's heart was sore as she watched him.

As though on cue, Damien appeared just when Rose felt the stirrings of panic.

'Hi, Dad,' he said easily, offering Ben his hand.

Rose watched as Ben took in every detail.

'Hi, Damien,' and his mouth registered disapproval as he saw the ponytail.

Rose noticed with shock that Damien was now taller than his father. That couldn't have happened in just over two weeks. Had she somehow missed out on all of that, too? Ben handed Damien an envelope, saying, 'Thought you'd prefer this.'

Damien acceped it with grace, all his movements showing the confidence of one sure of his place, his status.

Rose felt very powerfully that Damien was challenging his father. Don't, Damien, please don't, she pleaded silently; he'll think I've turned you all against him. For now, Damien was the man and Ben the boy seeking his approval. She could sense his unease, his unsureness. For the first time since she had known him, Ben Holden was at a loss.

'See you later, Ma.'

This, on his way out, sealed the special bond between mother and son which Ben must have been sensing since Damien's almost arrogant entrance.

'Would you like coffee?'

Rose was already moving towards the kettle.

'Yes, just a quick cup. I have a meeting later on this morning.'

Rose was glad her back was turned. She wanted to throw the kettle at him and scream, You bastard! You run off for two weeks without a word, cry on mother's shoulder and now you don't even have the time to face your own wife!

She knew that losing her temper was a bad idea. He would have reason to feel offended, aggrieved, and any control she had in this situation would be irrevocably lost. She could feel it slipping away already. She made herself take a deep breath as she plugged in the kettle.

She returned to the table, standing beside him, resting her hands on the back of a chair while he sat.

'I think that what you and I have to talk about is an awful lot more important than going to a meeting. I have made myself available all day today. You have said, more than once, that we need to talk. I agree. Now let's talk.'

The struggle between them was an almost physical presence. Neither spoke. Ben just looked at her, and she returned his gaze steadily. She felt that if the air between them could be seen, it would be a deep, purple mass. She could read in his eyes disbelief that she had anything more important to do than wait for him.

'When I said we needed to talk, I didn't have here in mind. I wanted to see you and the children this morning, but I think we need to arrange somewhere more . . . neutral to discuss the future.'

'And what about the past? Specifically the recent past?'

Rose's voice was soft and controlled, but anger, molten like lava, was beginning to rumble.

Ben stiffened.

'We need to discuss everything, of course, but it's going to take time. I need a lot of space to decide whether . . . what

I'm going to do. In the meantime, this house is not a suitable place for us to meet.'

Whether it was his prim, business-conference manner, his awful sunburned forehead or his assumption that the decision was totally his, Rose never knew. All she knew was that the purple mass began to deepen and widen and she had never felt angrier in her life.

Boiling water, sharp scissors, carving knives. She stood up carefully.

'Get out, Ben.'

His face, against his ludicrous forehead, was dead white.

'Get out, now.'

He began to bluster, not yet angry, just taken aback that he was no longer in charge.

'Calm down, Rose. This is my house too, you know.'

'It may be your house, but it is my home. Now, get to fuck out of it.'

He hated women swearing, Rose knew that. At that moment, she also knew with astonishing clarity that she never wanted him back.

He, too, became angry.

'Where is your dignity, woman?'

'I'll tell you where it is! I'll tell you! My dignity is lying somewhere on a beach in Málaga! My dignity has been stamped on by a stupid, arrogant, selfish man who didn't even bother to let his family know he was alive! My dignity has been shit upon by a man who didn't even have the courage after twenty years to tell the truth! That's where my dignity is! Now fuck off!'

For the first time in twenty years, Rose had had the last word.

Ben left, slamming the front door behind him.

He was right. This was not the place to discuss the past, present or future. They would have to find neutral territory. Rose's anger subsided very quickly, and she felt cleansed.

She would contact David O'Brien tomorrow to discuss what to do next.

Meanwhile, there were Damien, Brian and Lisa, waiting.

She went to each of them, cautiously. Lisa was willing to be reassured; Damien was angry: 'What does he think I am, a kid? Nothing for nearly three weeks and what does he give me – a lousy tenner!'

Rose listened without comment. Brian was playing his computer.

'I don't care if he never comes back.'

The opened parcel lay thrown on the bed, ignored.

She let them all do their own thing for the rest of the afternoon, too exhausted to play happy families.

She removed the cling-film from her bread doughs and began to knead them savagely. Amid all the pummelling and punching, stretching and flattening, Rose held on to one thing:

That was the moment of absolute clarity when she knew that she did not, ever, want Ben back.

'Calm down, Rose,' he'd said. 'This is my house, too,' he'd said.

She had stayed calm for twenty years. Now it was time to be angry.

Friday, 28th April; 4.30 pm.

Money was getting tight. The ESB and the gas were due. Ben knew that. Rose had thought of writing to him at his mother's; she did not want to speak to him over the telephone. She would keep the tone of her letter reasonable and calm and suggest that he choose some neutral meeting-ground. She had decided to be conciliatory, to tell him that he was right, that the house was not a suitable place to meet.

Her money from the Bonne Bouche was not nearly enough to meet the bills. Rose was now waking up at four o'clock every morning, exhausted and panicking. How were they going to live? If Ben didn't help out . . .

In many ways, his return had been worse than his leaving. She had learned to cope with hurt and humiliation, to live with guilt and self-doubt. But this was different. She felt trapped in a game whose rules she did not know. Her marriage now existed as a sort of economic bargain for survival; the interest rate was her dignity.

Late in the afternoon, she sat down to write to him. She was unable even to form the first sentence. For the first time since he had left her, Rose was filled with a great sadness. Not the grief or anguish she had suffered at first, not the anger or resentment she later felt, but a pure, simple feeling of loss.

After twenty years of shared living, and three children with a man she had loved, she was not able to find even the simplest words to reach him. She wept silently, tears flowing freely without restraint, washing away any last, faint hopes of reconciliation.

The telephone rang. Rose wiped her eyes with the back of her hand, smearing black all over her face.

It was a brief, brutal conversation.

With shaking hands, Rose replaced the receiver and immediately rang Ben, desperately needing his help.

Mrs Holden answered the phone and Rose tried to make her voice sound normal. To her surprise, her mother-in-law's voice was full of warmth.

'Of course, Rose love, I'll get him for you now.'

She ignored the cold formality of her husband's greeting.

'Ben, you've got to meet me straight away. Brian has been caught shoplifting.'

His tone changed instantly.

'Where are you now?'

'I'm at home; we've got to go to Pearse Street Garda Station right away.'

'Stay where you are; I'll come and get you.'

Rose grabbed her jacket and handbag. She rang Jane to ask her to hold on to Lisa until later. Damien would look after himself.

She ran down the driveway to wait for Ben. She was still shaking. God, she was right to have been worried about Brian. Stealing computer games from Virgin. Maybe, maybe if Ben was willing to come back they could try again. She had to do something for Brian's sake.

Maybe they could work something out. She had to try.

Saturday, 29th April; 10.00 am.

The doorbell rang at ten o'clock. Rose rolled over, willing Damien to answer it. Her eyes were heavy and hot. She had still been awake at four am, reliving in sharp detail the scene at the Garda Station. The Garda said he had given Brian 'a good fright'.

When Rose and Ben arrived at the station, she had been shocked to see people coming in and going out, doing ordinary business. Men and women in uniform walked around casually, carrying files. Others adjusted their uniforms and made their way quickly to the cars waiting outside. It all looked so busy, so normal. But this was not normal; this was no place for her son.

'This way, please, Mr and Mrs Holden.'

Even that was abnormal, Rose thought. Was she Mrs Holden any longer? Everything had an air of unreality about it. As they got up to follow the Garda, Rose's legs were still shaking.

Inside the interview room, Brian was sullen. He would not look at her as they sat down beside him. He kept his eyes down, staring at the table.

The young Garda introduced himself. Rose couldn't remember, didn't hear his name. Her heart was pounding.

'. . . And it's a very serious offence,' she heard. 'Do you realise that?'

Brian's expression didn't change.

Rose put her hand on his arm.

'Brian, please answer.'

He shrugged her hand off angrily. Rose turned to Ben for help.

'Brian, I want to know why you've done this. If you don't co-operate, you could be in big trouble. Now start talking.'

Ben was hunched forward, elbows resting on his knees. Rose noticed that his knuckles were white.

She saw the sullenness on Brian's face change to uncertainty. The Garda was talking again. Rose began to feel that she would wake up soon.

'. . . And I'm sure you don't want to have a criminal record, do you? It never goes away, you know, just follows you around for the rest of your life. Your name is never clear. Is that what you want?'

The tone was getting harder now, the same phrases repeated with an insistence that terrified Rose. But it was working. At least Brian was looking at him now, making contact. He was listening to what the Garda was saying. Rose noticed with relief that he was beginning to be really scared.

'I didn't mean to,' he suddenly pleaded.

'Did you think you could get away with it?'

Ben's voice was angry, humiliated. For the first time, Brian looked at his father directly. His eyes filled with tears. Oh my God, thought Rose. What a mess. This can't go on.

Brian shook his head, a few tears escaping.

Suddenly, the atmosphere in the room relaxed. There was an air of release. It was over. Rose heard the words 'official caution'. Brian nodded, listening as the Garda explained to him the seriousness of being given a second chance. The Garda made him watch as he wrote something down slowly, deliberately. He made Brian sign what he had written. Then he was sent to wait outside.

Rose remembered nothing of what the Garda had said to

them, except that nothing further would happen as long as Brian behaved himself.

Immensely relieved, she expected to find a penitent child waiting for them. They would work it out. Instead, he was furious, jerky, tight-lipped.

She felt that they had got nowhere with him after all. Rose was deeply depressed. This had not been a way of bringing them all back together. If anything, it was driving them further apart.

The journey home from Pearse Street had been a tense, silent one. At the arches in Fairview, Ben finally spoke. His tone was cold, clipped.

'I think it's very foolish to let a twelve-year-old child into town without adequate supervision. I don't care if all his friends do it. He shouldn't be allowed.'

My fault again, thought Rose. But she kept her mouth shut. She was not going to fight with Ben in front of Brian.

When they got home, she sent Brian to his room at once, saying they would discuss it in the morning.

Ben did not come in. Her territory, her problem.

She sent Lisa to bed early, told Damien not to worry, she'd explain everything tomorrow. Shortly after four o'clock, she took a sleeping-tablet and went looking for oblivion.

Now, she really did not want to get up. She wanted to sleep. Dimly, she was aware of someone answering the door. She hoped that the caller was not anybody looking for her. There was a soft tap at her bedroom door. She struggled for a moment with the desire to ignore it, to feign sleep.

After yesterday, she could not.

Damien opened the door gently.

'Ma, it's Granny.'

Dear God, let me die now, thought Rose.

'Tell her I'll be down in a minute.'

Rose forced herself to sit up. Sheer willpower placed her feet on the floor. She pulled on leggings and a shirt and splashed her face with cold water.

She looked awful. She was not going to make any effort to look better. Why should she? Let her see what her son had done.

Rose immediately felt guilty at the thought. The poor woman was no more responsible for Ben's behaviour than she was. A comforting thought. At least they now had something in common.

Damien had already put on the kettle. The old lady stood up as Rose entered the kitchen; she walked towards her and enveloped her in a big, maternal hug. Rose was astonished. Even after all these years, she still didn't know what to call her. 'Mrs Holden' sounded ridiculous, an echo of herself. 'Granny' was patronising; 'Maureen' was too familiar. She usually solved the problem by addressing her directly. On the phone, she would say brightly: 'Hello, it's Rose here. How are you?'

Now, here she was uninvited. Was she a messenger for Ben? Had she come to do some of his dirty work for him? Rose was instantly ashamed of the thought. Her mother-in-law's hands were trembling and Rose realised that she was deeply upset. The older woman's distress made her kind. She returned the hug and said, 'Sit down, and I'll make us both a cup of tea.'

The old lady sat, still in her coat, her handbag clutched firmly in front of her, like a shield.

'Give me your coat and I'll hang it up for you.'

She relinquished the coat, but held on firmly to the handbag.

'Ben doesn't know I'm here.'

OK, thought Rose, play it by ear.

She waited.

'I don't approve at all of the way he's behaving.'

That makes two of us, thought Rose, but I'll not say that or you'll spring to his defence.

'He used to be a very selfish little boy, and it seems that he hasn't changed.'

Rose still said nothing. She thanked God for the ritual of teamaking.

Eventually Rose had to face her. She brought the cups and saucers to the table, poured the milk into a jug and sat down opposite her mother-in-law. She gave the tea a final stir before pouring.

'What can I say? Things are very difficult at the moment.'

Rose wondered whether she knew about Brian, and hoped not. She couldn't go over all that again. Not yet.

'I can't get anywhere with Ben; his father won't discuss it, either with me or with him. I've told him he can't stay with me any longer than a month. Either he faces up to his responsibilities or he finds somewhere else to go. He'll have no soft option with me.'

It was the longest speech Rose had ever heard her make. She tried to respond to her mother-in-law's efforts to be kind, but the cloud of sleeping-tablet was weighing heavily on her.

'I'm sorry, I didn't sleep well last night. I really don't know what to say to you. He left me three weeks ago. I've no idea what he's going to do. The kids are confused and I'm at the end of my tether.'

It was true. All the illusions of strength and independence had suddenly shattered. She was behind in her baking, had no energy to work. It looked like she was going to make a mess of that, too.

'I want to help. I can babysit if you need, and I want to give you this.'

She reached into her handbag and withdrew a large white envelope.

'And please, call me Maureen.'

Rose smiled at her and waved away the envelope.

'You're very good, Maureen. Really, please, I'll be OK.'

'I insist. If you feel that way, then take this for my grandchildren. Please.'

Rose could not refuse her.

'Thank you,' she said simply.

Maureen nodded, satisfied. Over the tea, Rose told her what had happened, finding in her a surprisingly good listener.

'Consequences,' she said grimly, once Rose had finished her story. 'Ben never had to face the consequences of anything he did. He was always shielded.'

Rose looked at her in surprise. Maureen's words felt right. She had a sudden vision of herself, all through their years together, picking up after him. Picking up the pieces. She wondered who had done it before she came along.

'His dad thought he could do no wrong. Ben has always got what he wanted.'

Rose felt a new respect for her. She knew her son well; her comments were perceptive.

After an hour, Maureen got up to leave. Rose had enjoyed her company, and told her so.

'Call on me if you need any help. This visit is absolutely between us. Neither Ben nor his father knows I'm here.'

Rose nodded.

'I'll keep it that way.'

'Keep in touch.'

Another warm hug and she was gone.

Removed from the company of her husband and son, Maureen was different. Rose saw her as an individual personality, no longer part of a monolith to be endured at Christmas and Easter.

Damien walked his grandmother to the bus stop. Rose waved until the old lady was out of sight. Then she opened the envelope.

Inside, in crisp notes, were five hundred pounds.

She was not a rich woman; this was real generosity, real sacrifice. Rose felt the relief of the execution reprieved. This was breathing space, not just buying power.

Rose hid the envelope in her wardrobe and went off to tackle Brian.

Brian was unsure of his ground. He was less hostile than the previous day, but still jerky, abrasive.

Rose sat on the little wicker chair, he on the end of the bed. Somehow, this scene felt very familiar.

'Brian, I want to talk to you about yesterday.'

He was crumpling the duvet cover, making a fist over and over again.

'I want you to look at me.'

There was an edge to his mother's voice that Brian had not heard before. He looked up at her quickly. Rose could see fear in his eyes.

'That was a very dangerous and foolish thing you did yesterday. I think you know that now.'

The small, white face began to tighten. God, he was so like his father.

'I want to understand why you did it, Brian. Have you any idea?'

He shrugged.

'It was just a dare.'

Rose took a deep breath. Softly, softly, catchee monkey.

'Have you always done what your friends have dared you?'

He shrugged again. Silence.

'Answer me, Brian.'

Rose's voice was deliberately hard. He would *not* grow up believing that consequences were only for other people.

'Not always.'

'And why this time?'

Both small fists were now occupied with the duvet.

'They kept at me and at me.'

Rose could picture it. The group of them, standing around, coveting 'Streetfighter'. The nudging, the pushing, the group pressure. If you're so good at games, how about playing this one? She could almost hear the taunt. It held out the promise of acceptance, belonging, a sort of love. She could see why he had done it.

'But *you* did it. You were responsible, and you got caught.'

'I didn't mean to do it.'

The voice was only a whisper, the tears were welling.

Now Rose moved from the chair to the bed. She took the small, unhappy face in her hands.

'I know you want your dad to come home, but this is not the way to do it.'

He was not resisting her now.

'We are working hard to sort this out, love. Your Dad and I love you all very much.'

She kissed the spiky hair at the back of his head.

He pulled away from her suddenly.

'Is Dad still talking to me?'

Rose's heart missed a painful beat.

'Of course. He is upset and angry that you were dishonest. So am I. But we'll work it out.'

She let him move away from her.

'Until we do, you are not allowed into town, on your own or with anyone else, until I say so.'

Brian didn't respond.

'You have to earn my trust again. I want you to think about what you've done. I want to be sure you understand the seriousness of it. Until then, you're grounded.'

He nodded. Rose could have sworn he was relieved. She had no idea how else to punish him, how long to make the punishment last, how to drive the message home.

She'd have to think about it. This was all new to her.

She went back into the kitchen to make strong coffee. She couldn't go back to bed while there was all this chaos around her.

She cleared away the dirty cups and saucers, filled the dishwasher, and sat down, wondering how she was going to face what remained of the weekend.

Friday, 19th May; 9.00 am.

The morning after Ben moved into his rented apartment, he drove past Caroline's house. He had taken to driving past her house late at night. He was often tempted to call in, if Barry's car was missing. But common sense told him they could both be out together. Barry's was, after all, the better car.

Seeing the lights on downstairs, or a shadow passing the front door on the way upstairs, would fill Ben with unreasoning anger. It all looked so normal from the outside.

He was not prepared to give her up; she still wanted him, he knew that. Her flight from him in Spain was understandable, in hindsight. He had been a little heavy.

He cursed himself for having rushed it. She'd need more time. There were her children to consider; she would find that very difficult.

This morning, Barry's car was gone. Caroline's was still there. Good. He knew her habit of arriving after Barry at the office most mornings, and of staying later in the evenings. She was at home in the mornings until Eoin and Aoife left for school, and Barry was there most afternoons. Caroline hated cooking; Barry didn't mind. Ben had always found it an odd arrangement, but had never commented. Such details were really not important.

What was important was that he reassure Caroline he still wanted her, needed her badly. She could, of course, take as much time as she needed. But they would be together.

Ben drove off quickly. He decided against using his

car-phone. He'd go back to the apartment. He parked in the courtyard, right outside his front door.

He found his hands were sweating as he dialled Caroline's number. She answered; cautiously, he thought. Good; she must have been expecting him.

'Caroline. It's Ben.'

He couldn't help the relief in his voice. They could finally talk.

'I asked you not to call me again.'

Her voice was still sharp, but not as much as before. He was right. Barry had been there the first time.

He was not going to push her now.

'Caroline, we have to talk. We can't just leave it like this.'

'We're not just leaving anything. Our relationship is over. There isn't anything else to be said. It was a mistake and it's over.'

He'd have to play along with this. She was obviously upset, he knew by her voice.

'I don't want to force you to do anything. But there are lots of things unfinished. Don't you think I deserve to understand why you decided to leave?'

Ben stopped. He felt he'd said enough for the moment. He knew that she hated loose ends.

'I don't see any point in meeting, I really don't.'

Good. She hadn't said that she wouldn't.

'There's a point to it for me,' he said. 'I need to see you to believe that you really mean it. I'll meet wherever and whenever you say, and then I'll leave you alone.'

He could hear her hesitation.

'Look, Caroline, if you don't want to meet in public, I have my own place now. You can take a taxi, it can all be very discreet. A couple of hours isn't much to ask after two years, is it?'

He knew she hated to feel she owed anyone.

'All right. Give me your address and phone number. I'll see what I can do.'

But he knew that he'd won.

Ben finished his unpacking, such as it was. He'd have to go home and pick up a lot of stuff soon. The thought of another confrontation with Rose put him off. She had made him very angry on the last two occasions. Perhaps he could arrange to go sometime when she was out. Damien or Brian could let him in. It would be easier.

He knew that Caroline would come sooner rather than later. A little time together was all he needed to convince her. He tidied away the remaining cardboard boxes. The furniture was comfortable and plentiful, if a little frilly for Caroline's taste.

Before he left to face his bank manager, Ben put on the answering machine. With a little luck, Caroline might call back today.

He'd be ready.

Tuesday, 23rd May; 10.30 am.

Early the next week, Rose received a curt letter from Ben. It informed her that the mortgage had been paid, as had other outstanding bills. It expressed hope that they might meet soon to 'regularise their position'. Rose felt like the subject of a memo, no longer a human being. She had spent all weekend catching up on her work for the Bonne Bouche, preparing extra samples in the hope of increasing her earnings a little.

Ben's letter only intensified the sensation of doors closing all around her. She was beginning to hate him consistently, rather than in short bursts. It frightened her, the narrow range of options left open to her. If they split, where would she live? How would her children be educated, clothed, fed? But she wanted nothing from him, would take nothing from him. His letter hinted at serious business difficulties.

Six months ago, she would have rowed in behind him to organise paperwork, to photocopy documents, to make appointments with bank managers. Now she was suspicious, she trusted not one word.

Was he paving the way for meagre maintenance? Was he in collusion with his accountants? She could imagine income being hidden, outgoings exaggerated, profits minimised. She remembered once that he had laughingly referred to 'creative accounting'. She had felt a little uneasy at the term. But she had ignored its implications in the pursuit of her own comforts. Don't rock the boat. She regretted again her passivity, felt once more the stirrings of the new strength which she believed had deserted her once Ben came home.

She had specific instructions from David O'Brien. She was

to itemise and cost every expenditure she could think of. A sort of lifestyle balance-sheet to sum up twenty years. She was to open the business post; she was to take a copy of every piece of paper she could lay her hands on. She was not to speak to her husband.

She had almost finished photocopying the documents from the filing-cabinets. David had emphasised that everything was important – bank statements, share certificates, correspondence, memos. She was sure Ben would take all that away when he moved from his mother's. She did not even try to distinguish the important from the unimportant. Knowing her meticulous husband, she photocopied the lot.

There were now two boxes of envelopes in the attic. Maybe, in one of them, was security for the kids.

Rose finished ironing the last of the school shirts. This morning had been a rush to organise everyone. She didn't want that to happen again tomorrow. Damien had done his own, which she would continue to encourage and then, eventually, demand. Lisa fussed, afraid she'd be late for school. Brian had stood there, tight-lipped; he hated the chaos all round him. Rose didn't care. She was beginning to realise that disorder in the home was not a capital offence.

She, herself, had been relaxed about it. It was getting harder to keep the household routine together. She was not going to pretend to be Superwoman. She was aware of giving out the message, to Brian particularly, that she was looking at life a little differently. That the whole world did not revolve around an absolutely ordered household, whose wardrobes were filled invisibly, effortlessly, thanklessly.

She also had the five hundred pounds, which had removed some of the weight from her shoulders. She tried to think of a way to be kind to Maureen. But self-preservation made her hesitate. It could be a dangerous alliance for her, Rose. Blood was thicker than water. Ben's mother seemed to have few illusions about her son, but he was her son, after all.

Rose folded the ironing board and rinsed her coffee-mug. She didn't feel like baking just yet. She needed to get out of the house. She felt somehow threatened, in dread of an unnamed event. She pulled on a light anorak and stepped out into the still-chill sunshine.

Since Ben's visit, her own home disturbed her. She could not open the door without imagining him, angry, on the other side. His clothes in the wardrobe upset her, in a way they hadn't before. Every time the phone rang she imagined it was him.

Rose crossed the road at the lights. Making her way towards Dollymount, she was reassured by the familiar scenes all around her. This, at least, hadn't changed. The tide was full and the sun glinted everywhere. Grandparents pushed buggies; the occasional jogger sweated past. Rose wondered for a moment if she would see the woman with the Walkman, the man with the two greyhounds. All those years ago. Michael would have been fourteen now. Rose took comfort from the speed of her walk, the strength of the sea-breeze.

Back home, she hung her anorak in the wardrobe. Seeing Ben's things again made her sad, as though she was clearing out after a dead person. But he wasn't dead; he was very much alive and making her life unhappy.

She wanted him to come and take away all the reminders of whatever it was they had shared.

The rooms had long since lost their hostility for her. All the dark shadows she had seen there after Ben had left were gone. But each of them had also lost its warmth, its personality. There was no longer any room in which she could feel really comfortable. She had the feeling of having moved out a long time ago.

All that remained was to close the door.

The first thing Rose did when she arrived at the house was to turn on the oven. She had four hours to get everything perfect, and she was nervous. Jane helped her carry in the boxes from the car, dying with curiosity.

The house was empty. It had an unlived-in feel to it. Not even the expensive furniture and tasteful decor could disguise the fact that this was not a home.

'I've never seen such a clean fridge!'

Jane was stocking its shelves rapidly.

'There's absolutely nothing in here – does anyone actually use this kitchen?'

Everything was spotless, sterile.

Rose felt uneasy. What was this set-up? An expensive, discreet townhouse, tucked away in a very quiet corner of South County Dublin. No children playing on the street, no sign of life anywhere. Fancy cars outside every gate.

When Annie Cartwright had phoned, Rose had been eager to take the work. She needed the money and the Bonne Bouche had been good to her. Annie's confidence in her had helped her once more through a bad day. Rose hadn't paid a lot of attention to her insistence on complete discretion. Now she wondered. She hoped this wasn't anything illegal.

Annie had told her not to worry about the wine, it would arrive later. There would also be someone to set the table and to serve. Her job was exclusively to prepare and cook the food. Annie had discussed the menu in detail with her.

Rose had already tried out all the dishes. Now she was

terrified. She had to cook for twelve unknown palates. She was glad Jane was with her.

By five-thirty, the preparations were well underway; Rose relaxed a little. She had made the lemon sorbet the day before; all that remained was to soften it in the fridge for an hour before serving. It was Jane's job to shape and decorate it.

Rose stuck the different task-lists on the freezer door with Blu-Tack. She crossed off each item as she dealt with it. Jane was the perfect 'gofer'. She did absolutely as she was asked, cleanly and efficiently. She even stopped joking for the next hour.

Rose had partly cooked the braised duck in brandy early that morning. Now it was time to transfer the two huge cast-iron casseroles to the oven. She pulled out all the shelves, juggling for space until everything fitted. Mushrooms had to be added near the end, and the glaze made. A final thickening of the sauce with beurre manie just before serving, and it should be perfect. She prayed that it would.

Spinach with nutmeg and new potatoes with parsley butter were the accompaniment. She and Jane prepared them together, making sure the potato balls were perfectly shaped. The spinach had to be washed leaf by leaf. Once cooked, it had to be tossed in butter, black pepper and nutmeg. Rose began to sweat. All these hours of preparation and everything could still go wrong at the last minute.

For now, they concentrated on the starter – Pain de sole; layers of lemon sole and herb forcemeat. At least one and a half hours to prepare, and serve with Mousseline-hollandaise sauce. Despite all her meticulous planning, Rose felt panic. There were too many things that could let her down. The surroundings intimidated her; the guests were unknown quantities and left behind was a life that was falling apart.

Damien was babysitting, but there was a great deal of bad feeling between him and Brian. Rose was worried about the two of them being left alone together. Damien had given him a hard time over stealing the computer game. Brian's reaction was more than anger. He hated his brother, he said, for acting big, 'like he was in charge'. He hated Damien for usurping Ben's position. Rose continued to define the thin, almost invisible line which existed between treating Damien as an adult, and relying on him as a substitute for Ben. She felt so tired.

Here, in this kitchen, she had everything necessary from sprigs of tarragon to camellia leaves for her sorbet. But even this did not guarantee success. She had failed before despite working hard.

Jane handed her a mug of tea.

'Tea cures all ills.'

Rose smiled. About to reply, she hesitated, hearing a key in the front door. Jane looked at her in mock amazement.

'How many keys are there to this place?' she whispered.

The kitchen door was flung open. An apparition in tight jeans and a black T-shirt stood before them, chewing gum, pushing back a mane of dyed blonde hair.

'Hi girls. I'm Debbie. Annie told me to expect you. Which of you is the great cook?'

Jane jabbed her thumb in Rose's direction and introduced both of them.

Debbie nodded, satisfied.

'I do the table and the serving and the dishes; Tony will be along soon with the wine. Annie must really trust you two. She's never contracted out the food before.'

Rose felt absurdly proud. Her self-esteem soared. She *would* get this right.

Debbie busied herself pulling dishes and bowls out of the kitchen cupboards. Jane watched her.

'God, that's an awful lot of dishes!'

'C'mere.'

Debbie opened a door leading off the kitchen, which

Rose had assumed to be a cupboard. Inside were two dishwashers, a large sink, a microwave and an espresso machine.

'How the other half lives!' exclaimed Jane.

Debbie looked at them curiously.

'Didn't Annie fill you in?'

'Of course,' said Rose quickly, 'but she didn't mention *two* dishwashers!'

She thought that Jane was going to burst with curiosity; she frowned at her just as she opened her mouth again. Jane shut it obediently, eyes glinting with mischief.

They both went in to see the table when Debbie was finished. It was a picture; stiff linen tablecloth with matching napkins; fresh flower arrangements; the best in gleaming cutlery and crystal. Rose and Jane nudged each other and retreated to the kitchen to giggle uncontrollably until their task-lists sobered them up.

Just after seven, everything seemed to happen very quickly. Tony arrived in a cloud of bottles and efficiency, immaculate in white shirt and black tie. Debbie suddenly appeared in a demure black dress and white apron, blonde hair tied back with a satin bow, unrecognisable, except for the chewing-gum.

Suddenly, there was the sound of voices raised in laughter and discussion. The hall was crowded with people. Rose and Jane became so busy that they did not even look up, but there was the definite sensation of the rooms filling. Tony moved silently and rapidly from room to room, dispensing drinks. Debbie, minus the chewing-gum, brought around trays of the delicate canapés which the three women had just finished decorating. The volume became louder, uproarious laughter gusting at intervals.

At exactly half-past eight, Rose presented Debbie with the starter, crossed her fingers, and hoped. They had fifteen minutes to perfect the main course – thicken the sauce, glaze the mushrooms, cook the spinach, and drizzle parsley butter over the potatoes. They did it, with two minutes to spare.

Debbie took a quick drag of a cigarette before serving the main course. She waved the smoke away violently.

'Don't tell Tony – I'm supposed to be off them.'

Rose waited anxiously until everyone was served. The buzz of conversation was steady, less frantic. Once this part was over, she could relax. The dessert was a breeze.

Suddenly, silent Tony was beside her.

'The host's compliments to the chef. What would you ladies like to drink?'

Rose was so relieved she almost burst into tears. Jane answered for both of them.

'Large gin and tonics, please, Tony.'

He served them both with a flourish; for the first time that evening, he smiled.

'Large they are, ladies, and congratulations.'

Rose raised her glass to Jane.

'I couldn't have done it without you. Thank you.'

Jane raised hers in return.

'To friendship.'

The volume had begun to rise again next door. Jane eased the door open a little with her toe and beckoned to Rose.

Neither of them could believe their eyes. The table was like a who's who of Ireland's political and business worlds.

The host had just begun to speak. Around him, the hush was complete, almost reverential. Rose recognised him at once. Not as substantial as he looked on television, he was none the less imposing. His bald head gleamed in the candlelight. He was looking relaxed, at ease; a man sure of his importance among his peers. Leaning back slightly in his high-backed carver, his hands folded loosely across his stomach, he was telling his audience the *real* story behind the latest scandal.

'Murtagh, isn't it?' Jane whispered, close to Rose's right ear.

She nodded. 'Foreign Affairs.'

Jane started to giggle and had to move back quickly into the kitchen. There was an outburst of laughter around the table; the story was finished and appreciated. Tony moved silently again among the guests. Glasses were refilled.

At the host's right sat one of the most arrogantly beautiful girls Rose had ever seen. She kept pushing at her wild, fair hair with her fingertips. It was her birthday that was being celebrated.

'Speech! Bernadette! Speech!' was demanded noisily by a man Rose was sure she recognised, but could not place. His colour was high; an enormous cigar burned between his thumb and middle finger. He was holding it away from him delicately, as though it might explode. He half-turned to speak to the man beside him, still keeping his eye on the host. In that fleeting expression, Rose recognised him.

Jane was at her shoulder again, recovered.

Rose pointed silently in the direction of the man who had just called for a speech.

Jane shrugged her shoulders. Rose whispered to her.

'The one who made all the money? The one the Bar Council are investigating?'

Rose nodded, putting her finger to her lips. Jane's eyes were round.

As the very young woman stood to thank the guests for their gifts, she revealed the tightest, briefest black lycra minidress Rose had ever seen. She was pretending bashfulness, tugging at her skirt, letting her blonde hair fall across her face so that she could make extravagant gestures to push it back. She twisted blonde wisps between her fingers, her red nails glowing. Her long, tanned arms gleamed with jewellery as she piled her hair upon her head to show off her lover's gift – a pair of diamond earrings.

She smiled down at him.

'I want to thank all of you for coming. I particularly want to thank Brendan for this lovely surprise party.'

He watched her indulgently, never taking his eyes off her. The scrutiny of the other men was more discreet, but no less complete.

'And of course, for these lovely earrings.'

Bernadette leaned down and kissed the Minister's bald head.

Cheering broke out all around the table. Rose noticed glances passing among the three other young women. A sardonically raised eyebrow here, a secret smile there. Rose would have given anything to know what they were thinking. There was a coldness in their silent reaction, a cruelty in their gaze.

Rose watched the birthday girl as closely as she could without opening the door any further. She was terrified they would be discovered. Behind the girl's vulnerability there must have been a core of steel, of calculation. Her coyness, her dramatic dress, her exquisitely made-up face were created to impress, to captivate and to ornament the man who gazed at her with undisguised longing.

The guests continued clapping and cheering long after Bernadette finished her speech. The host basked in their attention, his hairline and portly figure of no importance tonight. He radiated power and money; his guests were close to fawning. It was no accident, Rose was sure, that the most beautiful girl was so obviously and so definably his.

Rose was shocked to the depths of her middle-class soul.

'Do you see who's out there?'

Jane nodded.

'The cream of Irish leadership – and hardly a wife in sight.'

It was true. Rose had by now recognised three of the eight

men; she could match their names and faces; the Minister, a handler, a barrister. Two with ponytails she did not know, but recognised a type; they had been seen everywhere after the last Government media campaign. One man, his back to Rose, was a complete mystery. He was deep in conversation with the men on either side of him. All three were totally absorbed in their discussion. Rose felt a pang. She had seen this sort of thing before. This was a business deal; this was money.

All four women present were young, stunning and self-confident. Rose recognised none of them. Whoever they were, they were not in the public eye as she knew it.

'Is the whole world at it?' she whispered to Jane.

Jane shrugged.

'An eye-opener, isn't it? At least half of those hypocrites would vote against divorce. No wonder Annie emphasised discretion.'

They were so overt, so blatant. Granted, they probably all had something to lose. Maybe that guaranteed secrecy.

Rose wondered was it just her. Was this well-known to everybody, except her? Was she the only one to believe what people said when they were interviewed on television? Rose wondered if she was the only woman in Ireland not to have grown up.

And now that she knew, what was she going to do about it? A few short weeks ago, she'd have been appalled at the thought of anyone she knew working in such a set-up. She would have been quite certain that the right thing to do, the moral thing to do, would be to refuse to have anything to do with it.

And now it seemed that she couldn't even afford her own principles any more. When she'd had money, right and wrong were very clear. Now that she had nothing, or almost nothing, things weren't so black and white. She needed to support her children, she needed to do something for herself. If she didn't take this job, someone else would, and they'd earn the very good money that came with it. What difference would giving it up make to anyone, except herself? Her responsibility to her children had to be greater than her sense of shock at other people's sexual morality.

She and Jane made ludicrously expensive coffee in their luxurious surroundings. Rose had a sense of her profound ignorance about life. She felt she had a lot of catching up to do.

'Are you OK, Rose?'

Jane's question made her realise that she had not spoken for some time.

'I'm fine; just a little older, that's all. Another g and t when we get back will do the trick.'

Debbie was rinsing dishes and stacking the dishwashers. Rose and Jane packed up and said goodbye to her quietly. Tony insisted on carrying the cardboard boxes to the car. As they left, there was a steady buzz of conversation from the dining-room. The doors were closed. Rose didn't want to see any more.

'That was quite something,' said Jane as they drove off. 'No wonder they pay for spin-doctors.'

'It's all about image, isn't it? I find it all quite depressing.'

Rose felt a huge sense of let-down after her success. Perhaps she was just tired. She didn't want to replay the evening, didn't want to talk, didn't want another drink. She felt guilty at being such bad company.

Jane yawned loudly as they approached home.

'Let's call it a day. I'm knackered.'

Rose was grateful.

'Thanks a million, Jane. I'll call you tomorrow.'

'My pleasure. Wouldn't have missed it for the world!'

And she was gone.

Rose couldn't put words on what she was feeling. All she was conscious of was a great need developing within her.

Saturday, 3rd June; 7.30 pm.

Ben had moved out of his parents' home two weeks before. He had rung Rose to tell her to forward his post. It was their first conversation since the afternoon in Pearse Street Station. He had not returned the calls she'd made to suggest that he see the children. Damien had shrugged it off. Lisa had asked Rose, more than once:

'Why can't we go and see Daddy?'

Rose had done her best, but she knew Lisa was not content.

Brian had become more sullen and unco-operative, both at home and at school. He would do nothing except play 'Mortal Kombat', 'Virtua Fighter' and 'Tekken' on his computer. Rose was desperate, unable to reach him, unable to stop him retreating into an increasingly violent and destructive fantasy world. His attitude to her was one of silent contempt, obeying her instructions but entering into no discussion. He even avoided eye contact.

Yesterday, while changing his bed, she had come across his school journal, wedged between the headboard and the mattress. Heart sinking, knowing already what she was going to find, Rose opened it. She flicked through the most recent pages. 'No homework done – rude and disruptive during class – refuses to participate.' And then – 'Please make appointment to see class teacher.'

She replaced the journal where she had found it. She needed time to work out how to tackle this one. God, she was tired.

Rose was working harder than ever now, accepting

everything Annie put her way. Maureen came to the house every day, Monday to Friday, and made lunch for Brian and Lisa. Rose felt torn, pulled in all sorts of directions. She had to work out some solution with Ben; they couldn't go on like this.

Why was he playing this waiting game?

It was now summer. Kids did things during their summer holidays that cost money. She was feeding them each week and trying to save something, anything, from her earnings. But she couldn't afford any extras. Nor could Maureen continue babysitting for nothing. It wasn't right.

She came home late that Saturday evening, having delivered a dozen fresh pizzas to a party in Howth. She was exhausted, pre-menstrual and angry.

Brian met her in a towering rage.

'Damien wouldn't give me the money to go to UCI, and *everyone's* gone except me!'

'You cannot go to the pictures, Brian, because I simply don't have the money. Damien has some money which I gave him for emergencies, but you going to the pictures is not an emergency. Damien was doing what he was told.'

'If you let Dad come home we'd have plenty of money. It's your fault he left! It's all your fault!'

For a split second, Rose wanted to thump the angry, miserable twelve-year-old who glared so spitefully at her. She kept her hands at her sides, afraid that if she started, she would not stop hitting him. Suddenly, she wanted to direct her anger where it belonged.

'Get your coat; you're coming with me – now!'

Rose had not shouted since Ben left; she had tiptoed around everyone, minding feelings and trying to fulfil impossible needs. Brian actually looked frightened, and Rose was glad. For a vicious moment, his fear was more satisfying than laying out all around her. Pressure was building up inside her; her head felt ready to explode.

'Get into the car, *now*.'

Brian was silent and obedient. At least the sullen look was gone. Rose screeched the car down the driveway towards the main road, barely checking the traffic.

'Where are we going?' Brian's voice was suddenly small, childlike.

'We are going to see your father so he can tell you himself why he won't come home. I am sick of being the bad guy, sick of your attitude and behaviour, sick of trying to make things up to you.'

This anger felt good. Rose only hoped that she would not cry. She wanted to be strong and bitter and raging, to demand respect and acknowledgement for herself.

The BMW was parked in the apartment carpark; good, he was home. Rose stopped her car, abandoning it in the middle of the courtyard, engine running.

'Get out, Brian.'

Brian did as he was told.

Rose rang the bell of the ground-floor apartment. She kept her finger on it until Ben's shape hurried to answer. He looked dishevelled, as though he'd been asleep in a chair. Good; all the better. There was the familiar smell of wine as she got closer to him. She pulled Brian towards her, more roughly than she intended. The child was crying, and Rose nearly weakened.

'Here's your son, Ben. Maybe you can tell him why you left home and why all of this has happened. Maybe you can get him to stop stealing, to stop treating his mother like a piece of dirt. Take him; he's yours too.'

Rose turned and walked away, ignoring Ben's astonished shout. She rammed the car into gear, forgetting the engine was still running. It made a most satisfying scream as she reversed quickly towards the exit, ignoring Ben's figure running desperately towards her.

She sped home, allowing the tears to well and fall. She

checked that Lisa was asleep, sent Damien to bed with a curtness that cut him, and took the phone off the hook. Then she sat down in the darkened sitting-room and proceeded to get drunk.

Saturday, 3rd June; 7.30 pm.

Ben ran his hands in frustration through his thinning hair.

'But Caroline, when we were together, we . . .'

He was interrupted by the doorbell ringing shrilly. Some-one was keeping their finger pressed hard against it. Caroline went dead white and dropped her glass. It seemed to take ages for the red stain to seep across the white rug.

Ben opened the door, cursing.

Caroline could hear every angry word.

'Here's your son, Ben. Maybe you can tell him why you left home and why all of this has happened. Maybe you can get him to stop stealing, to stop treating his mother like a piece of dirt. Take him; he's yours too.'

Jesus. It was Rose. Caroline felt suddenly sick. She looked around her wildly. Did she have time to hide?

She heard a car engine gunning loudly, protesting as gears were slammed. Ben shouted angrily and she could hear him running.

In the meantime, she heard a child sobbing. Caroline felt paralysed. The door slammed and Ben walked back into the sitting-room, one arm around Brian's shoulder. The child's face was twisted with crying.

Caroline took her coat off the back of the door. Ben was red-faced and furious. He brought Brian through into the kitchen, without a word. Caroline heard him say he'd be back in a minute.

She put her coat on quickly and stood by the door. She shook her head at him and raised her hand although he made no attempt to approach her.

'Don't ever contact me again. I never want to see you again.'

There were tears in her eyes. He knew they were for Brian, not for him. He made a gesture of resignation.

Caroline let herself out.

Ben filled his glass again and returned to the kitchen, the sound of sobbing increasing his anger at Caroline and at Rose. He sat down heavily beside his son.

He ruffled the spiky hair at the crown of Brian's bent head.

'Stop crying, son.'

Brian gulped and tried to do as he was told.

'I'm sorry, Dad. It's been really hard since you went away.'

Ben poured him a glass of water. Brian sipped at it, crouching over the glass. Ben noticed that his fingernails were dirty.

'Are you going to come home – ever?'

Ben was at a loss. How could he expect a child to understand?

'We'll see. Maybe . . . there are a lot of things I need to sort out. In the meantime, you're to behave yourself. I don't want to hear of you causing any more grief.'

Brian didn't answer.

'Are you hungry?' Ben asked him, looking for neutral ground.

He nodded.

'You don't fancy any of the stuff inside, do you?'

Bitterly, Ben remembered the care with which he'd prepared the smoked salmon, the brown bread, the salad.

'If you don't like it, you can have a take-away.'

Brian went off to have a look. He was back almost at once.

'Can I have the take-away?'

Ben nodded and pulled the phone towards him. He gestured towards the living-room.

'Sit down on the sofa and turn on the telly. I'll be with you in a minute.'

Brian disappeared. Ben drained his wine-glass and punched in the local take-away's number which he knew by heart. He wondered what he was going to do next.

Sunday, 4th June; 9.30 am.

Rose woke with a dreadful headache. As she opened her eyes, she heard the doorbell. In her troubled sleep, she had been expecting it, was waiting for it. She called out to Damien as he made his way downstairs.

'It's all right, Damien, it's your dad. I'll deal with it.'

Damien retreated wordlessly to his bedroom. Rose knew that he was hurting over the way she had begun to exclude him. But she was doing it for him. Maybe later on today she'd try to explain this to him. She missed him, too.

She took her time in answering the door. Apart from her head, her back ached and her stomach was killing her. She was bleeding heavily and she felt weak. But at least the pre-menstrual madness had gone. She felt able to face Ben and Brian.

She was also glad that her biology had allowed her to react in the way that she had. Women were good at making the best of the worst, she thought, at putting up with the intolerable. Sometimes the only safety valve was the anger and resentment at the world in general which built up just before a period. Normally, Rose would feel tetchy and close to tears for a few days beforehand, angered by the assumptions of all around her that she was made happy by looking after everybody else. Then the anger would disappear as the period arrived, and Rose would marvel at how she never learned to recognise it for what it was. The anger felt real every time, the resentment justified every time.

Because it *was* real, she now realised, it *was* justified. Just because it went away when the peculiarly heightened emotions of menstruation subsided, did not mean it didn't exist. All it meant was that she didn't have the heightened understanding to feel it any more once she had returned to 'normal'.

She opened the door to Ben and Brian, calm and controlled. Brian looked utterly miserable, Ben was pensive and white-faced.

Rose decided she wasn't going to take any more crap.

'Go to your room, Brian, we'll talk later.'

Her tone was firm, but held out the promise of reconciliation, of love. Brian nodded and sped upstairs, without a backward glance at his father.

'You'd better come in,' she said to Ben, matter-of-factly, determined that he was not going to take the advantage from her. Their relationship had been reduced to this, a game of tennis, or better again, a hand of poker, each one unwilling to reveal their tactics.

'That was rather dramatic last night.'

Rose heard the implications of that statement, rather than the words. She filled the kettle and swore to hold on to her temper.

'It was a pretty dramatic situation. Picture it: adolescent boy, abandoned by father he adores, takes to stealing in order to get attention. But attention is not forthcoming. Father buggers off again and adolescent boy is utterly miserable. So what does he do? Takes it out on mother who now becomes the guilty one, responsible for everyone's unhappiness – everyone's except her own, which nobody pays any attention to, anyway. So, self-absorbed twelve-year-old pushes all the buttons he knows how. No contact, no father, no money, no certainties any more. Result – explosion. That is why he ended up on your doorstep last night, because you have done nothing to reassure him that you are still his dad. And I'm not having it any more, Ben. I am sick of shielding them from you. If you are a total shit, then at least let us all know it so that we can get on with our lives. But I am not carrying your can as well as my own any longer.'

It was the longest speech Rose had ever made. Ben had watched her in amazement throughout. Her lack of concern about what he thought of her had made her eloquent. She no longer cared about his disapproval. She did not need his esteem. She felt detached and hungover, in equal measure.

'I just want you to accept responsibility for your kids, that's all. For myself, I don't care about you any more.'

He looked up at that.

'I don't think I can come back, Rose.'

Rose decided to go for broke.

'You're not listening to me, Ben; I wouldn't have you back if you were the last man in the world. I just want us to sort out a way of life that means I don't have to see you again.'

'I'll do my best, Rose, but business is very difficult just now. You'll have to be patient.'

'I've been patient for twenty years, Ben, waiting for life to begin. Bad business doesn't seem to stop you having good wine and expensive female company, though, does it?'

Rose's shot was not completely in the dark. Ben's appearance when he'd opened the door last night had registered something she hadn't thought about until now. He hadn't been asleep. His flushed appearance and dishevelled clothing were not due to a snooze after work. He was with someone; she had smelt wine from him, a smell that she had forgotten until now. Was it Caroline, or someone else? Who cares, thought Rose wearily. Brian's arrival must have put the kibosh on that romantic interlude, whoever it was with. Rose felt glad, glad, glad.

Ben's face had gone even whiter.

'I'm not prepared to discuss my private life with you.'

He stood up stiffly, pushing the chair back carefully.

'I'll ring you to arrange a time to collect the rest of my

things. My solicitor will contact you with the arrangements for maintenance.'

'Your solicitor can contact mine, Ben, and negotiate to all our satisfaction. I am not prepared to have terms dictated to me.'

Ben was clearly astonished.

'You have a solicitor? Since when?'

'Since you walked out, you bastard. And what's more, I have a photocopy of every contract, every share, every memo you ever wrote. Now get out. I'll contact you when it's convenient for *me* for you to collect your things. I don't expect to hear from you in the meantime.'

Rose virtually threw Ben out. All through the conversation, she had been edging him towards the front door. Now she slammed it with satisfaction, right in his angry face. She couldn't be responsible any more for his relationship with his children. If he chose, then it would continue, and she would encourage the children to see him. If he chose not to, then it was not something which she could make happen. She had enough responsibilities of her own.

Damien hesitated in the hall after the front door slammed.

'Are you all right, Ma?'

He was anxious, uncertain.

'Yes, love, I'm fine. Come here to me.'

Rose put her arms around him and rocked him, as though he were still a child.

'Everything is going to be OK. I think we're going to be on our own now.'

She kissed his face tenderly.

'We'll be fine.'

Damien nodded. Rose began to climb the stairs and said, over her shoulder:

'We'll have a family pow-wow this evening.'

She closed her door and settled back into the luxury of

a still-warm bed. She felt a contentment that was entirely new to her.

The red stain from Caroline's wine was still there when Ben got back to the apartment. In a way, he had expected it to be gone. The remains of last night's supper were also there. In the tiny kitchen, the dishes he had piled up were still there. The aluminium take-away containers were resting on the lid of the bin, filled with ash and cigarette butts from several nervous evenings on his own.

The flat no longer looked attractive. There was a film of grime everywhere. Ben carried the last dishes into the kitchen and closed the door.

He pulled his briefcase out from under the stairs and sat down at the coffee-table.

Sunday, 4th June; 12.20 pm.

It was well after midday when Rose woke. Her headache was gone; she felt light, refreshed. Pulling on her dressing-gown, she went immediately to Brian's room. She knocked and waited until he let her in.

The room was tidy. The computer was switched off. Rose got the sense that he had been waiting for her. She sat down in the wicker chair. It was beginning to feel like an old friend. She crossed her legs and wrapped her dressing-gown tightly around her. She felt suddenly cold.

'I'm sorry if I was rough on you last night. But I don't regret what I did.'

Brian looked at her. For the first time in a long time, there was no hostility in his gaze.

'The last few weeks have been hard. But I cannot allow you to behave badly at home, in the street, at school.'

She stopped, seeing his guilty look.

'*Have* things been bad at school?'

He nodded.

'Well, perhaps you'd better tell me so there'll be no more surprises. If you tell me the truth, I'll go much easier on you.'

Brian put his hand between the mattress and the headboard and pulled out his school journal. He handed it to his mother, wordlessly.

Rose opened it carefully, as though she had never seen it before.

She looked directly at Brian.

'This is bad, Brian. This is very bad. But I'll do a deal with you.'

She didn't care that he hadn't spoken. She knew he was listening to every word she said.

'I am not going to let you make a mess of things. I know you want your dad home, I know you miss him.'

She leaned towards him.

'I also know, more or less for certain, that things can't be like they were before. It's hard for all of us, but we have to get used to it. Now, here's the deal.'

He was waiting.

'You cut out the computer games during the week; you spend more time on homework. At the weekend, you can play for a time which we'll both agree to. It will depend on how hard you've tried during the week, and I don't just mean at school. Are you with me so far?'

'Yes.'

'In return, I will not go off the deep end about these comments in your journal. We'll put all the fights of the last few weeks behind us. Deal?'

He nodded.

'I'm not interested in punishing your bad behaviour; I want us to change it.'

He seemed about to speak. Rose waited. Then she said, softly:

'This is not all my fault, Brian. I didn't choose it. I have to live with it, too.'

He got up off the bed and came towards her.

'I'm sorry, Mam. I didn't really mean it.'

His hands were white and shaking. She held out her arms to him.

'I know. Come here to me. We'll work it out.'

He started to cry. Rose held him tighter. He didn't pull away. Eventually, gently, she sat him on her knee.

Softly, softly. Sufficient unto the day.

Monday, 12th June; 6.30 am.

Rose had had just about enough. Ben's answering machine had been on all weekend; he had returned none of her calls. In spite of her best efforts, she was short of money. Today's cheque at the supermarket would bounce. She would not touch Maureen's money until she absolutely had to. Schoolbooks and uniforms would swallow most of it anyway.

Now she was outside Ben's apartment. His curtains were still drawn; he must be asleep. Rose looked at her watch. Six-thirty. Half an hour later than his usual rising-time. That had obviously changed, too.

This was her third visit. On Saturday night, she had sat, from midnight to two am, waiting for his return. She hadn't intended to wait so long. After the two hours, her own sense of humiliation at having to beg overcame her, and all she wanted was to go home.

Last night at ten, she had tried again. Ben always liked to go to bed early on a Sunday night. By eleven, when there was no sign of him, she was embarrassed and angry. It was as though she was invisible. He had discarded them all like an old sweater. Once thrown away, they no longer existed.

This morning, Rose's sense of humiliation had abated. Now, she was just mad.

She wasn't waiting any longer. It was time to demand, not beg. She got out of the car and closed the door quietly. She had practised her speech. She wanted to be cold and assertive; she did not want another confrontation.

She rang the bell and waited. The car was there. The

apartment looked as though there was someone home. She didn't even care if he was with somebody. This was business.

She rang the bell again, stepping a little to one side so that her shape would not be distinguishable through the glass. Finally, she heard movements inside.

The door opened. He was unshaven, sleepy.

'I need to talk to you, Ben. I've been trying to contact you all weekend.'

'I've been away,' he said, standing squarely in the doorway.

Rose knew it was a lie.

'May I come in? I won't take much of your time.'

Reluctantly, he opened the door just wide enough for her to enter.

Inside, she stayed standing.

'I need money. I can't support the kids on my own. I've had nothing from you in weeks; I need housekeeping money.'

He made no move.

'This isn't for me, Ben. I've told you I want nothing from you. This is for the kids. Until all this is sorted legally, you've left me with no choice but to come here.'

And beg, she added silently. But this morning she didn't care. She knew it was just a tactic on his part. It was business.

She looked at her watch.

'I have to get to work. Can we get this over with?'

He had folded his arms.

'I don't keep cash around. You know that.'

Rose looked around her for a chair. She sat, crossing her legs, getting comfortable.

'I'll wait here while you go to the Banklink. There's one at Sutton Cross. It shouldn't take you long.'

'Can't this wait until tomorrow?'

'No, it can't. I'll sit here until you decide to support your children. I don't care if it takes all day.'

The humiliation of the last two nights was cleansed. This felt good. Her instinct also told her that he would be keeping cash around, now.

Ben turned abruptly and left the sitting-room. When he returned, his face was tight. He pushed a handful of notes at her.

'I've got troubles of my own, Rose. Money doesn't grow on trees.'

'Tell me about it.'

Slowly, deliberately, she counted the money.

'There's only a hundred pounds here. That's barely enough for this week.'

He shrugged.

'It's all I can spare. Business is dire at the moment.'

Rose put the money in her purse.

'I'll just have to come back next week, and the week after that. They're still your kids, Ben.'

She stood up. She was glad she hadn't lost her temper.

'I'll see you next week. You might give the kids a call. Particularly Brian, he's really missing you.'

Ben opened the door.

'Don't tell me what to do. I'll call them when I have the time.'

Rose didn't reply. She felt no sadness, no anguish, no pain. It was just business.

Ben closed the door behind her.

She pulled out into the light traffic and headed towards the city centre and Greystones.

Monday, 26th June; 11.30 am.

David O'Brien had gone over all of Rose's documents and figures very carefully. Rose had waited patiently as he made quick notes, leafing backwards and forwards through the sheaf of pages she had prepared for him. He worked intently, occasionally running his hand through his thick, grey hair. Eventually, he looked up at her, over the top of his half-moon glasses.

'These seem to me to be very low estimates, Rose; all your expenditure is trimmed to the bone.'

'That's what I've been living on for the past twelve weeks. I can manage, if I'm careful.'

David put his pen down carefully on the desk in front of him. His office was crammed with manila folders, all neatly stacked. Rose wondered if he knew what was in all of them.

'That's not the way we do it, Rose. What I want from you is a comprehensive estimate of all your expenses while Ben was still living with you. What was your lifestyle like? How often did you go out? How often did you take a holiday, a weekend away?

'You have got to continue to spend like that, or the judge will simply award you the lower figure. He will give you what you need to maintain yourself and the children. If you say that you can do it on, let's be ridiculous, fifty pounds a week, then it's likely that that's all you'll be awarded. Ben will be laughing – maintaining himself and his apartment at your expense.'

David waited, watching the conflicting emotions on Rose's face.

'But if I don't have the money in the first place, how can I spend it? Ben has paid the mortgage and the bills, but I can't pin him down for cash. He keeps promising, but it just never happens.'

'That's exactly the point. If he can show in court that you can manage without a lot of maintenance from him, that you are able to support yourself and the kids, that he has big business difficulties at present, what do you imagine is likely to happen?'

It all rang horribly true. This was obviously a strategy, probably worked out between Ben and his solicitor. She had just barely suspected it before; now David's words seemed to confirm it.

'Have you still got a credit card?'

'Yes, unless Ben has cancelled it. I don't have one in my own name.'

'Use it; for everything you buy, keep receipts and details. Summer is an expensive time with children. So is going back to school. We've got one shot at this and we've got to make it work. It could take a long time and a lot of money to get Ben back into court again if we don't get what we want this time.'

'I don't want anything from him, David. What I want is for the children.'

David shrugged.

'He deserted you, Rose. Your life and lifestyle have changed dramatically through no fault of your own. You are entitled to financial compensation for that. Don't forget, your husband is a very wealthy man. So far, he's got away with murder.'

Rose looked at the kindly, elderly man sitting in front of her, glasses perched on the end of his nose. Jane had warned her not to be fooled by his benign appearance.

He leaned towards her.

'Take my advice; it costs a lot. Let's pretend that the

more of it you take, the more expensive it will be; and your husband will be footing the bill.'

Rose laughed.

'It's awful; it's just tactics now, isn't it?'

David spread out his hands.

'It's nothing personal, Rose, it's just business. Believe me, that's the way your husband is looking at it right now, judging from the letters I have here from his solicitor. Go ahead, spend, spend, spend. Think of it as an investment in your children's future.'

She nodded, not trusting herself to speak. Ben was punishing her, she knew, for dumping Brian on him that night. For the past two weeks, he had been elusive, always busy, always promising to lodge housekeeping money, never quite delivering. Her response had been to work herself to the point of exhaustion. She couldn't continue like this, too tired and preoccupied to spend any time with her family, too ashamed to tell anyone what was happening.

It was a relief that David knew. Now, at least, her perspective was a lot less personal. It was business.

'Just business. Isn't that what the Mafia say when they kill each other off?'

She stood up.

'Thanks, David. I'll do exactly what you tell me.'

She pulled a bundle of photocopies from her bag.

'Here are copies of all the correspondence Ben got over the last couple of weeks.'

David leafed through them quickly.

'You being listed as a director is a double-edged sword, you know that. If he really does have difficulties, you are technically liable as well.'

Rose threw her hands in the air.

'Well, they'll have to put me in jail. At this point, I don't think I have anything else to lose.'

David walked her to the door.

'We can get you what you need, Rose, but you must trust me. Don't even speak to Ben without consulting me, and don't allow him to manoeuvre you into any sort of negotiations. There's no room for sentiment.'

Rose shook hands gratefully, and left, feeling that yet another landmark had been reached, and survived.

She was going to bring the kids out for the day tomorrow. A hamburger, bowling and the pictures. Maybe even Damien would decide to come.

The one ray of sunshine in all of this was Brian. Since the day after she dumped him on his father, he had been behaving better. Slowly, tentatively, he was responding to her. He was keeping to his part of the bargain, she to hers. He was less explosive. She needed time with him to make that contact real, solid. She hoped to God that Lisa wouldn't become difficult now, or, God forbid, Damien.

She needed a breather.

And now she was going to spend money.

Part Four

Saturday, 1st July; 11.00 am.

Rose couldn't believe it. She was actually *late* leaving for the airport. At the last minute, Lisa had whined about not wanting to stay at home with the boys. Rose could see that the child was frightened; the whining was a cover for something darker.

She almost weakened. She could see that Lisa was afraid that she would go and not come back.

Rose took her on her knee and said all the right things, one eye on the clock. There was a deep pull of guilt starting just beneath her heart.

A flashback of Ben on *that* morning and the steaming saucepan of eggs decided her. She would put herself first.

'Lisa, honey, I'll be back in two hours. If Martha's plane is late, I'll ring you.'

She resisted the urge to say, 'And I'll bring you back something nice.'

She stroked her daughter's hair.

'I've promised you we'll all go out to lunch tomorrow; we'll have the whole day with Martha.'

But now, she thought, I'm having an hour on my own with Martha and I'm not weakening.

'Have the kettle on at one, won't you?'

From the sitting-room, there was uproarious laughter.

'Quick, Lisa, look at this!'

Lisa fled.

Thank God for television. Rose put her head around the door.

'Bye, all! See you soon. Be good!'

'Bye, Mam!'

'Bye, Mam!'

Rose glanced at her watch.

'God Almighty! I'm gone.'

She felt like a child on Christmas Eve. Everything was going better. Annie had given her two weeks off; the kids were happy to be on holidays; and now Martha was almost here. Rose was sometimes frightened at how much she was looking forward to seeing Martha. She had invested this visit with so much, in her own mind. It was as though everything would be all right, once she discussed it with Martha.

But what if Martha had changed? Rose was afraid that they mightn't be able to find their old friendship after so many years. What if they couldn't talk to each other any more?

When she'd finally slept the night before, Rose's dreams were full of planes crashing and strange women insisting they were Martha when Rose knew that they were not. Nightmares had filled her sleep and she had woken exhausted.

Two whole weeks. The time stretched out in front of her like an eternity. No matter what happened, she had to get off the treadmill for a while, if only to get back on it again more productively. Things were holding together. It was good, this new feeling of independence. Rose decided she liked it.

She opened the car window and pulled the parking ticket out of its slot. The plane should have landed by now. The barrier lifted. Five minutes later, she was cursing the new carparks at Dublin Airport. There had always seemed to be spaces in the old one. Now she was right at the top level, out in the open again, before she spotted a space. There was a silver BMW beside her and Rose laughed as she remembered herself and Jane that day.

That's the second time I've laughed in the last few days, she cautioned herself. Better watch myself. I might be happy.

She felt very light and free as she made her way towards

the Arrivals terminal. A good sign – there was only a trickle of people coming through the automatic doors, all with Heathrow Duty Free bags. There was no one standing around, looking lost. Not that Martha would look lost . . .

Rose spotted her.

The moment Martha saw her, she knew it was going to be all right. She signalled frantically to an uncrowded spot away from the barriers.

Martha made her way steadily, politely through the hugging, shrieking crowds.

She held her arms out and Rose hugged her tightly, tears soaking Martha's velvet collar. Neither of them spoke for a few moments.

Rose had the strong feeling that Martha was not the only one coming home.

Saturday, 1st July; 10.30 pm.

'I don't believe you and I have ever got properly drunk together before.'

Martha made the statement gravely as she produced a large bottle of Jameson from the Duty Free bag she had put behind the sofa earlier.

Rose loved the way she had melted into her surroundings, her family, without any feelings of strangeness on anyone's part.

Brian had taken to her immediately; Rose had been puzzled at this. He had looked surprised, then pleased, when Martha shook his hand. What had he been expecting? She filed it for later.

Rose noticed how carefully Martha had chosen her gifts. She must have read, with great care, the letter Rose had written all those weeks ago. She had a sudden, vivid, memory of the thirteen blue airmail pages, and silently thanked Martha for reading beyond them.

Brian's computer game was complex, demanding; a complete shift from shoot 'em ups. She watched as he became absorbed in the large manual. It was the first time she had seen him sit still enough to read since Ben left.

Now they were finally on their own, Brian and Lisa happily in bed, Damien out until one. Rose took off her shoes and curled up in the armchair opposite Martha.

'Do you know, Martha, this is the first day I've felt at peace with myself from the moment I got up? I'm really glad you came.'

'So am I. Your kids are great, you've come a long

246

way since you wrote to me, and you look lovely. You must be doing a lot of things right, Rose. Congratulations.'

Martha raised her glass and Rose had a blinding picture of twenty years before, when Martha had made that same gesture. Its suddenness and its clarity made her eyes fill.

'You never did like Ben, did you?'

Martha nursed her glass carefully.

'No, I never did like Ben, but that's not to say that I was *right*, or that Ben's walking out on you proves anything. I could have thought the world of him, and he'd still have left you.'

'A lot of it is luck, isn't it?'

Martha nodded.

'I think so. I'm still trying to find out!'

Rose was unsure of her ground.

'Are you involved with someone?'

Martha waved her hand to say maybe yes, maybe no. Her face looked suddenly uncertain. Rose had the strong feeling she didn't want to continue. She decided she wouldn't push it.

She held out her glass for a refill. Whether it was the whiskey or Martha, or a combination of both, Rose felt she was getting closer to understanding the heart of what had happened to her.

'Tell me what happened, Rose, from the beginning.'

Rose was surprised at how easily she put a structure on the past three months. She thought and analysed, made connections and made sense out of the chaos.

It was dawn before they went to bed. Rose felt very sober, yet elated. The patterns of her life were vivid and she was beginning to understand what had brought her to now.

Calm and clear-headed, she knew what she had to do.

Sunday, 2nd July; 9.30 am.

When Martha came down the following morning, Rose was cooking breakfast.

'Hey, I was coming down to do that for you!'

Martha gave her a quick hug. Rose didn't take her eyes off the rapidly congealing scrambled eggs.

'Why change a tradition? Every significant moment of my goddam life has been spent in this kitchen, at this cooker. The morning Ben left I was boiling eggs, now I'm scrambling them. I wonder if there's a message in there somewhere?'

'Maybe,' Martha said lightly, 'you prefer them scrambled. Maybe that's the message.'

Rose turned off the gas and reached into the oven where the toast was being kept warm. She pulled two plates out.

'Here, get that into you, it'll do you good.'

Martha groaned. 'You know the other half of that? "Get that up and you'll feel better"! Go easy – I'm a little delicate this morning.'

'Well, I'm not. I'm starving. I feel great, and I know exactly what I want to do.'

Rose made a jug of strong coffee.

Martha waited.

'Talking to you last night was the best I've been in years, Martha. It was like all the fuzzy-headedness was gone. I can see where I've been, and now I'm beginning to see where I want to go.'

Martha nodded. Her face assumed the grave expression which Rose had so often loved. There was always something so solid about Martha; she was never flighty, never distracted.

When she listened, her whole body listened. She allowed no interruption. While you spoke, she was yours.

'Do you remember us talking about the ferry-boats last night?' Martha asked this with a smile.

'Every word of it! I felt as though I'd discovered a universal truth! Yes I remember – I said that men and women were like ferry-boats. They're very alike on the outside – in where they start from and where they're going to. The tragedy is that one is always on the outward journey when the other has just started the return.'

Rose paused for a minute, her eyes filling up again.

'It actually makes me feel better to believe that that's what happened to Ben and me. It makes sense, it has its own logic. And it doesn't hurt as much. Maybe that's really why I like it.'

'Does the "why" really matter?' asked Martha, who seemed by now to have recovered her appetite.

'No. But the result of it does. I don't feel bitter towards Ben any more. I feel I don't have to pretend. I can let him go. But I want to make sure that the kids have their dad.'

Damien walked in at that moment. His body followed his eyes to the large plate of toast, before he remembered his manners.

'Go on,' said Rose. 'Help yourself.'

He folded four slices rapidly.

He looked at Martha. She shook her head at him. Rose let it go. She felt a ridiculous pride that her son and her best friend had a secret.

'Later,' Martha said.

Now Rose was curious.

'Go away, Damien, we'll talk later.'

He obeyed Martha without question, taking a banana and a handful of plums on his way past.

Rose's chest tightened. God, the amount they ate. Ben had given her nothing. Everything on the table had been put there by her earnings. She was beginning to feel desperate. That, and her recent sense of letting go made it all the more urgent to finish with him.

'I don't want to live here any more, Martha. It reeks of Ben. I want to start again, on my own, with the kids. He's made no effort to see them, but I can work on that. I want to see him again to show him I'll be reasonable. I want nothing from him, I only want him to help support the kids. I'll get work – cooking, cleaning, whatever. What I really want is a divorce so that everything can be cut and dried. I don't want to go on like this.'

Martha nodded, while Rose wiped away the tears. Tears of release, this time, better, healthier, cleaner tears than they had been in a long time.

'That's a big change, Rose, and you need to think about it. Which brings me perfectly to my good news.'

Rose looked at her. She felt like a child, looking expectantly at the parent from whom all good things come. She knew that something happy was about to happen.

'I've booked a house in Clare for the five of us for a week, starting next Saturday morning. We'll be leaving at ten.'

And Martha calmly refilled her coffee-cup.

'Then, with a clear head, rested bones and fortified by Arthur Guinness, you can tell your husband to go fuck himself.'

And she raised her cup for a toast.

Laughing, gulping, grateful like a delighted toddler, Rose raised her cup in return.

Tuesday, 4th July; 6.00 pm.

Ben was not making this any easier.

He had spoken sharply to Rose earlier, by telephone. He had no money, he said. She was living in his main asset. *She* had access to everything he owned.

'You're the one with all the comforts. I've barely enough to get by on. The bank is crawling all over me.'

Rose fought back.

'Then let's agree to sell up and pay off everyone's debts. Then we can make a clean break and I won't have to hassle you.'

Ben's voice became more clipped.

'I've told you. This is not the time to sell. The house is my most valuable asset. I'm not going to be rushed into selling it.'

Rose noticed the singular pronoun. She felt anger prodding.

'Well, if it's *your* house, and *your* car and *your* main asset, aren't they *your* children, too? They need food, and clothes and security. I don't want anything from you.'

Children couldn't be discarded like old clothes, when you got tired of them, when they were no longer in fashion, when they no longer felt comfortable. It was Rose who had slammed down the phone this time.

Angrily, she got the stepladder and went up into the attic. She flung down several cardboard boxes, boxes that at one stage had been full of *his* expensive wine. *She'd* only begun to drink it since he left.

Angrily, she filled each of the boxes. She made decisions

as she went along. He'd spoken stiffly of not even having wine glasses. He implied that she lived in the lap of luxury, his luxury, because *she* had them.

She stuffed a dozen red-wine glasses into the first box. Each one into the section where a bottle of wine had once been.

Let him ask.

She pulled out the partitions from the second box and shoved in the ship's decanter, the one he liked. After a moment's hesitation, she pushed the crystal ice-bucket in along with it. She hated all of them. Into the third box she shoved six sherry glasses, six whiskey glasses, six port glasses. They had had a dozen of everything. Right down the middle.

Let him complain now.

Into the final box, she swept his bedside locker clean. Cufflinks, tie-pins, loose change. The only place he was never tidy. Was that because, in a bedroom shared with another, there was no place to hide?

Weeping with fury, Rose filled the car. Not his clothes, not the sweaters she'd bought him. He could come and face her when he did that. God, she hated his guts.

She longed for a gun. It would be such a clean end to all this. He was making their marriage dirty, he was leaving a mess for her to clean up. If he were only dead, then she could grieve properly for what they had once had, and move on.

Martha had come in from town as she was finishing loading the boot. She had Damien, Brian and Lisa with her. Watching them step off the bus, Rose's anger deflated like a balloon.

She closed the boot and ran to the bathroom. Running the cold tap, she washed her wrists, her face, willing her pounding heart to slow down.

She'd show him stress.

Rose put cold moisturiser on her cheeks and eyelids. Then she put on foundation, powder and blusher. Eye-pencil and lipstick.

She'd show him.

She was calm by the time she went back into the kitchen, where Martha had made tea. Rose gulped a cup, scalding her throat, hurting the lump there.

Too casually, she said she had to go out for an hour. Martha looked directly at her, but Rose would not return her glance, did not want to see her eyes.

She had to do this. Maybe it wasn't wise, but she was sick of trying to be wise.

'I'm going to cook. I have my three helpers organised, we've already bought the ingredients. It'll be a surprise.'

Martha winked at Lisa as she said this. The little girl winked back, happily.

Martha came out into the porch as Rose was opening the car door.

'You're very angry, Rose. Are you sure it's the right time for whatever you're about to do?'

Rose nodded.

'Yes. He can have some of his precious main asset back. And I'm not nearly as angry as I was before I packed them. I need to get rid of this bootload of shit.'

Rose gestured wildly to the back of the car.

Martha nodded, gravely. She put her arms around Rose's shoulders and hugged her hard.

'Then do it and come straight back. We'll be here, waiting dinner for you.'

Rose nodded in reply, biting her lip. God, why couldn't women marry women? It would be all so much simpler.

Ben was taken aback when he saw her. She was calm by then. She wanted to offload the glasses and the horrible, vulgar decanter and the last twenty years. Before he answered the door, she had a mad moment of calculation. Given the state of Ben's present values, how much did Waterford crystal represent? How many years of faithfulness, of cooking, of cleaning, of phone messages did her bootload represent?

Give me a gun.

Inside, he was cold, stiff. The apartment looked grotty to Rose, and she was glad. The furniture was cheap, the room was untidy and there was an ugly wine stain at her feet.

Clean *that*, you bastard, said the voice in her head.

'What do you want, Rose?'

Had she really once loved this pompous, balding, middle-aged man? She noticed he'd got fatter, softer around the middle. She was glad. She was at her thinnest.

The disorder in the room didn't escape her. Take-away trays, refuse sack in the corner, coffee-table strewn with papers.

Suddenly, out of nowhere, she felt enormously sorry for him. Her anger drained, flowing down through the top of her head, down through her bowels, out at the toes. The poor unfortunate gobshite.

Suddenly, she had the same feeling she'd had walking the prom in Clontarf all those years ago, the rat nudging at the base of her throat.

Only now, she knew the loss she'd been grieving for, all the promise turned sour.

'I don't want anything, Ben. I just brought you some things I thought you might want.'

Rose propped open the door and went out to the car.

He made no move to help her.

She stacked the boxes inside the front door.

Once she'd carried them in, she felt better. And hungry. She suddenly wanted to be gone.

'You said you had no wine-glasses, Ben. So here they are. And the decanter you liked so much.'

She watched as his face changed colour and expression. Rose was puzzled. What was the matter with him?

'Where is it?'

Rose looked at him, stupidly. She was aware her mouth was open, so she shut it.

'What? They're in the box. The glasses are in the box.'

She reminded herself of a beginner's class in Irish. *Tá na gloinne sa bhosca*, she thought, and almost giggled outright. She was beginning to feel a bit hysterical. Ben's face was so *peculiar*.

'The wine, you stupid bitch. The *wine*.'

What wine? And then she remembered. Of course. The wine that had kept her alive for the first two weeks. The wine she'd shared with Jane.

'I drank it, Ben. For Christ's sake, what's the matter with you?'

Ben's face had turned purple.

'It was an *investment*,' he hissed at her. 'That wine was worth a bloody fortune!'

Rose lost it.

'Another fucking *asset*, I suppose! Well, let's be consistent, at least!'

Before he could stop her, Rose bent down, and pulled glasses out of the box at her feet. Looking straight at him, she smashed them together, sending showers of light and colour into the grimness of his flat.

He grabbed at her. She pushed him away.

She pulled the ship's decanter out. What was this worth? Five years? She smashed it against the wall, feeling her cheek pierced by exploding splinters. She was past caring. This was nearly as good as killing him.

He pulled both of her wrists behind her back and she kicked him, hard, on the shin. With a yelp of pain, he let her go.

As quickly as it had come, the exhilaration drained, and Rose felt frightened. He had hurt her, he was coming at her again, lunging for her hands. She had managed to get her keys out of her handbag and she raised her hands to defend herself.

Somehow, Ben's face was there, mixed in with keys and hands and anger. She really hadn't meant to, but it was inevitable. Her car key gouged a long, wine-coloured exclamation down the left side of his face.

His eyes seemed to grow huge.

Then he hit her. Hard. Right across the face with all the strength of his right arm, all the anger of twenty years.

They both stopped, horrified.

Without a word, Rose took her bag off the ground, opened the door with a shaking hand, and left.

She used her blood-stained car key to open the driver's door.

She sat in and turned the key in the ignition.

She didn't even look back.

Tuesday, 4th July; 7.30 pm.

The smell of frying onions was halfway down the driveway. Rose was still shaking as she turned off the engine. Glancing in the mirror she saw a long dribble of blood along her right cheek, too close to her eye. She'd been lucky.

She was exhausted after her anger. The whole left side of her head was throbbing. It felt as though something had been knocked out of place. Her cheekbone was bright red. It seemed to swell as she watched. She couldn't face the kids like this.

She half-stepped, half-fell out of the car and stumbled down the driveway. She had to escape before they saw her. She made her way to Jane's house, praying she would be there. She pressed the doorbell. Jane answered almost immediately.

Her whole face lit up with pleasure for a second. Then her expression fell as Rose's face registered.

'Jesus,' was all she said.

She lifted Rose into the hall. Rose felt as though it was all happening to someone else. Her legs had turned to plasticine, as though she had just had a strenuous walk. She was beyond words. She could not form a thought, a sentence. She knew there was pain but couldn't locate it. Was it hers? There was a most extraordinary sound.

It was her teeth. They were chattering. Everything was shaking.

People at a great distance were doing things to her. It was like the hospital again. But instead of peeling layers away, they were piling layers on. Gradually, she began to feel warm. Her hands especially. Someone was holding them as they were wrapped around a mug. A child's mug. Something like 'My Little Pony'. Something pink and white, the promise of romance.

It was tea. Strong, hot tea, full of sugar. She began to focus. Words started to flood.

Jane stroked her hair. She whispered to Jim. White and shocked, he refilled Rose's mug.

The electric fire was on. She was safe.

'Please – ring home. Talk to Martha. Tell her to tell the kids . . . anything. They're not to worry, they're not to know.'

Jane sat on the arm of the shabby, comfortable chair. She kept her arm around Rose's shoulders. With her free hand, she dialled Rose's number.

'Do you want to talk?'

Rose shook her head. Minutes later, Jane hung up.

'Everything's OK. The kids are fine. They're cooking Chinese. She's told them you've been delayed. She'll keep them busy as long as possible.'

Rose realised, with amazement, that Jane was almost in tears. She must have looked a right sight. Probably worse than she was, really.

'We've called the doctor.'

'That's not necessary.' Rose found her voice, unsteadily. 'I'll be as right as rain.'

Where had that phrase come from? She hadn't heard it in years, had never used it herself, even. It was a voice of childhood, of skinned knees, ice-pops and home.

The doorbell rang.

'Well,' said Jane, 'he's here, so you might as well.'

Kevin McDermott came in seconds after Jane left. Rose felt suddenly too tired to protest. He brought kindness and efficiency with him. Rose felt like a little girl again.

Gently, he cleaned her face, removing tiny slivers of glass.

'You won't need stitches, Rose, they're only tiny cuts. Tell me how it happened.'

Rose told him, anxious to be clear that the cuts were her fault, her rage. Ben had not done that to her.

'And what about this lovely shiner? Did you do that too?'

Rose told as best she could about the keys, the hands, the anger.

He nodded. 'I'm going to take a photo of your face, Rose, so just sit still.'

The Polaroid whined.

'I'm giving you something to help you sleep, and something for the pain. That's going to hurt like hell tomorrow. I want to see you again tomorrow night. I'll call to the house after my rounds.'

Rose felt will-less; all she could do was allow things to be done to her. She no longer had any control.

She fought the sensation of lethargy, knew the danger of it, from before.

'I'll take it later, Kevin. I must go home and have dinner. My children are cooking for me.'

She saw the way he looked at her.

'No, I'm not mad. Still a bit shocked, yes, but my kids are waiting. After dinner, I can collapse all I like. But this is important.'

He nodded.

'OK. Have a couple of glasses of wine, no more. And take those when you're already in bed. They should knock you out more or less straight away. We'll talk tomorrow.'

And he was gone.

Jane was back on the armchair again. More tea. Rose drank it gratefully. She *did* feel better. There was a strong sense of an ending.

Not a happy ending but something clean and brutal. And over.

She smiled up at Jane.

'I'll be fine. Thank you. I need to talk to you tomorrow. Please come.'

Jane nodded, patting her hand.

'Of course I'll come. Whenever you're ready.'

Rose stood up. Quite steady now. Her knees were back in place.

'I must go home to eat Chinese with my kids. What did Martha tell them?'

'Nothing. She's leaving that until you go home. You can always say you were mugged.'

Rose smiled.

'That'll do fine for now. Can you walk me home?'

The pain was beginning again, the throb above her left ear. It felt as though something was growing inside her eye. She touched it. It was puffy.

She'd have to make as light of it as she could. The younger ones would believe her. It was Damien she was worried about.

'Let's go.'

Jim insisted on driving her the short distance while Jane sat in the back with her, ice-cubes wrapped in a plastic bag and a tea-towel.

She had been very stupid. She was as much to blame as Ben. She shouldn't have even tried to talk to him while she was still angry. For a mad moment, she hoped that she'd hurt him every bit as much as he had her.

At least she didn't have to sweep up the glass.

The smell of onions was still strong, mixed now with spices that seemed familiar, but which Rose couldn't name. Her stomach lurched from nausea to hunger.

She'd do her best.

In through the kitchen door. Once more with feeling. Would she die in this kitchen, too, when the time came?

'Hi gang. I'm back.'

A few minutes comforted the younger ones. But Rose saw

how Damien looked at her. His eyes were suddenly black in a dead-white face. She tried to signal to him that it was not what it seemed, to wait, that she'd explain.

He left the kitchen abruptly.

She had to let him go. Brian and Lisa were anxious, frightened at the sight of her rapidly blackening eye.

Martha was the reassuring doctor to perfection. She sent Brian for ice and Lisa for an extra sweater and all the time she kept up a wonderful, running commentary about it not being as bad as it looked. The busyness she created, the tone of her voice, the quickness of her hands calmed Brian and Lisa back to normality, to a stage where they could even be brave about it.

Rose said she needed to go to the bathroom. Cupping Lisa's face in her hands she told the little girl she was starving. Would she set the table for Martha?

Brian she brought by the hand into the sitting-room and opened the press door. Grimly, she handed him the last bottle of wine.

'Bring that in to Martha, and ask her to show you how to open it. I'm going upstairs for a minute. When I come down, we can eat. I'm looking forward to this.'

Brian nodded, eyes still looking in hers for a clue. Then, suddenly, he hugged her. It was agony; it was also the sweetest ache Rose had felt in a long time.

She kissed the top of his spiky hair.

'You're the best,' she whispered.

Now for Damien.

Play it by ear. Softly, softly, catchee monkey. Sufficient unto the day.

What a bloody day.

Wednesday, 5th July

It did hurt like hell the following day, and the day after that. She let Martha take over. It was a delightful feeling, doing nothing. Jane came and stayed for hours. She and Martha took an instant liking to one another. Rose was glad.

They sat on either side of her bed the following afternoon, drank wine, laughed uproariously at Ben's fury over his investment and all the dark feelings stayed away. Rose laughed and cried as she related the tale. *Tá na gloinne sa bhosca*. It wasn't so savage, so full of hate, laughing about it with Jane and Martha.

Between sips of wine and painkillers, Rose slept on and off throughout the day. It was all still a little bit unreal.

Damien was relaxing gradually as he watched her recover. Throughout the waking day, she was conscious of making a great effort to show him – look, I'm OK, I'm surviving this. I am not a victim here.

I am Rose. I will survive. All those years.

He had wanted to kill his father.

Rose was very clear as she told him what happened, over and over again. She waited until he made sense of it. She waited until he understood that nothing was expected of him, or needed from him.

She and Martha worked hard during dinner that night. Pictures of the cottage were produced, plans were made.

Rose had never felt so grateful to anyone in her life.

It was a good omen, she decided. Things were going to get better.

Saturday, 8th July; 10.00 am.

Rose locked up and put on the alarm, hoping everything would be all right in her absence. Just before leaving, she went to check her bedroom. Windows closed, bits and pieces of jewellery hidden. For a moment, she was tempted to take the rest of the money that Maureen had given her. She resisted. She had enough from her Bonne Bouche cheque.

If she brought more, she'd spend more. And the kids had to learn how to enjoy themselves with less.

Closing the boot of the car and driving away was like leaving her life behind. Martha wouldn't let her drive. Rose didn't protest too much. Her face was still very sore, her eye an interesting palette of blues and purples. She was still stiff and aching.

Strangely, it was an ache she enjoyed. It was physical, she knew the reason for it. Painkillers sent it away.

She preferred it to the rat which had lodged at the base of her throat for the best part of twenty years. All the heaviness was gone. Her head was clear, she could breathe easily. With a shock, she realised that the sensation was happiness.

The first day in Clare set the pattern for the week. The weather was hot and sunny. At ten, they all went for a long walk, pushing against the wind, enjoying the physical challenge of hills and rocks.

They came home to the cottage for lunch.

Every afternoon, they drove to somewhere recommended by the guide book, usually chosen by Lisa or Brian.

Home again for dinner.

Each night, they went to a different pub, enjoying the music and the welcome given to children. Rose thought she could live there for the rest of her life. The simple daily structure which became like an old routine almost immediately, the complete tiredness each night made her feel that her life could be different. The old patterns *could* change.

And somewhere in between all of this, Martha taught Damien how to drive.

It was only on the Saturday morning that Rose became depressed. She had to go back and face that other life. She felt uneasy all day, as though things were happening at home, spiralling out of control.

It was a feeling of dread that couldn't be explained by just reaching the end of the holiday.

'It's natural,' Martha reassured her as they packed up. 'You've been through a hell of a time. Some depression, some let-down is natural now. It'll pass. If it doesn't, you can get help. There's nobody out there handing out medals for doing it all on your own, you do know that?'

Rose smiled.

'Yes, I'm sure you're right.'

Quietly, they tidied up together. Martha was going to Galway next week; then three weeks in London. Then home to Sydney.

Rose didn't know what she was going to do without her.

'I'll be back, you know, and we'll be keeping in touch this time.'

'I know. I'll miss you.'

Martha nodded.

'Me too. Rose?'

Rose looked up from her packing. Martha looked a little embarrassed.

'If anything goes really haywire financially, will you let me know? You can't work any harder; let me help if you come unstuck. I'd like to, OK?'

'I will, I promise. And you've already helped.'

Rose felt her depression begin to lift as they drove towards Dublin. She felt calm, at peace again.

Saturday, 15th July; 9.00 pm.

The minute Rose put the key in her front door, she sensed something was wrong. Quickly, she punched in the code to stop the alarm from sounding. Everything seemed OK, but her gut told her something different.

Martha and the kids went into the kitchen to put on the kettle. Rose said she'd be down in a minute.

Outside her bedroom door, she froze. It was open. She had closed it, she was sure she had closed it. But the alarm . . . how?

Ben. She didn't know how, but she knew it must be Ben.

Cautiously, she opened her door wider, still standing outside on the landing. She couldn't call the bedroom untidy, but it was not as she had left it. The bed was creased. The air was different.

Everything seemed to be there. She opened the wardrobes. With a sick, sinking feeling, she saw that Ben's side was empty. No suits, no jackets, no shoes.

How had he got in? She felt violated, as if a burglar had been while she slept.

Suddenly panic-stricken, she opened the central door to the shelving unit.

The sweaters. Gone.

Quickly, she ran her hand across each of the empty shelves in turn. Surely he wouldn't have stolen money from her. She must have put Maureen's envelope some-where else. She must have put it somewhere safe. She tried desperately to remember. She forced her hands to slow down. Methodically, she searched every shelf, every drawer, every pocket.

It was gone. The envelope with the two hundred pounds was gone.

Rose sat down heavily on the bed. She should have taken it with her. At least she would have enjoyed it.

There was a quick tap at the door.

'Are you right – tea's made.'

Tea. The symbol of all that was normal.

Martha poked her head around the door. Rose's face made her close her mouth. Her smile vanished.

'What is it Rose? You're like a ghost.'

'I've just seen one. He's been here.'

'Who? Ben? How do you know?'

'All his clothes are gone. I don't know how he got in. All the locks are changed. But he's been here. And I know I was stupid, I know I should have put it in the bank, but it was my emergency money.'

'What did he take, Rose? Tell me, what did he take?'

There was an edge of anger to Martha's voice; Rose was surprised. She could not remember Martha as having been angry, ever.

'Two hundred pounds. What was left out of the money his mother gave me.'

Martha knelt on the floor and brought her face level with Rose's. She put her hands on Rose's elbows.

'Rose, look at me. Look at me, Rose.'

Rose obeyed. She had that distant feeling again; this was happening to someone else, not to this Rose.

She tried hard to focus on Martha.

'You'll make up the loss of the money. It's just another ending. You're finished with him. He can't do anything else to you. Are you listening to me?'

Rose nodded. The strength of Martha's hands began to ground her.

'You've three kids depending on you, and you've never failed them. Don't let this destroy all your good work. What was it you used to repeat to yourself after little Michael died? Say it, Rose.'

The tears began to flow.

'I am Rose,' she whispered. 'I will survive.'

'You're not his wife any longer. You're beginning again. Let this be the last thing he does to hurt you.'

'It's not even the money . . .'

'I know. I know. Come on, wash your face. The kids are waiting.'

Rose stood up and obediently went into the bathroom. She washed her face and brushed her hair.

She heard Martha say cheerfully, 'We're coming!' She heard her go downstairs, to stop Lisa coming up.

Rose stood up straighter and had a physical sensation of, literally, pulling herself together. She made her knees bend, her legs move, her face smile.

And she went back down to the kitchen.

Monday, 24th July; 12.15 pm.

Rose waited until Martha had gone to Galway on the following Monday before she went looking for Ben. She had a feeling of finality about his leaving, this time. Now that he had stolen her money, Rose knew that he would never have the guts to face her. This time, he was gone for good. With a detached sense of curiosity, Rose wondered had he gone away with Caroline, or with someone else. Had he gone far? It didn't matter to her, in any real way, but she would have liked to know.

Early on Monday afternoon, she called on Jane. As usual, there was no problem. The weather was glorious and a visit to the beach suddenly took shape. Brian and Lisa were happy.

'No point in thanking you again, I suppose?' Rose said. 'I feel like the Angel of Death, the constant bringer of bad news.'

'Quite the opposite, you were the constant bringer of very good wine. I'm very glad now that I enjoyed it so much! Take your time. We'll have a picnic.'

'See you later then.'

'Good luck. Are you sure you don't want to wait until I'm with you?'

'Positive. There's nothing left to fight about.'

Rose was calm as she drove out towards Ben's apartment in Howth.

There were quite a few people sitting out on their little bal-conies, others in the courtyard under some brightly coloured parasols when Rose drove up. She parked outside Ben's door and knocked. She hadn't really expected any answer; this was just a matter of form.

There was a woman sitting on her own, reading. She looked a bit older than the others. Rose approached her.

'Excuse me. I'm looking for the occupant of Apartment 9. His name is Ben Holden?'

The woman closed her book.

'So am I. Who might you be?'

Rose was taken aback at the directness of her manner.

'I'm Rose Holden. His – ex-wife.'

The woman nodded. She picked up a large canvas bag off the ground.

'I think he's moved out. Will you come with me?'

Rose followed her. The woman rooted in her bag and took out a large bunch of keys.

'I'm Geraldine Kenny. I own a couple of the apartments here.'

Very nice, too, Rose thought to herself.

The woman opened Ben's front door.

'I cleared out all the refuse sacks this morning when I got no answer. The place was beginning to smell.'

The room was well and truly empty. Only the wine stain remained to show that Ben had ever been there.

'He left these,' she handed Rose a bundle of envelopes. 'I was going to post them, but some have no addresses. Only names. I figured someone would call. Do you want to take them?'

Rose got the sense that the woman was uneasy. What did she suspect? Suicide? Murder? Maybe she had seen some of the comings and goings around Ben. Whatever she had seen or sensed, the woman was definitely suspicious of something.

'Yes, I'll take them.'

Rose was on the point of asking, when the woman intervened:

'He doesn't owe anything, everything's been paid up.'

She wanted to be rid of him. You and me both, thought Rose. All the old feelings of resentment, stilled for some time, began to well up inside her again. Here she was, once more, picking up after him. She held out her hand for the letters.

'Good. Well, I'll take care of these.'

Her money had probably taken care of his rent, too, the bastard.

'Do you want me to forward any post?'

'No,' said Rose. 'I have absolutely no idea where he's gone. Thanks for your help.'

She waited until she got home to open the envelopes.

One to Barry, one to Jack Morrissey at the bank, one to her, one to his solicitor, two others to names she didn't recognise.

She opened them all.

When she finished, she got five new envelopes and wrote the addresses on them. The sixth letter she took over to the sink.

She rummaged in the drawer for matches. She lit one and held the letter by one corner, setting fire to another. She watched with satisfaction as it burned. Then she washed it down the sink. It made her feel tired. Her failure, her fault, his need to find himself. It would have been better, much better, if he'd left without saying anything at all.

She pulled the remains of Martha's whiskey out of the press in the sitting-room. She didn't bother to lock it again. There was no point. There was nothing left.

She punched in the new alarm code.

Then, bottle under her arm, she made the now familiar journey down the road to sanity, and to Jane.

Tuesday, 25th July; 9.10 am.

'So what are my options, then?'

It was early on Tuesday morning. Rose was talking to David O'Brien.

'Slim and none, I suppose?' she answered herself.

'If we can't trace him, there's not a lot we can do, Rose. Have you any idea where he might have gone?'

'No, not right now. Maybe if I keep thinking, I'll remember something. But to be honest, I have to make plans assuming he'll never be found. In fact, I hope I never see him again. It'd be a lot easier if he was dead.'

There was a moment's silence. 'I can only guess how you feel, Rose. I'm truly sorry.'

Rose shook her head violently to stop the tears. This was no time for self-pity, for anyone's pity.

'Send me the five letters,' David said. 'I'll make copies and forward them. But from what you've said, Ben has not left any financial security behind him. Don't talk to anyone, don't do anything until you hear from me. I know Barry Herbert is a personal friend, but don't tell him anything yet. Do you hear me?'

No point in telling David that Barry was a good man, an ethical businessman. No point in saying that her hunch was that if anyone could salvage anything out of Ben's disastrous business deals, he could. David was suspicious by nature and by profession.

She agreed. 'OK. I'll wait to hear from you. Can you make it soon?'

Rose was learning that the law was very slow. For ordinary

people and their problems, for divorce, Irish-style, it had nothing to offer. She felt that she had no rights. She was no longer half of a respectable, solid, middle-class couple. Instead, she was half of nothing. Everything now depended on Ben, on finding him, on clearing up his mess, on getting his agreement. Without that, she was in the no-woman's land of separation. And she was waiting, again. She didn't want to spend any more of her life waiting.

'I'll be back to you by Friday. Hold on until then. Let me make the enquiries.'

Enquiries. What a neat word. Her life would be summed up, shaped by enquiries. The future of her children, her home, herself. She had the feeling that these enquiries would go on for a very long time.

Rose made coffee and sat down in the quietness of the kitchen. She would like to leave it – the kitchen where everything seemed to have taken place – to go to another kitchen where the events would be defined only by herself.

She would paint it a different colour. The presses and shelves would hold only simple things. She would get rid of the complex machinery of cordon bleu cooking from her home. She would find somewhere else for it, somewhere called work, not home. She began to plan a second space, another kitchen where she might begin to earn her living. Cooking, for love or money.

Rose pulled her notebook out of her handbag and began to list the ways she could earn. There was the Bonne Bouche, four hours a day, say from six until ten every morning. There was the dinner-party once a month for twelve. There was the party catering, if she could increase that to once a week.

With a sudden flash of insight, Rose knew what else she could do. Why not? Why shouldn't she take the initiative and believe in herself. She figured Jack Morrissey would do anything to get his money back.

Rose's head was buzzing. She made dinner for six o'clock,

273

on auto-pilot. Dinnertime was rowdy, summer holidays in full swing. Brian and Lisa, particularly, were freckled, healthy. How was she going to tell them that their father was gone for good?

She had a moment of panic. Was she mad? How was she going to handle all of this alone? The moment passed.

After dinner, she closed herself into Ben's office and worked well into the night. By four o'clock she was finished. The office was littered with papers. Bound securely in a blue folder were fourteen sheets of neatly written paper. She'd have to learn how to use the computer.

Rose was so elated she couldn't sleep. She decided to anticipate the Bonne Bouche's needs. She baked for the next four hours, trying out two new middle-eastern doughs. She could do it, she knew she could do it. And she *would* do it.

As she waited for the doughs to rise, she thought about her life. As a young girl, she had wanted only what she believed her mother had. And her sister Ellen would say she had been wrong even about that. Then she had wanted only what Ben wanted. She had never taken the time to find out what she really wanted, independent of anyone else. But then that would have made her a different person at nineteen, and how could she have been that? Rose wondered how a child could try to turn into a different adult. How can you learn to mould yourself?

For the first time in her life, Rose felt grown up.

It was as though scales had fallen from her eyes. She saw her next life as very different, her second chance. Her new beginning. There was nobody to protect her. Nobody even to give her the illusion of protecting her. She was responsible for herself and three other people, whom she would not shelter as thoroughly as her mother had sheltered her. That was the difference. That was how you learned to put shape on yourself. She would protect them only by exposing them to all the options she had never had, had never created for herself. She hadn't wanted them only because she didn't know that they were there. With her own children, she would do better. She would teach them that there were choices to be made, not simply roads to be followed.

She would feed them, clothe them, educate them or die in the attempt. If anyone tried to take away her home to pay Ben's debts, she would fight them. For now, she was not going to worry about that. Sufficient unto the day.

I miss you, Mother. I wish we'd had the chance to understand one another. I hope I don't die before my children and I can be adults together.

Gritty, eye-aching exhaustion finally hit at nine o'clock. The children filed in looking for breakfast. Bare feet, pyjamas, unwashed, unbrushed. Rose smiled to herself. What a thing to worry about.

Damien promised to be there during the day for Brian and Lisa. She handed him the blue folder when the children had left the kitchen.

'I'm knackered, Damien. Let me sleep until three, then call me. Otherwise, I'll be up all night again.'

Damien was looking through the folder.

'I'll do a spreadsheet on this for you. We learned, at school. It'll look the business.'

He was all eagerness. Seventeen, nearly eighteen. He could play his part. It was time.

'Do that,' she said, 'and later you can teach me.'

Finally, she rested.

Before sleep came, in the last moment before unconsciousness, Rose felt her chest expand with a feeling of optimism, of looking forward.

Softly, softly, catchee monkey. She had done it; she was free.

Friday, 15th September; 9.00 pm.

Martha was calling every couple of weeks now to see how Rose was doing. Sometimes she caught Rose on a bad day, but more and more, Rose was buoyant; keeping it all together.

Martha encouraged all her plans. She believed in Rose, and Rose was grateful.

One Friday in the middle of September, she called to find Rose in a state of great excitement.

'Guess what!'

'Tell me,' said Martha patiently. 'Come on – we deserve good news!'

'It looks as though the bank is going to give me the money! Not only did they like the spreadsheet, but my order book is nearly full and, boy, did that impress them!'

Rose went off into peals of laughter. It was infectious. Martha found herself joining in.

'I don't know why I'm laughing, Rose. You deserve this, you're going to make a success of it. Why are we laughing?'

'Because you'll never guess what I'm being paid a fortune for – well, a fortune for me!'

Martha forced herself to be serious, ignoring the gurgling delight in Rose's voice. She decided to be very firm.

'Tell me. Come on, you must come clean.'

'Wedding cakes! I'll be making my living from wedding cakes!'

And she was off again. By the time she had stopped laughing, Martha was ready for her.

'Rose, that's wonderful. In less than a year, you've turned everything around. Now you're not just surviving – you're starting to live again. I think you're great.'

There was a long silence. Martha wanted to reach her again.

'Rose? You're playing a blinder. I mean it. You're doing great.'

When Rose spoke again, her voice was calmer.

'They found him, you know.'

'Who did?'

Martha didn't need to ask who 'him' was.

'Maureen and Bernard. They traced him. Or rather, his father did. Poor Maureen. She said she'd never seen her husband so angry, in over fifty years.'

Martha waited. She knew there was more.

'Ben was in London at the time. They found him in a cheap hotel. Bernard got so angry that he hit him, punched him right in the chest. Maureen said she was terrified. She said the lamp went flying, there was glass everywhere.'

'Go on,' said Martha gently.

'Then they left. Bernard was insisting that Ben face his responsibilities. Maureen said she knew it was years too late for that. They left, and they haven't seen or heard from him since.'

'How are the two of them?'

Martha could almost feel Rose's shrug of sadness.

'Devastated. Maureen says she has finally got Bernard to start talking again, but the man is diminished. He's about half the size he was. I really think Ben has broken his heart.'

Martha allowed a long pause to happen.

'It's not your fault, Rose. None of this fallout is your fault. You must believe that.'

'I do, I do. It's just all so . . . sad. I feel like I'm at a long, slow funeral. Only I have no body to bury.'

'That'll come. In the meantime, keep doing what you're

doing, and write to me. There's a letter in the post for you; it should arrive next week.'

Not for the first time, Rose was grateful for her friend's solidity. She thought of Ellen in London, and of Grace, just down the road from her. Blood was not thicker than water; she was sure of it.

Saturday, 6th April, 1996

'Good morning; Bonne Bouche Catering.'

Rose cradled the receiver on her left shoulder and reached for her notepad.

'That's right; this is Rose Kelly.'

She was getting used to the sound of her own name. She liked it.

'For Saturday, fourth of May; that's four weeks from today? Yes, we can manage that. For one hundred and twenty. What sort of buffet did you have in mind?'

Rose always said yes these days. She worried afterwards about how she would fit it all in.

She wrote rapidly on the page in front of her.

'That's the tennis club, isn't it? No, no, that's all part of our service.'

Our service. Rose still felt grateful to Barry and to Annie whenever she said that. Together, they'd come up with a package which Rose still imagined as wrapped in a ribbon marked salvation.

The Bonne Bouche name, the finance, the van in the driveway. What a year.

And Caroline. Still recommending clients. The atmosphere was easier between them now. Rose had told her long ago to stop feeling guilty; Ben was responsible for the hurt; maybe Rose was too. Caroline was not.

Brian and Lisa were quietly doing homework, in the same room. Damien was doing the Friday deliveries.

She worried all the time about him driving.

And in June, new premises, nearer than Greystones.

Rose was happier than she had been in several years; perhaps ever. She seldom thought of her other life with Ben. Sometimes she could not recall his face, no matter how hard she tried.

She was grateful for the weekend stretching ahead of her. Two mornings without getting up at half-five. Luxury.

She took a pizza out of the oven and called the children for dinner. They were well, they were happy, they had shoes and clothes and schoolbooks.

Rose looked at them with a great rush of love. She paid her bills, worked her hardest, minded her children and needed her friends. And that, for now, was enough.

Sufficient unto the day. Thank you, Mother.

She put their plates on the table, poured herself a glass of wine, and another weekend began.

Epilogue

Ben's attention is caught by the same child every morning. Crushing on the platform under the anonymous leaden skies, the child's bright face shines in a just-scrubbed-schoolboy way.

It has taken Ben a while to focus on this child, rather than on any of the others. He has usually been on his own, just apart from the group. Some mornings, he plays with a hand-held computer game.

He gets into the same carriage every morning, as Ben does, as everyone seems to. He rarely looks up, intent on the killing machines that buzz their way around the tiny screen.

It is the bent head that does it. Ben realises with a shock that almost takes his breath away, that the child's hair is permanently in a spiky peak at the back of his head. The first time Ben sees this, he is made almost dizzy with grief.

Now the pain is less, but Ben has to still the impulse to reach out, to smooth down the crown of his head.

He was tempted to phone at Christmas. But what would he say? It was better to leave things as they were.

He remembers how his father and mother found him, months back, while he was still in London. His father's rage still chills him.

He had left London that night, too weary to confront the parents who would see nothing but his selfishness. They did not understand that he did not want what they had.

He does not want to end up dry and wasted, letting life pass him by. He wonders if they even speak to one another any more. He wants more out of his life. The next stop is his. Hull isn't such a bad place.

Ben stands up, tucks the cheap briefcase under his arm. He walks up the hill, away from the station, towards the centre.

Right in front of him, the boy walks with his mates. Ben's last sight of him, before the children turn in the gates of the huge comprehensive, is the bit of spiky hair.

It bobs up and down gently, keeping rhythm with the boy's light step.